MONSTROUS

Book Two

SAWYER BLACK

DAVID W. WRIGHT

STERLING & STONE

To YOU, the reader.
Thank you for taking a chance on us.
Thank you for your support.
Thank you for the emails.
Thank you for the reviews.
Thank you for reading and joining us on this road.

MONSTROUS

Chapter One

FORTY-ONE DESCENDED the stone stairs for the first time, heart pounding in his ears, eyes fixed to the sliver of light fanning through a gap beneath the thick mahogany door. Water seeping up through the sandstone for a century had left a glittering film of salt on the landing's uneven surface.

He pressed the tray of steaming food into his hip and dug through the front pocket of his robes. An iron ring of fourteen keys hung heavy, tugging at the neck of his garment, digging into the soft flesh at the top of his shoulders. He fished out the keys, gritting his teeth against the pain.

Iron repelled demons, especially minor ones like him who lacked the strength to defend against its touch.

Forty-One slowed his descent, easing his toes past the rounded edges of the final few steps. Standing firm at the bottom, he found the largest key, unlocked the door, dropped the heavy ring back into his pocket, then stood with his eyes closed, forcing his shoulders back and his head up. He breathed through his nose, wondering if those before him had done the same.

His throbbing hand fell on the latch and opened the door, wincing from the rusty howl and squinting against the bright lights that hung from the ceiling. A stone hallway stretched away from him, thirty feet to end at an iron door with a narrow slit at the top. Six matching doors on either side for a total of thirteen cells.

Forty-One drew a deep breath then stepped out of the stairwell and into the light.

He sent a silent prayer to Naburus and clung to the tray's edges, staying in the center of the hallway.

The last cell was the only one that mattered.

Moans and indistinct shouting. The ripe scent of prisoners rolling past his nostrils. Fluorescents swayed from their chains and sent shadows in and out of the corners. Forty-One kept his eyes on the final door, breathing through his mouth.

"Is someone there?" The voice from the first cell, thin and weak. A virgin being held for her blood, nearly depleted. Cells two and three were empty. Four held a man with no eyes.

"I *seeee* you," the no-eyed man whispered.

Forty-One shook his head and continued.

A demon wrapped in chains, hanging suspended in the center of cell five, sent a glamour through the door. The hall became a garden path, morning light now beaming through rustling leaves overhead. Sprites and fairies flitting among the motes of dust and pollen.

Forty-One smelled honeysuckle and jasmine. He breathed deep, but didn't stray, passing where he knew the door to be, and the glamour crumbled like a wall of smoke. The demon bellowed rage into the corridor, piercing his ears, making him duck and forcing him to flinch. Still, he carried the tray to the end.

It was quiet after the demon, with only the last two

cells occupied. Cell twelve held the body of a vivisected Englishman. Forty-One didn't know what he'd done, or to whom the man might have done it, but there was cruel anger apparent in his punishment.

Torn open from chin to pelvis. A bladder of Ambrosia hung from the ceiling, dripping into the cavity holding his heart and keeping him suffering at the edges of death.

"Excuse me, good sir." The man's voice was thin and reedy. Airy like the push of a pair of bellows. "I'm quite thirsty and in an awful lot of pain. Could you be a dear and get us … just a *sip* of water?"

Drip.

"I cannot."

Drip.

"A shame. I would very much have liked to taste some again. Before the end."

Drip.

"I am sorry. Truly."

Drip.

"Not at all. I'm sorry for bothering you. Just … you know …"

He left the man to his misery.

Forty-One removed the keys from his pocket, rolling the mess around the ring until he stopped on the one that burned. The key tingled as he slid it into the lock on the thirteenth door. The man in cell twelve whistled a jaunty tune in time with the drips.

The door to cell thirteen clanged shut, silencing the insanity of the Englishman's happy tune. Forty-One sighed in relief then set the tray of cooling food on the table in the near corner. He busied himself with pocketing the keys and straightening his robes. He was loath to turn and face the inhabitant of the final cell.

Chains rattled behind him. He jumped at the sudden

noise, a yelp escaping his compressed lips. A final deep breath to settle his nerves, and he turned, hands behind his back and eyes on the floor.

The boy sat on the edge of his bed, dirty robes riding high enough to expose his filthy ankles. An iron chain trailed away to a bolt in the wall, and the skin beneath the manacle was dark and blistered. Grit filled every crease in his fingers, running around the edges and under his nails. He touched his fingertips in endless fidgeting repetition. His slender neck led to a face framed by pale hair. Nearly white, wild, and falling across his forehead to brush his cheeks. A sheen of platinum as he tossed his head and exposed his eyes. Forty-One returned his gaze to the floor.

"Are you here to free me?" the boy asked.

In his ears as lilting music, and behind his eyes where it set off colorful sparks, a shiver traveled through Forty-One's body. He caught his breath then sighed. "No, Adam. I am here with your meal."

"You're not here to help me?"

"I am afraid not, young sir."

"Afraid?"

The quiet question made Forty-One look up into the boy's face. Small eyes set in the shadow of his brows were bright, practically glowing from within. Forty-One had to stare into their depths. Curiosity or compulsion, it didn't matter. He took a half step forward and reached into his pocket to keep the keys from jangling.

He snatched his hand away from the burning iron and looked down in a daze. He drew his foot back and cast his eyes to the corner. The boy almost had him. Anger bubbled up at his carelessness. He turned his back on the boy and lifted his bowl of soup from the tray. The boy's voice made him pause, its music filling the cell. "Why are you afraid?"

Colors danced in Forty-One's mind. "I am not afraid. It is polite."

"Oh."

Forty-One turned with the bowl held in front of him with both hands. He kept his eyes fixed on the liquid inside, keeping it level with sliding strides. At the limit of Adam's reach, Forty-One lowered the bowl and turned his head. He lightened his voice as one does with children. "Chicken soup, young sir. And there is cake still on the tray."

Adam shot his hand from his lap and swatted the bowl. It sloshed from Forty-One's grip, the greasy broth splashing the front of his robes as it tumbled, then shattered, splattering soup up onto his down-turned face. He jumped back, sputtering as he lifted his gaze to the child's face, angry reproach filling his mouth.

He looked directly into Adam's eyes, and Forty-One's pointing finger froze in front of him. His face relaxed, and his hands fell to his side. He stared.

Weird and beautiful, the eyes were unlike anything he'd ever seen. One blue and the other gold. Both lit with an internal fire that sparkled like gems in a cave. Adam smiled, and Forty-One faltered, joy rising into his heart. Bringing happiness to this boy was his brand new mission.

"Free me." Adam's mouth hadn't moved, but Forty-One still heard the voice as before, in sweet concert with the dancing colors. Gold and blue like the child's eyes. Jingling chimes and the rush of a breeze through the reeds. A distant horn, rising pure into the air, echoing off the hills and rolling down to fill the ears of those fortunate enough to hear it. "Free me."

Forty-One gasped and raised his hands to clasp them in front of his chest. Sorrow swelled within him, and he blinked back tears. "I cannot, young sir."

"Why not?"

Forty-One pointed at the chain, bitterness rising to greet his sorrow. "They will not give me *those* keys."

"So, you can't help me?"

Forty-One fell to his knees. Sadness and disappointment filled Adam's eyes, and Forty-One curled into the nausea already twisting his gut. He shook his head and shrugged, begging the boy to understand.

"Then what good are you?"

"Please," Forty-One gasped. "How else may I serve you?"

"It doesn't matter." Adam's eyes glistened with unshed tears. "You'll leave and betray me like the others."

"No!" Forty-one shuffled forward, grabbed the boy's foot, and brought it to his cheek. Closing his eyes, he said, "I will not. I *swear* it."

"I wish I could believe you." Adam's whisper trickled like the splashing of a brook, sun dappling off its rippling surface. "You're just like the others."

Forty-One looked up into the boy's eyes. "Please. Let me serve you."

"Unless you can free me, you're no use. Just like the others. Bad."

Forty-One reeled back from the verbal slap. His feet scrabbled beneath him and he rose, staggering until his back hit the door and knocked his breath away. Adam lowered his eyes to the floor, and the dismissal sent a crippling shaft of shame through Forty-One's heart. He regained his balance and turned to face the side wall.

His feet pounded and his arms pumped. Forty-One darted across the cell. His forehead connected with the stone. Pain exploded behind his eyes, setting off a bright flash that replaced the dancing colors of Adam's voice.

He stumbled back, blood flowing into his eyes and

down into his mouth. Vertigo sent the room into a crazy spin, and Forty-One fell to all fours. Blood dripped into a red inkblot on the floor under his eyes.

"Look at me."

Forty-One twisted his pounding head until he could see Adam's face. The boy's eyes were wide, the light inside them dancing like reflected flames. Forty-One fell into them, and the pain subsided. He walked on the shore of a rushing creek in the middle of a spring shower, raindrops pattering on the leaves like blood onto stone.

Adam grinned, his teeth shining out, and Forty-One felt his own mouth stretch into a smile. The boy tapped the tips of his fingers together in time with a song only he could hear. "Again."

Forty-One rose to his feet and charged the wall. The impact cracked like splitting wood.

Light and music swirled above him. He turned to see the boy watching with glee. Happiness filled him to match what he saw in the child's eyes, and Forty-One struggled to stand.

"Again," Adam said.

Forty-One ran at the wall with his own voice filling his ears as he cried out with effort. A wet crunching, and the light in his right eye went out.

"Again."

Forty-One struggled to obey, and the impact sent a shard of freezing cold down his spine. On his back looking up at the ceiling. His left eye went dark. But he could still see the dancing colors of Adam's voice with every command.

"Again."

Forty-One rolled to the side, feeling for the floor with numb hands.

"Again."

The cold stone floor pressing against his back, his feet splayed out.

"Again."

His robes heavy with blood, slick under his probing fingers.

"Again."

Forty-One drifted down into darkness, swirling in a current made of his own blood, the small shower becoming a heavy storm. The creek becoming a river raging toward the crashing waves of an ocean glowing with the fires of Hell. A black boat raced by, and the boatman reached out a skeletal hand.

Again.

Chapter Two

HENRY STOOD atop the Burg-Heartstone bridge.

Three hundred and ten feet above the water, the east tower afforded the harbor's best view and kept the city at his back. Lights from the boats ferrying the city's trash to the landfills were a glittering constellation of garbage along the coast. A rancid, reeking rot rose into his nose. One of the peregrine falcons nested in the crooks of the bundled cables that kept the bridge out of the river flashed by, her screech on repeat.

Henry sent her a big red bird of his own and tipped the bottle to his lips. The glass clicked against his fangs as he drained the second half of his cheap whiskey in one long pull, hoping to dull the ache of Boothe's betrayal.

He blinked away his tears and flicked his empty into the dark. The bottle hummed as it spun. A falcon cried as it dove past his shoulder. Henry ducked and watched the bird turn into a shadow outlined by the sliver of setting sun.

"Fuck you, Chelsea!"

The newspapers had named all the bridge falcons as

some kind of celebration. They survived the encroachment of man, digging out a little place of their own in this new modern ecosystem, and since Chelsea Park was next to the 3rd Street entrance on the east side of the bridge, the old girl buzzing the tower of Henry's horned head had received a fitting name. Her little tufted mate was named Leo after the lion statue at the center of the park.

Henry rolled his eyes.

After watching the predators wheel and dive, snatching meals from the air and pavement with their razor claws, Henry determined their survival was a foregone conclusion. After man spent the next thousand years destroying himself, the falcons would emerge from the ashes to feed on the survivors until there was nothing left. Then they would die, too.

Fuck.

Henry pushed off the edge and spread his arms. The wind whistled past his horns like the scream of a plummeting jet. Tears squeezed through his slitted eyelids, and the city lights dotting off the waves broke into blurred fragments. The flapping of his hood trailing out behind him sounded like applause.

He imagined people lining the shores of the East River, watching him fall with wonder in their eyes. Children pointing. The entire crowd clapping and holding their breath in anticipation.

From the corner of his eye, he saw Chelsea in a dive, keeping pace. Henry laughed, and the rushing air stole his voice. His field of view filled with chopping water, and an air horn split the night. One of the children in his dark suicide fantasy looked up in delight. Amélie, her mouth open and her eyes wide.

Ladies and Gentleman ... the Amazing Henry!

Henry broke upon the water, and the blackness swirled around him as he sank beneath the surface.

THE SCENT of pepper stung his nose. Sticky moisture like snot along his upper lip. He opened his eyes and squinted into the open square of sunlight beating his face and heating the fabric over his thighs and chest. He licked the ropy fluid oozing into his mouth and smiled as memory flooded through him. Salsa verde from Rocko's Tacos.

He'd done some open mic stuff at The Reginald Comedy Showcase, a dump in the basement beside the Hyatt on 72nd and Clarke. The air had been thick with smoke, but Henry still managed to see Samantha sitting at the table with the spotlight shining through her raven hair. He felt punched if not gutted. Pain rumbled from his nervous stomach. He started sweating, feeling fatter and balder with every glance her way.

After stumbling through the first two minutes of his set, Henry had found his rhythm and finished strong with the bit about the doughnut hole. Roaring laughter and applause drowned his pounding heart, and he looked down to see Samantha wiping tears from her eyes. He went straight to her table and stammered through an awkward conversation that ended with her holding his hand as they ran across the street through honking traffic.

They sat in front of Rocko's until the awning lights flickered off for the night and finished their first date with a handshake that Henry felt lucky to get. But a woman like Samantha would never want to be with a slob like him. So eventually Henry came to his senses, staying up until five in the morning sucking the rest of the salsa from the tops of soggy tortilla chips.

Then ice cream after that.

He saw her the following Friday. She waved and smiled. He vented a breath that had felt trapped for a week. Reggie yelled at Henry for going over his ten, but that hadn't mattered. Samantha laughed until tears were back on her cheeks. Applause washed over him, like the flap of his clothing in the wind as he fell.

Henry sat up in a crinkle of plastic and a tinkle of glass. Orange metal walls with rust at the top. The wet scent of old food and filthy grease. Diesel exhaust and fry oil. He craned his head, trying to gather his bearings, recognizing the fluttering awning peaking around the corner of the building barely visible above the rim of the dumpster. He was in the alley behind Rocko's Tacos, and he'd been right about the crap on his upper lip. He'd know that salsa verde anywhere.

"Motherfucker!"

Henry pushed slimy trash bags off his lap and rolled to get his hands beneath him. Why hadn't he splattered against the water?

I had to have been going a hundred miles an hour.

He planted his feet and rose to peer over the edge. Traffic roared by at the end of the alley. Taxis and buses. A bike messenger and pedestrians dressed like tourists off the Redding Trail from the beach.

"What the fuck?"

Henry dug his feet into the piled garbage and reached for the top of the dumpster to hoist himself out. He would flee from the light then figure out his failed suicide from the shadows, aided by another bottle of booze.

A bag burst beneath him, rolling his foot and making him pinwheel his arms on the edge of balance. A slick of used oil spread under his toe, and his legs spread in a seam-ripping split.

Henry fell forward, smashing his face into the side of the dumpster, making it ring like a gong.

On his back again, staring at the open square of light above him, driving his fists into the trash at his sides.

Glass shattered under his right fist. Henry snatched his hand back then held it up in front of him, warm blood dripping into his eyes. He dug his fingers into the broken glass, tears washing blood from his eyes. A wicked shard stuck out about seven inches from his bleeding fist. He plunged the makeshift knife into his neck and raked the glass across his throat.

Blood sprayed in an arc. It spattered the dumpster, running down to mingle with the fluids dripping through a hole in the rusted metal onto the asphalt below. He lost his breath in a wheezing gasp bubbling up from under his chin. No pain. Only pressure. And heat radiating into his face.

Henry opened his eyes as the sun dimmed, the square of sky above the dumpster compressing and narrowing. His energy and will pumped out in the fountain of blood that slowed with every heartbeat. He stared at the pinprick of light in the center of his vision fading into the distance.

The trash could no longer hold him up, and Henry fell into the dark.

Heat across his chest felt like Amélie's embrace.

I'm here, sweetie. Daddy's here.

SOMETHING DUG into Henry's back. He shifted to the side to ease the discomfort and rolled down the side of the tree where he'd been leaning. He opened his eyes. His breath puffed the dry pine needles away from his face in little swirling tornadoes.

Rustling in the leaves above him swelled as a fresh breeze sent the dry underbrush skittering into the shadows. Light danced across the worn path before him in a tidal pattern of limbs bending and retracting in the wind. He reached up and felt for the wound at his throat.

No torn flesh. No blood. Even the cuts on his hand were gone.

Henry sighed and pushed himself up off the ground. He sat with his hands in his lap, leaning forward over his spread knees, and cried until tears and snot made a glistening puddle in the dirt.

He couldn't get Amélie out of Hell. He couldn't join her. He apparently couldn't die, but he sure as hell wasn't living. He couldn't do shit, and that's exactly what he felt like.

Fucking Boothe and his fucking … *shit.*

Henry looked up and saw the city through the trees. Above the north side, he sat on one of the hiking trails in Bradford Park. There was a liquor store a block down from the entrance. A nice dark alley behind it. He wiped his nose with his sleeve that still reeked of old tacos, waiting for night to fall. He would get good and drunk again, then he'd throw himself off Treyton Tower. Fifty-two floors to the pavement. Better than water every time. Maybe one of his attempts would finally take and whatever force that was keeping him alive would just say fuck it and release him.

Henry threw the third bottle and watched it shatter in the corner along with the others. Then he turned his head to the rain and spread his arms to invite the lightning.

He walked forward and pressed his knees against the half-wall along Treyton Tower's roof's edge.

The bustling city sprawled in every direction.

Arms out at his side, he stretched to his full height. Another dive from the Amazing Henry.

Now with fifty percent more splatter. You gotta give the people what they pay for.

He took a breath and held it, leaning forward ready to let gravity take him.

"What's wrong, fella?"

The voice made his knees unhinge in frightened shock. Henry gasped as his weight pulled him backward, away from his record-setting jump. He landed on his back, the force driving the air from his lungs in a groaning whoosh.

He blinked the rain from his eyes, drew in a whooping breath, and a shadow fell across his face as someone bent over his fallen body.

Boothe!

Chapter Three

BUT IT WASN'T BOOTHE.

Henry spun away and jumped into a crouch, fangs bared and claws flashing. "About time you showed up, fucker!"

"Whoa there, fella." The demon stepped into the light of the security spot over the roof access door. He was beautiful. Carved from a stone that didn't exist here on Earth. Celestial alabaster smoothed by a gifted hand. Heartbreaking symmetry, and a lean, powerful body packed into a tailored tuxedo. A tan overcoat open at the front, with the man's hands buried in the pockets. Henry felt dirty and grotesque just being near such perfection.

His collar was turned up, although the rain didn't touch him, and a black fedora with a white band crowned his slick black hair. His shoes gleamed like mirrors, and his ebony eyes glinted like swirling mercury. He rolled a toothpick across his lips, smiling in what appeared to be genuine pleasure. He removed the toothpick, holding it like a cigar, his brow furrowed with concern. He walked to the spot where Henry had been perched, ready to fly, and pointed at the city with the toothpick. "You weren't trying to … kill yourself, were you?"

His voice sounded like some old-time radio actor.

Henry looked around for another bottle — he'd brought plenty — and spotted one laying on its side in the corner. He scooped it up and squatted to his heels. He took a long pull, and belched heat back into the air. "So what if I was?"

"Only a dame can make a man hot enough to murder another. Or himself." The man walked away from the ledge and leaned against the wall next to Henry with a dancer's grace. "What about it, fella? Lady problems, right?"

Henry grunted and looked away.

"I knew it. Money and dames. What else can make a man want to end it all?" He pulled the toothpick out of his mouth and frowned at the chewed end, shaking his head. He flicked the pick into the corner and pushed off the wall, reaching into his pocket for a fresh one. Before putting it between his teeth, he paused and pointed it at Henry.

"There's other fish in the sea, you know? Don't end it all over one dame."

Henry, sick of the man's prattle, shattered the bottle on the wall and jumped to his feet. He hunched forward and thrust his chin at the man's face. "You really think the dames will like *this*?"

Instead of pulling away, the man leaned in for a closer look. Curiosity, sympathy, then pity. He shook his head and slid the toothpick between his lips, sighing through his nose. "Poor, poor Henry. What did Boothe do to you?"

Henry reeled away, pressing his fist into the wall for support, grinding tiny shards of glass into the skin of his knuckles. "How do you know my name? Did Boothe send you?" Henry raised his bloody fist and jabbed a finger at the man's face. "You tell that fucker he's dead when I see him."

The man's pity transformed into mirth, and his gleaming teeth shone out through the beacon of his grin. He extended his hand. "The name is Mandyel, and it is my esteemed pleasure to meet you at long last."

Henry's hand fell on instinct. He clasped hands with the stranger. Trumpets rang in the distance and the rain slowed to a drizzle. He pumped Mandyel's hand and the rain stopped. Clouds parted. Moonlight spread across the roof, setting puddles ablaze, swirling light like eyes beneath the brim of a fedora.

Mandyel loosened his grip and leaned back against the wall. He shook a handkerchief from his coat and wiped the blood from his fingers. Henry let his hand drop and shook his head. "Who are you?"

"Let's just say I work for the boss."

"What, God?"

"The only boss there is."

"Good. Then *you* can tell him I'm trying to get into Hell."

Mandyel looked out into the night, rolling the toothpick in his mouth. "Why would I do that?"

Henry stepped to the side to break into Mandyel's line of sight. "Because Boothe tricked me into killing the men who murdered my daughter." His voice hitched, and the pain hit his shoulders. Henry curled into it, clutching his stomach. "And now my baby girl is in Hell, and Boothe's bitch lover is back in his fucking arms. Amélie is all by herself. She doesn't deserve to be in Hell. Or alone. I need to be with her. Please. You tell him."

"Ah, but that's not how it works. Hell is not a night club. Nor a place to plan a family vacation. You go there, you get punished. *Eternally*."

Henry wiped his nose. "It's not fair. She's just a little girl. She's innocent."

"The kind Lucifer likes best."

Mandyel glowed white in the red heat of Henry's rage. Henry roared, lunging with a vicious swipe of his black claws, but Mandyel was a whisper and gone in a thought. His slash hit only air, and Henry lost his balance, crashing into the wall where the man had been standing.

"Is that how you treat a friend?"

Henry spun toward the voice. Mandyel stood with his hands behind his back, shaking his head, eyes full of sad regret.

Henry leaned his head back, caught his breath, and said, "Never even see you before and suddenly we're fucking *friends?*"

"Every friend I ever had was a stranger at some point. Besides, I came bearing gifts." He slid his hand into his front pocket and brought it back out with something pinched between his forefinger and thumb. He flipped it like the pre-game coin toss, and it spun through the air, humming and winking, singing along an arc into Henry's palm.

Not a coin, but a ring. "The fuck is this?"

"It's a ring, fella."

"No fucking shit it's a ring. What's it do?"

"Put it on."

"What's it *do?*"

"Come on, Henry old pal." Mandyel's voice fell to a seductive whisper. "Put it on."

He narrowed his eyes and stared at Mandyel's smile. He nodded and shrugged. *Fuck it.* Henry slid it on but nothing happened. "Great. I put it on. Now what?"

Mandyel swept his arm to the side, indicating the small window in the stairwell door.

"What? Does it let me walk through walls?" Henry walked to the door and caught a man staring at him from the darkness of the stairwell.

But it wasn't someone on the other side, the window's surface was mirrored.

Henry saw his face in the reflection. Well, not *his* face, but a human face. Handsome and trim. All of his hair. A short beard without any gaps and patches. He reached up and touched his forehead. He could see his horns in his periphery, but not in the reflection. He couldn't feel them under his fingers. "What is this?"

"The first of many gifts." Mandyel walked over to stand behind Henry's shoulder, eyeing him through the glass. "You put it on your right hand, and people will see this construct. Handsome but normal. Free to move in the daylight, with nobody screaming when you step from the shadows. On your left hand, you go back to the monster. The *true* you."

Henry snatched the ring off and flung it into the corner next to the broken bottles and chewed toothpick. "Fuck you! I don't want your fucking gifts. I want my daughter back."

"What if I told you I could help you get her out of Hell?"

Henry froze. His anger cooled. "You can do that?"

"Boothe did it for his lover, didn't he?"

"Yeah, but so can you?"

Mandyel smiled and pulled the toothpick out of his mouth. He dropped it then ground it under his foot like a cigarette butt. "I'll be back in a few days with an offer."

"Fuck a few days. I want her now!"

"Don't worry, pal. They're not hurting her yet."

Henry slumped in relief. "How do you know?"

"They're not hurting her because they want her for something else."

Henry covered his eyes with his hands. He imagined the terrible things they could do to a little girl, and his stomach roiled. His thigh muscles quivered. He fell to all fours. "What do they want her for?"

"She's being groomed."

Henry nodded. He rose to sit back on his calves, still on his knees. He looked up into Mandyel's face. "Grooming her for what?"

"To be an agent of Satan."

Henry's shoulders lifted with a bitter chuckle of resignation. "Well, that's just fucking fantastic."

"Well, pal, given the alternatives, I'd say *so*. The point is, you're playing for the winning team now. Enjoy your gift, and give it a couple of days. Or not. It's *your* choice."

Henry looked at the glittering ring in the corner then back at Mandyel. He couldn't tell the man to go fuck himself because he was already gone. Henry stood and plodded to the corner. Then he dug through the bits of glass soaked with rain, bourbon, and blood. He pulled the ring into his palm and shrugged. "Why the fuck not?"

He put on the ring and the rain returned in full force. Thunder in the distance. Maybe trumpets.

Chapter Four

EVERY TIME HENRY had passed the banana vendor on his way into Burg Foods back in the days before he'd found fame, and long before he'd been murdered, he'd felt a pang of guilt tighten the skin on his neck. Like the guy was watching him pass by all that farm fresh goodness for the shiny crap from the conglomerate produce machine. Guilt made way for anger. Who was *that* guy to judge someone for doing what they could for their family?

Fucker.

Henry could always feel the man watch him go into Burg Foods with that judging glare. And each time he went through, he had always wanted to spin around, stick his head through the narrowing gap, and shout, "Hey pal! I'm broke, and they got watermelons for a *goddamn* quarter!"

Henry walked down 26th, spinning Mandyel's ring on his finger in nervous repetition. He wondered if the banana guy would even be there tonight. Maybe a different fruit would be in the cart after all these years. Maybe he would stop and talk to the guy. Learn about his family. The struggles of selling produce in a crumbling market. Probably not.

He and Samantha had shopped at Burg Foods in the early days of ramen and flavored water. They made the seventeen-block trek from the apartment with paper thin walls and the perpetual funk of kimchi, into the bright light of savings. Burg Foods specialized in dented cans, wilted lettuce, and prices that fit the budget of a struggling comic and an ER nurse working the swing shift.

They hid behind the toilet paper, watching shoppers compare prices and consult coupons. Making up ridiculous conversations with the accents to go with them until they were howling with laughter. She had always been more comfortable acting like a fool in public, while Henry had always felt a creeping self-consciousness that quickly blossomed into embarrassment. But he would die for her laugh.

He never told her, but channeling Sam's easy comfort on-stage had been the only thing to swell the crowds. Her oblivious self-assurance had become a character he'd wear during shows. Down to her half-shrug and eye-roll that later became *his* trademark. Clueless self-deprecation endeared him to so many fans. The critics gobbled it up.

He imagined her grabbing his hand as he turned the corner onto Deveroux. She would swing his arm and laugh at his scandalized expression. He would rein her in with an arm over her shoulder, her cheek pressed against him.

Henry swallowed the grief and shook his head. Forced a smile and glanced at his reflection in the window plastered with weekly specials.

Who is that handsome man?

His smile became a grin, and he walked through the wheezing automatic doors to stand bathed in a rush of memories that left him breathless. That wet cardboard smell. Dirt pushed into the corners with only the high spots truly clean. Dated pastels, and crackling jingles bleating from the dated sound system. Like a time warp.

But Henry hadn't checked out the vendors outside, so he spun around and stepped away from the other shoppers on his way to the stack of baskets. He pressed his nose to the glass and cast his eyes right and left, but there was no one out on the curb. No vendors. Graffiti, traffic, and garbage. Just like the rest of the city. And he felt a pang of sadness for the lost vendors he'd once been annoyed by. He shook his head and turned to go deeper inside. His eyes caught a guy doing a hyper two-step with a harmonica jammed into his mouth.

An open cardboard box on the ground at his feet.

Homeless dancing vet.

A little helps a lot.

God bless.

Not a single person so much as glanced the vet's way. Heads down and hustling. The box skittered away in the wind, empty. He could turn shit like that into five minutes that would have the audience laughing at their own shame, and it would make him feel better about also being one of the people who walked by without looking.

Henry grabbed a plastic basket with a broken handle and headed to the right, past the registers and the cooler full of wilting flowers. Through the two rows of greeting cards, and into the fruits and vegetables. That cheap vitamin smell prickled his nostrils. Bright colors arranged in a wet rainbow. Dribbling mist shining the tomatoes.

Henry stopped in front of the apples. The nearest one was fat and red, glistening with a coat of wax. He scooped it up and rubbed it on the front of his hoodie. Fourteen times. He pulled it away and examined the burnished spot with a critical eye, swallowing the saliva threatening to pour from the corner of his mouth. When was the last time he had eaten good food? Fresh food? Standing beneath a bright light for all to see while he satisfied a craving or two.

He crunched into the crisp flesh. Juice burst into his mouth. He tilted his head back to keep the tears from spilling. Tart sweetness flooded his senses. Memories flashed like snapshots.

The caramel apples from the lobby at the Guzman Theatre making his goatee sticky. Samantha picking drying bits of sugar from his mustache. Burned apple pie from the first Thanksgiving at the new apartment after Henry recorded the new special. Comedy album of the year. Instead of celebrating, he sat on the kitchen floor with her pregnant ass in his lap as she cried her apology into his neck.

Feeding Amélie applesauce from a tiny rubber spoon while she giggled and bobbed in her pumpkin seat, smearing baby food into her hair.

He swallowed and blinked his eyes clear. He sighed and lowered his head for another bite, and caught the eye of a little blonde girl walking next to a woman leaning over a crate of avocados, her face obscured by the tumble of the bleached ponytail brushing her shoulder. She smiled and waved. He smiled and waved back. Then the girl bounced away as her mother tugged her hand and moved on to the bread.

With their backs to him, they could have been Sam and Amélie, walking hand in hand down the street.

The apple tumbled from his fingers. He dropped the basket behind him and fled. Pushing through the shoppers blocking his way, he went out through the 'in' door and ran past the dancing harmonica vet. Down a few blocks, dodging pedestrians and muttered curses, he angled into an alley and squatted behind a dumpster over a vent of oily steam.

He leaned in the shadow of the building behind him. The darkness that could hide his ugliness from the world and its pain from himself. He slipped the ring off and transferred it to his left hand. He became the monster, wrapping himself in night, and launched from the asphalt, swirling in and out of the shadows to outrun his memories.

But of course they caught up.

They *always* caught up.

He stood cloaked in the deep shadows of the stone wall surrounding his old neighborhood, the setting sun stretching and spreading his cover along his front lawn. Samantha stood in the front window, a glass of wine in her hand, looking up the darkening street as if waiting for something.

To be so close yet so far from her felt like blades through his being.

How much he wished he could walk through the front door and tell her he was still alive. How he wished he could step back through time before he died and was cursed to return in this demon form. How he wished their daughter was still alive and not trapped in hell.

Wishes were pain in their truest form.

Henry slid the ring from his left hand and held it in his fist. He could put the ring back on his right hand, become a normal looking human she wouldn't even recognize as her dead husband. He could go up to the front door and say he was lost. He was just looking for a bathroom. He was selling shower curtain rings. *Anything* for a look in her eyes without the terror inside them that would come seeing his true form.

He nodded and squared his shoulders. He'd think of something. He aimed the first finger of his right hand at the loop of silver. Samantha jumped back from the window and walked out of view.

The hum of an engine. He squinted into the headlights of a car that turned in front of him and pulled into his driveway. He shrank back and jammed the ring back onto the first finger of his left hand. He crouched down, dug his feet in for purchase, and prepared to rip out the throat of what better be the fucking pizza guy.

The beige sedan rocked as the door opened and the driver stepped out. The fucking cop. Mike Stone. He jumped out of the front seat and closed the door as Samantha appeared on the porch. She glided down the stairs with her arms held out in front of her. Stone scooped her up, spinning her bare feet above the grass.

He set her down and their lips met in a kiss. Henry leapt over the wall with a roar that split his lungs. He threw himself into the twisting shadows and ran away.

He knew they'd been together that one time, but clearly this was more than a *one-nighter.*

How could she move on so fast?

How could she have forgotten me so easily?

He ran until he couldn't breathe. Until every step felt like pushing through Play-Doh. He rested in the dark under the stairs next to The Shoeshine Pub, sweat pouring down his forehead to track with the tears. He wiped his nose on the cuff of his sleeve then took the ring off, holding it up to a sliver of light from a flickering street lamp.

A tiny sculpture stood out in relief, carved all the way around in exquisite detail. A frog eating the tail of a hissing serpent on its way to devour the frog. "Am I the frog?" Henry rotated the ring, following the image through the loop. "Or am I the snake?"

He jammed the ring onto the first finger of his right

hand and pulled himself out from under the stairs. He squinted against the light coming from the signs and windows then headed into the blaring music of the bar. He was sure he could find *somebody* to sleep with a monster in there.

~

HE FOUND a girl ready to get just the right amount of drunk then follow him to The Registry Arms just down the street. By the hour or by the night, there were no long-term rates at the Registry. Melisa *with one S* was a staggering goth with a black ribbon around her throat. Eyeshadow ran in black trails down her cheeks as she doubled over with laughter. "You are so *fucking* funny!"

Black stockings and blacker boots. A skirt that had barely covered her ass, and a black shirt so tight, the ridges of her nipples poked through the fabric. She had been directly behind him when he entered, merging with the crowd funneling into the pub. "Fuck Richard, you know? I'm gonna blow the first guy who buys me a drink."

On instinct, he jabbed her with his elbow while reaching into his pocket. "Oh God, I am *so* sorry. Please let me buy you a drink in apology."

She eyed him up and down, smiling over her shoulder to her girlfriends. "Richard who?"

"Excuse me?"

"Don't worry about it, honey." She grabbed his arm, falling into step beside him. She leaned in to whisper, "Cranberry juice and vodka."

True to her word, she had his pants down before the door latched shut, and he stood and looked up at the stained ceiling, unsure of what to do with his hands. Later, moaning and writhing beneath him, she dug her nails into the back of his neck. "I want you to choke me when you cum."

He paused mid-thrust, staring at her in confusion. "What?"

She drove her pelvis into him with a snarl, jerking his head down and biting his ear. "Choke. Me."

He pulled away from the pain, and his orgasm gathered at once. He pulled his hands off her breasts, closing his fingers around her throat. She bucked beneath him, gasping in pleasure.

Afterward, lying on his side in the dark, with her rasping snores rocking the bed, Henry rolled the ring between his fingers, watching the frog eat the snake eat the frog by the light of the Registry's neon sign. He fell asleep with the heat of guilt burning his cheeks.

Chapter Five

HENRY KEPT his eyes closed against the morning sun filling the room with its aggressive smile of light and curled into the sheet with a groan. He was not a *rise and shine* kind of guy. The bed rocked, and a draft shimmered across his back as Samantha threw the sheet back and rolled her feet to the floor.

Shuffling footsteps to the bathroom, and the soft click of the closing door.

She had always been an early riser. Even when she had stayed up late. At a show or a party when they were younger. Up most of the night when Amélie had strep throat. Sitting by her bed, reading Winnie The Pooh and doing all the voices. Waiting for the antibiotics and codeine to kick in.

When his grandmother had died.

His biggest doubter. His loudest detractor. Grandma. He'd told her he'd be somebody and she'd laughed in his face. All the terrible things he thought about himself, she threw back at him with oblivious cruelty. But the worst? She never thought he was funny.

"Your *friends* may think you're funny, Henry. But *I* don't think you're very funny. Me. Your *grandmother*."

"Grandma, I'm going on stage in front of ten thousand people."

"They're just *people*, Henry. They're not your family."

"Samantha thinks I'm funny."

"Jesus. She's a *Protestant*, Henry. They think *everything* is funny. Have you eaten yet?"

Every once in a while, Henry still picked up the phone and started dialing her number.

A stroke got her while she'd been hanging out her window, yelling at Saul Hines to keep his dog out of her flowers. Her neighbors hadn't exactly celebrated, but the tenants seemed relieved after she was gone, as if they had all exhaled a breath they hadn't even known they had been holding.

Nora Jenkins from across the hall had yanked Henry into an embrace, then pulled back to point at his grandmother's door. "When I was a girl, my father had a barn. Nobody would go into this barn. Because of the bees. A big hive!" She spread her arms to the limit of her five-foot-tall frame to illustrate the size, and her eyes had opened so wide, Henry thought they might tumble right out of her face.

"But the men came. Smoked the bees away and moved the hive to another barn. We could finally go inside. *That* was your grandma."

He never figured out what she was supposed to be in that story. The bees or the barn.

After the funeral, he sat on the edge of his bed, crying into his hands. She would never see him make it to that next level, the biggest one, the one where he could rub it all into her bitter face. The sobs only slowed when Samantha sat next to him, rubbing his back and whispering in his ear. "Shhh, it's okay. It's okay, baby."

They sat like that for hours. Henry crying. Samantha comforting. The next morning, she was up with the sun. The smell of coffee had roused him from a dream about his grandmother sitting in the audience, eating olives. Unimpressed.

He snuggled the sheet up under his chin and drifted down. Maybe she'd make bacon. Her and Amélie standing in the doorway with matching smiles. His jaw cracked in a yawn. He heard the bathroom door open. Footsteps stopped short of the bed. Henry floated up, worry creasing his brow, dream and memory in a war of confusion.

It wasn't Samantha beside him.

A gasping breath.

Then a scream ripped into his head like the swelling signal of an approaching train. His heart shot panic into his throat. He extended his body in a shocked line of rigid electricity, leaping away from the shriek.

He tumbled to the floor, the sheet tangling around his arms and legs. The scream continued to rise until it severed with a ragged inhale. Henry popped his head up to see *what in the world*, and saw Melisa standing at the edge of the bed, staring at him with horror that spread her face out like bread dough. Cords and veins bulged in her neck. Purple fists were clenched against her thighs.

Clinging sleep fought with his sprinting heart, and Henry rose up, staggering back when his feet got hooked in the sheet that pooled on the floor. He caught his balance. Focused on Melisa as she lost another breath.

She tipped her head back, but her eyes rolled down to keep Henry in sight. He held his hands up in front of him, wincing as her shrill wailing hit the frequency to shatter glass.

"Easy! What the fuck?"

Still screaming. A backward step.

"Come on, calm the fuck down before they call the cops."

Another hitching breath. Another scream. Another step away from him.

"Look," he said, pointing at Melisa with his right hand while trying to cover his red dong with his left. "*You* asked *me* to choke you. I just wanted some meat and potatoes."

He glanced down at his pointing finger. The one without the ring.

"Oh shit."

He held his hands with his fingers splayed like he was displaying his polish. Without the ring he'd converted back to a monster as he slept.

"Fuck!" He dropped to his hands and knees, jerking the sheet out from under him. It ripped in two, and he threw the remnants over his shoulder. Jeans and socks, shirt and hoodie. All pressed into a wrinkled pile against his chest.

Melisa's screams finally stopped. The room filled with her rough panting punctuated by Henry's grunts of frustration.

He snatched up his underwear, tossing them out of the way where they spun and flipped up past his forehead, hooking onto the horn over his right temple. They fell, hanging over his right eye until he swiped them away. The ring fell from a fold in his tighty-whities. It rolled away. He slapped his hand over it before it could get out of his reach. He sighed with relief and straightened to his knees, a smile of triumph freezing his face.

Melisa jumped to land on her knees on the bed. Leaning back in a wide stance, she dug through her purse with grimacing focus. Her eyes widened and she withdrew her hand, flipping the purse over her shoulder.

It spun in an arc, scattering its contents in a suspended nautilus before slapping into the bathroom door. The black satin choker bobbed as she swallowed, her pale tits heaving with her breath. Empty fist trailed behind her. Shoulders back. Hair in crazy anime spikes. The hand that emerged from the purse held a silver canister, the spray nozzle pointing at his face.

Henry chuckled. "Whatever that is, it ain't gonna work." He tossed his head to the right, and his underwear swung to the side like cotton bangs. Melisa's eyebrows drew down, her mouth twisted into a sneer of anticipation.

She shot Henry in the face with pepper spray, and Henry was wrong.

That shit *worked*.

He threw himself back with a howl. Burning and stinging filled his mind with panic. The pepper spray splashed into his palms, squeezing through his fingers in stuttering spurts that coated his face.

A flood of snot and tears.

The backs of his knees hit the threadbare recliner against the wall. He fell back into it, and his clothes jumbled up over his face, blocking the spray and soaking up some of the dripping acid ... *bullshit.*

Henry worked his hands together under the clothes and slipped on the ring. The hissing stopped, and the springs in the bed squeaked as Melisa stepped back to the floor.

He pulled the clothes away from his face, squinting through pain and tears.

Melisa's mouth hung open in confusion, the spray can dangling at her side. She fell back with stilted steps, sliding her feet through the crap from her purse.

He stood. With the ring on, he looked like a man again. He dropped his clothes on the bed and pulled the underwear off his head. He wiped his eyes with his forearm.

Goddammit! That just made it worse.

Melisa's frown deepened, and she took another step back, passing through the bathroom doorway. Henry pulled on his underwear, and the soaked pepper spray hit the sensitive skin of his testicles. He sucked in a hissing breath, then blew it out in a whooping holler.

He focused on the sink behind her. He rushed forward, pulling his underwear away, trying to lower them as he ran. Melisa's eyes sprang open. She gasped as she lifted the can, and Henry slid to a stop with, "Come on, woman!"

Pounding on the door. He turned, his distraction filled with fresh pain as Melisa swung a kick to his balls. A spike of agony stabbed Henry to his collarbones.

"GWAH!"

He screamed and fell to his knees.

She unloaded the rest of the spray into his face, and he threw himself back, bucking and kicking, vomit and snot spilling onto his chin.

Melisa ducked into the bathroom, then slammed the door as a pounding from the other side of the room ended with a CRASH — the door splitting from the jamb and smashing against the wall. Henry rolled to his knees, swiping sticky pepper spray from his face and sucking in rib-splitting gasps that threatened to launch puke into his throat. His pulse pounded in his temples, and his vision turned red.

Anger sent pain into the corner. Barely there, he stood to his full height and removed the ring. A fat sweaty hump in a tracksuit rushed in brandishing a bat. Another hump that looked like the first one's twin followed him in with a revolver pointed dead at Henry's chest. With an accent that sounded like he was speaking with a carrot cake in his mouth, Hump shouted, "What you do to the girl, hey?"

Henry slid the ring onto his left hand and let out a roar.

The Humps stopped short, wrapping each other up in their panic to escape from the demon that had just burst out of a man. Henry roared again into their gaping faces. Rage and frustration. Heat rising from his steaming breath.

The Humps disappeared in a clatter of slapping fat and stomping feet.

Henry followed them into the hall, echoing with slamming doors. He sprinted its length, moving in a blur that left a blistering wind in his wake. The window at the end grew as he neared. He was a rocket through the glass. He soared through the air in a freeing moment of joy, the musical chimes of shattered panes glittering in the morning light.

He floated into a roll that carried him into an alley, slamming the asphalt on the tops of his shoulders. He came up cloaked in shadow, then vanished into the city, using the shadows in the corners and doorways as shelter.

In the alley behind Boothe's apartment in Martinsburg, Henry switched the ring to his right hand and walked to the hanging fire escape. As he set his hand on the first rung, a voice floated up from the shadows from under a plain metal door. "Damn, son. What's wrong with your eyes?"

He squinted to see an old black man sitting on the concrete with a cigarette pinched between two fingers. He couldn't make out the name badge, but Henry had seen the man pushing a broom and scrubbing the sidewalk before. He grinned and pulled himself up the fire escape.

"Allergies."

Chapter Six

HECTOR'S BASEMENT was a comedy club in Bay South, right off the docks. A gentlemen's club from eleven to seven, they changed the color of the stage lights at eight and brought out the comics until they closed. Half-priced drinks and appetizers fried in the same oil that had been boiling since breakfast, and the membership *dues* they took at the door kept them exempt from the citywide no-smoking law.

It had been Henry's favorite place to try out new material. Crane operators and forklift drivers rubbing shoulders with law firm interns and dog hair stylists. The broadest audience he'd ever seen. Rolling the whole place into a grand laugh meant the joke couldn't get any better.

Henry loved the stage, too. Only about eight inches above the main floor, it had poly-carbonate tiles lit from behind with light wheels that put him in the mood to dance when the colors changed in silent rhythm. Some guys complained about the distraction, but Henry could have put Hector in his will for how much those lights had influenced his pacing.

Blue started the observation. Purple, and he would roll into the premise. Red for the body of the joke leading into the beautiful green of a well-crafted punchline. White would give him a break while he set up the next bit, but before the blue came back, some yellow for the callback, and he'd wait for the laughter to die before moving on.

Dodging the stripper poles got a little distracting, and he always left smelling like fish and beans, brushing glitter out of his hair for days.

The security staff had been a bunch of crushing gym bros. Friendly as could be, but always ready to jerk a knot in someone's head, and Henry had only seen things get out of control twice in all the years he'd played there.

His favorite had been Carl Iglesias, a juice monkey at the door who blotted out the sun. With a neck wider than his head and a Gorgon scowl, most of the static stopped before even coming through the gate. If you could get past Carl, there was nothing inside that could stop you.

After all these years, Carl still stood at the front checking IDs. Like a jacked grandpa ready to chase the kids off his lawn with the fury of an Aztec horde.

Henry stood in line, fingering the crinkling package in his hoodie pocket. Carl used to have a crippling addiction to chocolate sandwich cookies. Not the national brand, but the cheap knock-offs sold in the big club stores. Henry had scored a few sleeves at a bodega on 43rd, but it had been a long time since he'd been here.

Fame and marriage made it difficult to find time for a titty bar next to the river.

Carl waved a couple of giggling chicks through the door and held his hand out to Henry with a bored sigh. Henry slapped a package of cookies into a hand as big as a frying pan, and froze in expectant fear when his old greeting from years ago spilled out of his mouth before he could stop it. "*Que pasa, maricón?*"

Carl straightened with a low growl, but his eyes flicked down to the cookies. He paused in confusion, then looked up, squinting into Henry's face. "Do I know you?"

"Yeah, man," Henry said, his mind racing. "I'm Mike. Mike Serafino." Carl shrugged, shaking his head. "I used to work the mic waaaaay back in the day. Me and Henry Black and Paco Riggs. Grace Jennings and that chick who always came out in the apron."

Carl's face lit up. "That's right! She used to hold the mic and smoke cigarettes with those oven mitts on. She was fucking hilarious. Whatever happened to her?"

"She's living as a man now. Trying to be a cop in Seattle."

"No shit?"

Henry tilted his head. "All true."

"Well, right on. You working tonight? Coming through the front door?"

"Nah, just here to watch. Maybe some scouting. I wanted to bust your balls a bit and give you them cookies."

Carl smirked and brought the package up to his nose, peeling the cookies open with his pinkies up for class. He took a deep sniff, rolling his eyes and grinning. "Just happens to be my cheat day, too." He hitched a thumb at the door behind him. "*Vamos.* We'll catch up later."

"Good deal." Henry slapped Carl on the shoulder on his way by. Carl waved with a cookie before popping it into his mouth and held his hand out for the next ID.

Heading to the bar that stretched the length of the club on the left side of the room hit Henry with nostalgia hard enough to buckle his knees. Topless dancers gyrating to pulsing salsa. Grease hanging in the air thick enough to taste with his mouth closed. Worn carpet and flaking paint.

It was like no time had passed. Henry took a deep breath and hitched his leg over a stool. He caught the bartender's eye with an upraised finger then spun around to face the stage.

Henry was three drinks in by the time the second comic took the stage. The first guy had been a hype man. Hackneyed punchline crap to get the crowd to quiet down after the girls were gone. Henry thought he had even heard a couple of his *own* jokes, but the next guy was all original. His stuff was rough, but Henry could see the glimmer, and the kid had a good delivery, despite the quaver in his voice. A little rushed, but Henry didn't hate it. He tipped his glass in a quiet salute.

"You enjoying yourself, pal?"

Henry turned to eye Mandyel. Glossy black shoes under cuffs that fell right to the tops of his heel. Dark gray wool suit. Two buttons with the bottom one undone so the jacket broke over the hand resting in the front pocket of his pressed slacks. Crisp white shirt beneath a thin black tie. Red pocket square. A gold cuff-link sparkled as he poked a toothpick into his mouth, and his hair swept back from a sharp part at the side.

People were noticing. Henry shook his head. "Do you have *any* fucking idea how much you stand out? What do you want?"

"Try to be a little grateful, Henry. I gave you your life back ... sort of."

"Yeah. What do you want?"

The bartender leaned across the bar to slide a glass full of rocks and amber into Mandyel's hand. "Here you go, Mandy."

Mandyel slid a bill into the bartender's hand and lifted his drink, pausing at Henry's expression. "What?"

"That kind of smooth is just mind-boggling. You come here often?"

"No, this is my first time." He tipped the glass, knocking half the drink back in a swallow.

"Then how the fuck did he know your name?"

"That's what I chose."

He looked at Henry as if explaining something to a child, and Henry threw his hands up. "Fine. Just tell me why you're here already."

"For the same reason you are, Dear Henry. To stop Order From Chaos. They're bad news."

The memory of the gun pointing at his face. The beady eyes. Amélie's screams.

He slumped forward and stared at the floor between Mandyel's feet. "Why me? Why *my* family?" He scrubbed at his welling tears. "Who the fuck am I to anyone?"

"Order From Chaos are on a mission. Like the name of the cult would imply, they weaken the world's resolve so demons can have it all to themselves. They destroy faith."

"Why? Just to party?"

"No, Henry. If the will of humanity dies, they can align themselves with Hell. Create an army beyond count. And whoever is controlling the order will try to use this army to storm Heaven and kill God."

"Wait a second." Henry drained his glass and turned to give Mandyel his full attention. "God can be killed?"

"I don't intend to find out."

Henry recoiled from the heat in his gaze, and the intensity in Mandyel's squared shoulders. "What are you gonna do?"

"The important thing here is that humanity is at risk. Not just *your* family, Henry. Angels ... we don't have the strength here on Earth that we once did. Demons have the upper hand, and they gain strength every time they create chaos. Even a tiny little bit." He leaned on the bar and swirled his glass. "Every time they destroy good lives or stage horrible acts of violence that shake a community or a nation, their power grows. Every person they kill. The rich. The young. The *famous*. You kill those kinds of people, and you also kill something in the people that follow them. Demons *love* when they can kill someone famous, *especially* if they can drive them to suicide. Whispering to them in their dreams. From the shadows. If a star dies, someone who had it all, if somebody like *that* doesn't think life is worth living, then how can a *fan* possibly make it?"

"Wait, are you saying all my favorite rock stars and shit were tricked into killing themselves by demons?"

"Only the really good ones. Like you."

"Fuck you!" Henry looked around with flinching embarrassment, continuing in a lower tone. "You're saying it's *my* fault my daughter died because I was good at my job?"

"No, Henry. I'm saying your daughter died because you were one of the greatest of all time. Legendary. Nearly without peer. Have you happened to read a paper since you died? The outpouring of grief was incredible. Very touching."

Henry sat back as shame reddened his face and crushed his shoulders. He hadn't paid attention at all. "I've been busy. What do you want me to do?"

"There is an event being held at the Viazo Grand. It's called the *Draconis Arcanum*, and it is an auction of relics and objects, dark and forbidden items, that could help us stop this war before it starts."

"What? Am I supposed to buy something? I'm fucking broke, *Mandy*."

Mandyel smiled. "We give you the money and the list

of items to buy. Win the auctions for these items, and you will gain the attention of the Purveyor, the man we believe to have the item we are *ultimately* seeking."

"Whatever. I don't even care anymore. If I do this, you get my daughter back. Right?"

"Of course, Henry. But it's only the beginning."

"The beginning of what?"

Mandyel dropped his toothpick into his empty glass. "Pal, this is the start of a mutually beneficial relationship."

Henry leaned back and closed his eyes, his imagination already running wild with images of Amélie in Hell. Fire coming at her in waves. Her eyes wide with terror, mouth opening to scream for help.

The audience erupted in applause, snapping Henry out of his morbid reverie. He clutched at the edge of his stool to keep from falling to the floor. He looked up into Mandyel's eyes. "And what if I say no?"

The angel vanished.

Henry slid from the stool in shock, slapping his hands on the bar for support. Mandyel's words echoed to him as if coming from a long tunnel, and Henry felt a freezing wind ruffle his shirt.

You won't.

Chapter Seven

THE VIAZO GRAND was a moss-covered edifice in the middle of a vineyard in Fairmont Hills. A Scottish church until 1924, when Lord Ludlow Thompson floated the whole thing to American shores north of Burg City. Stone by stone, including three miles of cobbles, he even had a steamer dedicated to nothing but the ornate ironworks.

A hotel for the super-wealthy, it boasted award-winning sparkling wines produced on the grounds and a stable of world-renowned thoroughbreds. Of course, the Illuminati conspiracies had grown over the years, and Henry had even included some of it in his act when he'd taken a poorly-received political detour in the late nineties.

He looked at the beautiful people passing by his window as the limo slowed to a stop under the covered entry, and even in his Mike Serafino disguise, he felt plain and poor.

His driver was a thick Italian man with impenetrable eyes and a permanent scowl named Francesco. As Henry ducked into the limo, the driver leaned in. "Yo, I don't get paid to talk, so keep it down back here."

"Whatever, Oddjob."

The slamming door was his rebuttal.

Henry sat with his anxious hands stroking his tuxedo slacks. He wasn't exactly a stranger to money, but these people's wealth made him light-headed. Nervous with bile rising in his mouth, he cleared his throat for the hundredth time, cursing Mandyel, Boothe, and even the guy who had taken their toll at the head of the Fairmont Bridge.

"The fuck am I doing here?" he whispered.

The same feeling of unreality had washed over him when he won an Emmy for the writing on his first sitcom, *Bye Henry.* A show that had turned the shlub husband/hot wife trope on its head by putting the wife in a wheelchair for two seasons after a car accident in the premiere episode left her paralyzed from the neck down. Unable to support her, physically *and* emotionally, she divorced him. Writing himself as the bad guy had been *gold.*

Unable to hide from the industry any longer, he went to a tailor recommended by his agent, Herb Miller. Two grand on a suit that still hadn't hidden his gut. He'd stood in front of a mirror while Samantha and Herb fussed with the details.

"Why am I here?" he had asked.

"I've been trying to tell you how good you are for fifteen years, ever since you walked into my office with a notebook full of jokes." Herb was a small man. Sixty with the body and skin of a thirty-year-old, he always managed to sound offended.

"Yeah, but I just don't know what to say. It's like I'm gonna get there, and security's gonna throw me into the street. A bus'll come by and splatter me with a convenient puddle. A dog will probably pee on my head."

Samantha snickered, but Herb stepped in front of him,

adjusting his black tie, smoothing it flat and shaking his head. "Just tell the joke about the Brazilian doughnut shop. The one with the missionaries."

"That's not my bit."

"Really?" Herb shrugged. "Too bad. That's a helluva bit."

Under the pre-presentation lights, Henry had realized that everyone in the room had been playing a part. His role was the uncomfortable upstart whose overnight success took nearly twenty years. He sat back in relief. Imagined himself as an affectation. Made all his character traits the traits of a *character*. By the time he hit the stage, he'd been comfortable showing the world how little he belonged there, and it cemented his reputation as one of the industry's most genuinely nice guys.

Henry knew better.

"What am I going to see there?" he had asked Mandyel.

The angel looked at the floor, poking another toothpick between his teeth. "The worst."

"*Fuck.*"

He closed his eyes and thought about Mike Serafino. His history. How he felt about his family. The disdain for his own social circle. That same discomfort with the phony bullshit of people trying to impress each other with self-defined standards. "I can do this."

Francesco opened the door and stepped back with a bored smirk. "You coming out or what?"

Henry slid out and stayed to block the door. He buttoned his jacket and flicked imaginary dust from his thigh. Picked microscopic lint from his sleeve. Shot his cuffs and straightened his tie.

Francesco's laugh was sandpaper on stubble. "I see why he likes you so much, but get the fuck outta my car."

"You're not gonna get a tip with that mouth."

"Story of my life. I'll be around."

Henry walked with a calm certainty, as though he were getting settled on-stage. Reaching for the mic as applause washed over him. They owed it to him. Even if he *didn't* deserve it.

A woman on the granite steps leading into the grand entrance reached her hand toward Henry as he neared. He almost reached out to shake it, but realized she was waiting for his invitation before he could embarrass himself. His eyes fell to her skintight red dress as he slipped his invitation into her hand. Heavy parchment paper with a gold dragon spreading its wings across the header.

She took it with a wide, welcoming smile, and Henry shifted his eyes to the giants posted on either side of the door at the top of the steps.

Rooted like trees, their heads swiveled in security camera arcs. Matching black suits, sunglasses and haircuts. A coiled wire climbing from slab neck to ear. Black canvas slings holding weapons at their backs, barrels angled at the ground peeking out from behind their bulging thighs.

"Welcome to the Viazo Grand, Mr. Serafino." She handed him an auction card with the same dragon atop a list of items for sale. He took it, sighing as if he were put out by her speaking to her. Her smile widened, unfazed. "Drinks and food are provided the entire time, and if you need *anything*, just look for my sisters in red. They'll do their best to accommodate your needs."

She dismissed him by looking over his shoulder at the next guest in line. He ascended the steps, trying not to look like a yokel on his first day in the big city.

The front doors opened onto a lobby of marble and gold with giant stairs carpeted in red leading to the second floor. A moment of Mad Hatter vertigo enveloped him.

How could the inside seem so much bigger than the outside? The ceiling appeared to arch into clouds. Gilded frescoes and plaster molding. Henry closed his mouth and looked for the nearest drink. A woman in a red dress swirled by. She looked like the girl outside, to the smallest detail. He grabbed a glass of champagne from the passing tray at her hip, and she flashed the same smile he ignored on the front steps.

Henry mingled through the milling crowd with noncommittal nods until he landed in a quiet spot next to a nude statue of some muscular god. Henry looked over to find the leaf-covered dick right at eye level.

Perfect.

The staff behind the front desk stayed busy the entire time Henry hid himself in the corner. After his third glass of bubbly, they disappeared, and a hush carpeted the lobby.

The double doors at the top of the stairs swept open, and every eye rose to behold a beautiful woman in a silver dress slink to the marble railing. Red hair was piled intricately high upon her head. Silver bracelets trailed tinkling chains from wrists to tiny waist. Her neckline plunged, and her breasts, pressed in and up by shimmering fabric, sparkled with silver glitter.

She looked like a captured mermaid.

"Ladies and Gentlemen." Her sultry voice carried across the throng, echoing from the arches and pillars as if she spoke from a hundred mouths. "I am pleased to preside over this year's *Draconis Arcanum*."

She swept her arm to the side as she turned, indicating the doors leading into the heart of the hotel. "Shall we begin?"

The crowd compressed toward the stairs in a swelling bustle of fabric and hushed conversation. Henry stepped in among the people passing by and found himself pulled into the current then carried into a room with quartz floors and mahogany walls. Light washed out of the coves in the coffered ceiling, and a raised stage holding a granite pedestal and lectern stood in the contrast of a soft spotlight.

Most of the people wanted to be in the front, but Henry resisted the push, hanging back at the last row. An empty seat on the end next to a small lady in a sequined gown. Gray hair and wrinkles, she clutched her black purse to her chest and looked around with wide eyes, bright with the spectacle. Nobody sat on either side of her, and she fluttered like a lonely pigeon looking for food at the feet of passing tourists.

Most of all, she looked safe, so Henry took his chair with a smile, picking up the numbered placard from the cushioned seat before settling in beside her.

"Oh, good," she said with a wheezy voice soaked with wine. She patted his knee and smiled. "Now I have an auction buddy. I'm Thelma Wencsis from Oregon."

"Mike Serafino. Right here in Burg City."

"Oh? What do you do, Mr. Serafino?"

"Nothing," Henry chuckled. "I find as many different ways to spend my family's money as I can."

She threw her head back and laughed. Breathless and hollow like the town drunk in an old western, she flapped a hand in front of her face. "You sound just like my grandchildren."

"Really?"

"Oh, yes. You know, when my Paul died, I had such a hard time keeping the little leeches at bay."

"How'd you finally do it?"

"I had the youngest one murdered."

Henry stared, struggling to hold his smile of polite

interest. Thelma grinned and laughed again, holding a hand to her stomach. Again, she patted his knee. "Oh, my. I was only teasing, but you should have seen your face." She wiped tears from her eyes and fanned herself with her own numbered placard. "No, I just bribed them until they shut up."

"That seems a lot better."

"No, Mr. Serafino. I love my grand babies. I say *babies*, but to be honest, the youngest one is almost thirteen. Do you have any children, Mr. Serafino?"

"Call me Mike, and no. No children."

"They're a pain in the ass. You should keep it that way." She rested her hand on his thigh and leaned toward him. "Don't get me wrong, they're a *joy*. Like the youngest one I just mentioned. She goes to the Sanctum Glorianis."

She looked at Henry with the expectant expression of a bragging grandparent. He smiled and nodded. "Really?"

"Oh yes. She is scheduled to graduate the torturing portion of this semester at the head of her class."

Henry froze his smile again, his cheeks sending cramps into his forehead. "Really?"

"Oh, yes." She leaned in closer, and Henry bit on the urge to throw himself from the chair. "She opened a man from pubis to throat, and he barely even made a sound. She has a very steady hand. We're all so *proud*."

Henry was spared his reaction by the light rapping of the gavel. Thelma removed her hand, and he sagged in relief, following her excited gaze to the front of the room.

The mermaid stood behind the lectern, and a man in a black tuxedo over a silver vest and red tie carried a blue gallon jar full of murky liquid to the pedestal. A wrinkled cylinder of flesh coiled in a rising spiral floated inside it, drifting back and forth with the man's steps.

"What is that, Dillinger's cock?"

Thelma giggled. "Oh, Mike." She slapped him with her bidding placard and settled back to read the auction brochure. Henry pulled his out and read it.

The Apophis Tail: The evil lizard of the Nile brought forth to coil around the sun, removing the light and power from Ra himself, he was struck down in mighty battle, the tip of his tail torn free during his banishment to the underworld. Lying just under the horizon, he eats the souls of those foolish enough to wander from the path between worlds.

The possessor of The Tail manipulates from the shadows, protected by its mantle of darkness. The price of its use is yet undis-covered, but its power is immeasurable, even exerting influence over its surroundings without the blood offering required to activate its gifts.

It was long held in the collection of Samuel Easton, kept in a cavity beneath the floor of the Bethel Waterfront Trust and Loan. When Bethel burned to the ground, the only building which remained after the inferno raged through the city was Easton's bank.

Legend maintains it was the protection afforded by The Apophis Tail itself. Bidding begins at $4M.

Henry peered over the edge of the brochure as the bidding began, placards rising left and right. The mermaid's voice flowed through her auctioneer's stream with a magical lilt. Graceful and musical. Mesmerizing. A siren's call. She moved onto the next item. Henry sat up straight and took a deep breath. This was the first item on his *buy* list.

Ofskelor's Last Wish: Hand written and bound, this manuscript recovered from the estate of Regal Anthony, Marquis of The Sumerian Order, is believed to be written in an undiscovered demonic language by Ofskelor himself, after being trapped in his human form during The Great Confession. He was known to desire his knowledge be given to mankind upon his death.

Though often considered a fabrication, it may yet provide secrets *of great value, and would fit nicely into an amateur collection. Bidding begins at $127T.*

It looked like a plain diary. Heavy stitching and ragged leather.

Henry opened the bidding. Against a man on the phone, they were the only two raising their placards. Thelma looked up at him out of the corner of her eye, and he smiled down at her when the man on the phone shook his head and hung up.

"Yours at three hundred," the mermaid said with a smile.

The next item was a gnarled staff that shot fireballs. Thelma won it with a staggering seven-million-dollar bid. She giggled and clapped, leaning into Henry with bright eyes. "Wait until they see what their Grammy got!"

Thelma talked about her Paul through the next three items while Henry smiled and nodded at what he hoped were all the right spots. He interrupted her with a pat to the knee when his second item came up. She locked her lips with an imaginary key, throwing it over her shoulder with a smile.

A shining iridescent vial with a crystal stopper was set on the pedestal. The spotlight dimmed, and the bottom of the vial twinkled with a faint red light.

Kempf's Blood: While another Kempf rose through the Nazi ranks in 1941, Vernor Kempf was in South America, where he was negotiating for arcane power on Hitler's behalf. Betrayed during a meeting with what has been reported, but not confirmed, as Tezcatlipoca himself, his blood was rendered into brine containing the acidic bitterness of the Aztec god's power of dark entropy.

Able to dissolve any substance known to man, save for its impenetrable vial, it has been nearly exhausted through the years, its minute glow the only reminder of its former power. Bidding begins at $150T.

A three-way battle to win the blood pushed Henry into worry when the price went over five hundred grand. A woman in a blue dress too small for her quivering flesh sent a bloody gaze his way whenever he raised his placard. Finally, at five hundred and thirty thousand dollars, she sat back and crossed her arms with an audible *humph*.

Henry won the blood, but he had no time to enjoy his victory. The third item on his list came next. A small black knife with a stained leather handle. Coarse hair spilled from an iron grommet on the pommel. Black gems glittered, seeming to steal the light from the room for their own.

Heaven's Blade: In the forges on the shores of the river Styx, many weapons were made to aid in the defense of hell against the agents that would attempt to free the souls of the dead from their rightful place of damnation. Decorated by the hair of St. Margaret, harvested by Veltis during her persecution, and bound by the feathers of the dove that appeared to her, Heaven's Blade can make the bearer aware of the presence of the divine.

It has been rumored that the blade may even possess the power to kill emissaries of heaven. This theory has not been tested. Bidding begins at $17M.

The mermaid opened the bidding, and Henry's was the only placard raised. In the awkward silence that followed, Henry lowered his number, and the mermaid struck the lectern with her gavel. "Done."

The murmur of conversation resumed as the next item came out. Thelma clasped her hands together and looked up at Henry in reproach. "And why in the world would you buy *that*?"

"I don't know …" Henry tried to come up with something, but a hand fell on his shoulder. He flinched away, spun around, and found himself looking up into the smiling face of a sister in red.

"Peterson would like to meet you."

Thelma grabbed his sleeve. Henry jumped with a squeal, spinning to face the little old lady with the torturing granddaughter. "Ooh, Peterson wants to see you." She lowered her voice and ducked her head in conspiracy. "You must have impressed him."

Another tap on his shoulder, and Henry twisted back. The sister was still smiling, her hand out, inviting him to stand.

"Don't make him wait, Mike."

Henry touched Thelma's shoulder on his way to his feet. "It was nice meeting you, Thelma Wencsis from Oregon."

She snatched his hand up and held it to her cheek. "It was nice meeting *you*, Mike Serafino from Burg City."

He pulled his hand away and waved goodbye as he followed the sister to the back of the room and through the double doors overlooking the lobby.

Henry was surprised by his calm and smooth bearing. With every step into the unknown, into possible danger, he felt his confidence grow. It was easy when every step brought him closer to Amélie.

Daddy's coming.

Chapter Eight

PETERSON WAS a thin black man with close-cropped hair and sharp cheekbones. His red suit hung in crisp lines, the black shirt underneath shining like oil. The white buttons and red bow tie made him look like he was ready to take the stage as part of a soul revival act.

He looked at Henry with pale eyes through the lenses of a pair of wire rimmed glasses. He took a sip of coffee from a tiny crimson cup and favored Henry with a warm smile. "I've not seen you around here, Mr. Serafino." His accent was thick and British.

"Well, I only just started collecting, myself."

"As the items you won would suggest. Except for that last one. *That* one usually keeps 'em at bay."

"I'm not interested in what anybody else thinks, Mr. Peterson. I like what I like."

Peterson tipped his head with another smile. "Don't we all, Mr. Serafino." His brows wrinkled and looked up at the ceiling. "*Serafino*. Can't say that name's familiar to this group."

Henry shrugged. "I'd like to change that."

"Would you, now?"

"I would."

Peterson nodded like as if weighing his response, then he flashed his teeth in a grin that Henry thought was probably the last thing a mouse saw before being eaten by the family cat. "How'd you get started with this, then?"

"My uncle was a collector. Kind of the black sheep of the family. He and my dad were … *connected*, let's say."

Peterson nodded and took another sip of his coffee, all polite attention.

"My mother was very religious. Sheltered me growing up. Hid the family business from me, well, tried to. Not my dad so much. But my uncle took me under his wing and showed me …" Henry trailed off. He wanted to *sell* it.

"What did he show you, Mr. Serafino?"

"That Christ is the oppressor. True freedom lies in darkness. He showed me the *way*, Mr. Peterson."

"Ah, that he did, my son. That he did."

"Anyway, they were both killed last year in a war on the docks with some Russian gentlemen and the BCPD."

Peterson narrowed his eyes. "I think I may have heard of that one. A bad bit of trouble there. I'm sorry for your loss."

"Thank you."

"With *that* being said, would you be interested in selling anything from your uncle's collection?"

Henry laughed and shook his head. "Maybe someday."

"That's a shame. So, if not to sell, then only to buy?"

"What I'd *really* like to do is learn. I want to experience the darkness that my uncle told me about. As much as I can. To experiment."

Peterson set his coffee cup down and clasped his hands in front of him. And he was back to that mouse-eating grin. "I think I can help you with that, Mr. Serafino." He held up a finger and his face grew serious. "But the cost may be a bit steeper than today."

"Costs are no problem, Mr. Peterson."

Peterson reached into his inside pocket and removed a brown business card. "That's what *everyone* says before they've seen the menu."

He handed Henry the card. Thick and heavy, the back was blank, but the front held an image of a crowned man riding a camel. A phone number in Roman numerals along the bottom. A sense of antiquity ran through his fingers.

Peterson stuck his hand out, and Henry took it in a friendly shake. He ignored the chill slithering up his arm as Peterson looked into his face with eyebrows raised. Peterson nodded and released his grip. "Call that number and mention my name. They'll take care of you."

"Thank you so much, Mr. Peterson."

"No, thank *you*, Mr. Serafino."

Henry needed a piece of cheese.

HENRY SETTLED into the backseat of the limo. He rested his head against the leather and closed his eyes. The car rocked as the porter from the Viazo Grand put his purchases into the trunk. Francesco pulled away from the hotel, and light in the cabin faded.

Ice clinked in a glass next to him, and Henry flinched away, snapping his eyes open, heart hammering against his ribs.

Mandyel lowered the drink from his lips and regarded Henry with amusement. "Calm down, pal. It's only me."

"Holy shit, man. You can't do that." Henry leaned back and put his hand over his heart with a dramatic sigh.

"My humble apologies, Dear Henry."

"Yeah well, I got all the stuff on your evil wizard's shopping list."

"Did you, now? That's just aces."

"Aces? What the fuck?" Henry looked over and leaned back to get all of the angel into his view. "What is it with you? Where do you go when you're not here?"

"Wherever I choose."

"So where did you *choose* to go while I was in Castle Hellmouth just now?"

"I was stationed nearby."

"How near?"

"Earth."

Henry threw up his hands. "That's just great. Ma Kettle rolled a plus ten fire damage with that staff, and Bring Out The Funk Peterson acted like I would make a great appetizer, but you were nearby. On *Earth*."

"I'm but a thought away, Henry. I can be wherever and *whenever* … I *choose* to be."

"*Whenever?* How about you do me a solid and go back in time and save me and my kid before all this shit kicked off?"

"It doesn't work that way."

"Of course. So, what's the knife for, anyway?"

"Couldn't tell you."

Henry pinched the bridge of his nose. "You don't know why I was told to buy it?"

"That's not what I said, pal."

"Right. You said you couldn't tell me. Like, you're not allowed to?"

"No, like I choose not to."

"Why?"

"Because you don't need to know, and because I don't want to tell you."

Henry shook his head, watching the street lamps whiz by through the window. "Anyone ever tell you that your communication skills could use some fucking work?" He slapped his hands on his thighs. "You're just like Boothe."

Mandyel leaned forward, his eyes blazing. Henry drew back, pressing deeper into his seat.

"I am *nothing* like Boothe. Unlike that criminal, I will do *exactly* as I say. You give me what I want. First. *Then* I will give you what I promised. No trickery. I chose to give you a chance, despite my misgivings, and you chose to help. If you now choose to go back on our deal …" He leaned back and smiled. Just friends out for a ride. "I walk away, and you can find someone else to help you save Amélie."

Henry swallowed his tears. Battled the rage. Took a trembling breath and nodded. "You really *are* a bastard."

Mandyel swirled his drink, keeping his eyes on the whirlpool of whiskey. "So, you met Peterson?"

"Yeah, and he gave me a card."

Mandyel switched the glass to his other hand. "May I see it?"

"Sure." Henry fished out the card and handed it over. "I don't know what it means, but there's a number at the bottom."

The angel brought the card up to his eyes, squinting at the image on the front. "Paimon."

"Is he the Purveyor?"

"He may be. This depiction is of a demon that commanded legions. Before ascending to power he was a teacher of forbidden knowledge, often dealing with obscure and hidden things."

"What kind of things?"

"Better to not talk about it, pal."

"You're so fucking dramatic. So, is that the guy or not?"

"Maybe. The guy or a guy who knows him. Only one way to find out." He passed the card back to Henry and reached into his overcoat pocket. Then he pulled out his hand and tossed something over.

The brass box gleamed as it twirled through the air, landing heavily in Henry's surprised palms. About the size of a deck of cards, though heftier. Complex designs carved into its surface reminded Henry of old manuscripts at the museum. He turned it over and over, reflecting light into his eyes, seized by its beauty. A seam along its narrow edge caught his attention. "What is this?"

"Open it."

Henry looked at Mandyel, but saw nothing in the angel's eyes. He opened it like a box full of spiders, turning his face away from whatever might jump out. The brass block parted on invisible hinges. The carving continued on the inside, and there was a gold circle with a burning sun pressed into it. Glittering silver mesh covered a pair of holes along the outside edges.

Henry looked at Mandyel with a sarcastic tilt of his head. "What the hell is this? The Holy Cellphone Of Antioch?"

"Sorta." The angel tipped his head at the object. "Try it."

"How am I supposed to try it?"

"Press the gold button."

Henry rolled his eyes then mashed the button with a petulant thumb and brought the thing to his ear.

The pop and hiss of an open line, and the tinny voice of 1930s phone operator. "What number, please?"

"Um … never mind." He snapped the phone shut and dropped it into his lap, pulling his hands up to his shoulders. "What the fuck is that thing? Was Phil Robertson right? Do I have a direct line to Jesus?"

"Not exactly, but they'll get you into contact with just about anybody by name. By the number is even better."

The car came stopped and the motor died. Henry looked out the window. They were in front of his building.

"You know what?" He turned to finish, but Mandyel wasn't there. Just an empty glass with melting ice on the seat. "Fuck it."

Chapter Nine

HENRY SAT on the couch in Boothe's loft.

All that modern white and stainless steel gave him a headache. His stomach rumbled, and something pulled at his attention like a half-remembered appointment. He shook his head and flipped the brass phone open, pressing it to his ear and waiting for the operator.

"What number, please?"

He read the number on the card.

"One moment, please."

Henry sagged back into the cushion and closed his eyes. He held the phone between his head and shoulder and dropped his hands in his lap, twirling the ring on his finger over and over. He had always hated talking on the phone. Texts or emails were okay, but telephones sucked time and energy like a starving whore. A little bit of his soul every time he raised it to his face. "Can I get some hold music or something?"

A click and a hiss, then Johnny Cash's voice rose through the static. *When The Roll Is Called Up Yonder.*

"Um … thanks."

Henry rubbed his forehead and tried to ignore the hunger and that nagging feeling that he was missing something important.

"Yeah, man." The deep voice in his ear sounded thick and distorted, like the guy was eating a burrito. "What can I do for ya?"

Henry sat up, juggling the phone back to his ear when it fell from the crook of his neck. "Is this the Purveyor?"

"Maybe." The man ended with a loud yawn.

"Well, I'm looking for something."

"Whatcha looking for?"

Henry pulled the phone away and growled in frustration, looking to Heaven for some patience. He took a calming breath and brought the phone back up. "It depends on what you're selling."

The guy sighed. "Look, man. I'm not playing games here, okay? I need to know what you called for."

"A guy named Peterson told me to."

"Peterson gave you this number? Shit, man. Why didn't you say so?"

Henry pinched the bridge of his nose and shrugged. "I don't really know."

"So, check it out. I'm gonna talk to the dudes at the Viazo, and then I'll call you back."

"Whoa. No. I need to speak with the Purveyor."

The line went dead.

How the fuck's he gonna call me back? This magic phone actually have a number that shows up on Caller ID?

Henry snarled and slapped the phone closed with one hand. He drew it back to sling it across the room, but paused when he caught its gleam from the corner of his eye and thought better of damaging a relic. He sagged and dropped the phone on the cushion beside him and stood. He held his forehead in his hands and swayed as nauseating hunger rolled through him.

The pulling grew, and he couldn't think. He slid the ring from his right hand and slipped it onto the left. Hunger boiled over to a crippling punch to the gut, and the pulling in his mind became the howl of the city's unceasing pain.

Henry tore the expensive tuxedo off and threw it to the floor. He rushed into the bedroom and pulled his hoodie and jeans on in a frenzy. A quick stop in the kitchen to fill a pitcher full of cold water. He closed his eyes and drew a deep breath, tipped the water up, and with every swallow, the screaming pain washing over him from the shadows of the city compressed into a single point of agony.

The smell was intoxicating.

Henry set the empty pitcher down and pulled a full breath through his nose, savoring the sweetness that filled his mind with anticipation. He crossed the room to the window and pushed it open. Stepping through, Henry braced his feet on the stone sill and leapt into the night, wrapping himself in shadow, rocketing through the dark like a laser. The brightness of the pain he'd sensed from his apartment pulsed like a beacon.

He planted his feet on the edge of a roof above the pain and anxiety floating up from the alley below, then stepped out of the shadow to stand in the light and hunkered down to look at three hoods bent over a dirty hobo in the space between two dumpsters. One drew a foot back and launched a kick that Henry heard connect all the way from the top of the building.

Laughter and shouts. The three punks jumped back as fire sprang out on the homeless man's pants. His scream rose to Henry's ears, and though its flavor coated his palate, it wasn't what he craved.

Henry longed to taste the pain *he* caused. Not the pain of innocents.

He stepped off the edge and plummeted into a drop that billowed his hoodie out like gray wings, roaring with joy that screamed like a missile.

Three shocked faces looked up as one. Two light. One dark. Eyes wide and staring. Mouths hanging open, expressions twisting from mad glee to panicked confusion. Henry landed with his feet planted on either side of the hobo's hips. The wake of his fall washed around him. A deafening rush that blew the flames out and swept greasy trash into whirling eddies that filled the air with garbage.

"All right, fuckers!"

Before the haze settled, Henry roared again and lunged at the nearest kid.

The punk backpedaled, his red hair sticking up in gelled spikes. A clawed swipe to his thigh, and Red fell with a scream of pain. Blood spurted into his face as he toppled.

He attacked the next kid, the one who had put the boot to the homeless man. Henry delivered a kick of his own, his shin plowing into the kid's upraised arm, shattering bone and continuing into the side of his head. Boots fell in a marrowless heap, and Henry spun to grab the trailing hood of the third kid before he could make his escape.

He snatched the kid back and twisted, throwing him through the air.

The kid hit face first into the brick above the homeless man's staring face. He bounced back to land in the alley next to Red who was crawling back, pressing his hands over the spraying wound in his thigh.

Red's face glistened with sweat and blood, the skin pale and gray. His mouth spread in a pleading grimace as terror rolled off his body in waves. Henry inhaled a gust as he stalked the kid's frantic movement. Red's good foot kicked in useless arcs. Henry's shadow fell on him. He froze, his eyes widened to their limits.

Henry dropped to straddle Red's legs, sniffing at the kid's body like a dog as he rose to his face. He looked into Red's eyes and saw a spiraling darkness as his system shut down from blood loss. Then they closed, and he fell back.

Henry caught him by the shoulder and thrust his mouth into the kid's neck, nuzzling past his jacket collar. He bit down, and the blood flowed into his mouth. Terror and pain pulsed into his throat. Henry pulled Red's departing life force into his own body then reared up to roar into the night as electricity flowed into him.

His senses sharpened. Light and sound bursting onto his brain. The struggles of the terrified Hobo Bob behind him. The detached fear of the two unconscious kids on the ground. The millions of souls crying out all over the city.

He turned and lifted Boots by his shattered arm. His eyes sprang open in his dark face, and the scream of pain as he jolted awake was like the start of a second course. Henry shook Boots like a doll, then lowered him to the ground and stepped on his chest. The punk's cry died with a whooshing sigh, and Henry tore his arm from its socket, planting his foot deeper into his collapsing chest.

Blood burst from his mouth and nose, covering Henry's foot. A gout of blood shot from the kid's stump of a shoulder, and he died with his life force floating up into Henry's body, filling him with a spasm of ecstasy and strength.

He dropped the arm behind him and caught his breath, his heart pounding like he'd just done a bump of cocaine. While running a marathon. With a refrigerator on his back.

Hood scrabbled through the dirt and blood, struggling to reach the alley's mouth. His thoughts were fragmented with disjointed colors and flashes of his screaming face. Henry stepped over his flailing form and spun the kid to his back. His face was split and pouring blood, filling Hood's mouth in sputtering pools as he coughed his own life into the air. Henry squatted down and tore his jacket open, exposing his T-shirt.

He exposed the kid's belly … then stopped.

"What's a matter?" Hobo Bob was leaning forward, his sneakers still smoking, watching Henry with an unsteady gaze.

"What?" Henry said.

"Fuck that kid. He was gonna burn me up when you showed. I mean, you look kinda fucked up, but you put it out." The guy swayed, catching himself with an outstretched hand to the dumpster. "And then you stopped." He shook his head and furrowed his brow. "Why'd you do that? Stop, I mean?"

Henry looked back to the kid splayed in the alley. "Cuz he's wearing my shirt."

"He's a thief, too? God damn *kids*."

Henry Black's Comedy Monster Tour. Black with a red pentagram covered in cartoon blood. His most success-ful piece of merch ever. Twenty bucks and it went all the way up to 4X. He'd died on stage more times than he could count, but killed more often than not.

Just not like this.

Hood coughed a bubble of blood that broke out of his lips in a spray that splashed into his open eyes. They didn't blink. He drew in a ragged breath and let it out, trailing through the air with the wet sigh of his death. Henry scrambled forward, panic squeezing his heart. "No, no, no," he whispered.

He bent over to look into Hood's eyes, and the life force washed up, passing by his lowered head. His stomached heaved, and Henry sat back on the kid's thighs.

The fuck is wrong with me?

He let the power dissipate, drifting up and away. He didn't reach for it. The thought of filling himself made him sick to his stomach, even as the energy from the other two coursed through him.

Sirens screamed in the distance, and Henry's head snapped to the end of the alley. A crowd had gathered, smartphones aimed into the dim tunnel of asphalt, dumpsters, and blood. He spun away and staggered to his feet. Slapped the hood and rushed into the shadows. Away from the street lamps shimmering off the pools and spatters of crimson.

He curled forward and walked on numb feet. The kid's face swelled in his mind, and became something else in his imagination. Softening. Round and smooth. Blonde hair spreading beneath it. The face of his daughter.

Amélie staring into the sky with dead eyes, blood turning her garish.

He couldn't save her. She would be stuck in Hell, and they were going to turn his baby girl into a monster just like him.

Samantha. He needed to see her. Confess that it was his fault. Their precious daughter had been taken from them because of him. Stuck in Hell because of him. All those kids murdered at the Burg Spires Massacre. It was all him.

He wanted to hold them both. Tell them it would be all right. And it *would* be. If he could just talk to Samantha. The only woman who had ever truly understood him. Loved him for his flaws. Blind to how deep they really ran.

"Where you going, buddy?" Hobo Bob held out a sloshing bottle of cheap wine. "Let's have a toast."

Henry wrapped himself in shadow and flew into the night.

Then he would apologize to his wife for damning their daughter.

Chapter Ten

THE BEIGE SEDAN was back in the driveway. That meant the fucking *cop* was there.

Henry rose out of the shadows behind the bushes in front of the living room windows of the home he had died in. The shades were pulled, but he could see the shapes of the couple inside. Dancing.

Fucking dancing.

Music pressed against the glass. Frank Sinatra. Good music to dance to, but Henry had hated dancing when there was even the tiniest possibility that he would be seen. Samantha tried for years to get him over his fear of looking foolish when he started his flailing. A fat and sweating monster under the lights and scrutiny of everyone in the room.

Fuck that.

Another thing to regret. Samantha would come around the corner, twisting and rocking, her hips pulling his eyes to her waist. She would beckon him with a smile, and every time, a part of him had wanted to surrender. Step into her waiting arms and move with her. But Henry didn't understand that kind of freedom.

Now she was in the arms of another man. And Henry fucking hated that guy.

Their silhouettes swayed to the big band rhythm, probably coming from his fifteen-thousand-dollar McIntosh audio system. That remote had taken him a week to figure out, but it had also been his greatest purchase. The house. The Lexus he hardly drove. None of it had been as satisfying as sitting in his leather recliner with Rush rattling the windows.

The Mike Stone silhouette pulled away from the Samantha silhouette. Henry leaned forward and narrowed his eyes. The cop crossed the room and bent over to pick his phone up off of the coffee table. His dumb head nodded, then he jogged back to Samantha where she received him into an embrace, tipping her head for a kiss.

He let her go and she sagged back as he ran out of the room. Henry pressed himself down out of sight. Mike popped out from around the corner and ran to his car, his jacket trailing behind him as he searched for the opening of his sleeve. He peeled out of the driveway, his headlights washing over the glass above Henry's head.

Henry stood to look at Samantha, standing with her arms wrapped around herself, lonely shoulders slumping forward. He wanted to crash through the window and sweep her up, but Mike's siren pierced the air as he sped away, and Henry shot into the shadows, soaring into the night after his wife's boyfriend.

Following Mike Stone was easier than facing *her*.

Cloaked in the darkness that reached out to him as he passed, Henry followed the sedan, careening through the streets, blue and red lights flickering behind its grill. Over the Thompson Street Bridge along the path Henry had just taken. Anxiety crept into his gut when Henry realized where Stone was going.

At the head of the alley where he had killed three kids for setting a homeless man on fire. Where he had raged like the monster he had become. Or had always been.

Henry stopped in the deep darkness of a doorway under the stairs of a Chinese restaurant's lower entrance. The bare bulb above the door dangled from a thin wire, swaying in the socket as a breeze kicked up around his shoulders. He switched the ring to his Serafino hand and stepped into the flashing lights of an ambulance. A crowd milled in a ragged circle around the rear doors. Henry pushed himself into the crush of gawkers.

Stone was already out, talking to a uniformed officer next to the ambulance. Henry couldn't hear what they were saying, so he pushed closer to the thin wooden barricade and turned his ear to the conversation.

Scraps of words. Tone of voice. Anxious. Angry. A woman in yoga pants with a huge backpack on her shoulders looked at Henry with a sneer of disgust, sidling away in a hurried shuffle.

Whatever, bitch.

Henry turned back and a gurney rolled out of the alley steered by two paramedics. A third followed, huffing his fat ass to catch up. He looked like he might need an ambulance of his own. Hobo Bob sat up in the gurney, looking at the crowd like a starlet before her adoring public. His bandaged feet splayed out in front of him. He pulled his bottle from inside his jacket and saluted and the crowd cheered.

The fat paramedic caught up and reached for the bottle. The crowd booed. Henry joined them. Hobo Bob slapped the hand away and tipped the bottle up, fending off the fat paramedic's attempt to curtail his fun. Henry clapped with the crowd, and Hobo Bob bowed with the bottle held just out of reach of the fat paramedic's questing grasp.

God, if that guy falls, I'm gonna piss myself.

The gurney hit the end of the ambulance. Hobo Bob dropped his hands for balance and watched his bottle get snatched like a toddler losing his favorite toy. Henry added his voice to the disappointed groans.

Stone held the paramedics from lifting the gurney into the ambulance. He leaned in to ask Hobo Bob a question then reeled back when the answer washed over his face.

"The kid stole his shirt."

"Which one?" Stone asked. Henry leaned over the barricade to catch the words.

"The black one."

"The black kid? You know his name?"

"No, dammit," Hobo Bob shouted. "The black *shirt.*"

"You killed them because they tried to set you on fire after they stole your black shirt?"

Hobo Bob threw his hands up with a dramatic flair. The crowd laughed at his antics. "Not *me.*"

"Somebody else killed these kids and set you on fire?"

"No," Hobo Bob said, rolling his eyes. "He killed them *after* they set me on fire. Came outta nowhere and blew the flames out. Killed the little arsonist fuckers and took off when the cops showed up."

"You ever see him before."

"Hell, *evrybody* has. It was the Hooded Angel. Though, given the horns, I'm thinkin' Hooded Devil might be more like it."

Stone stepped back, shaking his head and waving for them to set the drunk inside.

"May God have mercy on your souls," Hobo Bob shouted through the closing doors.

The ambulance pulled away, and Stone turned to look at the crowd. He froze when his eyes landed on Henry.

Henry looked around and noticed the circle of empty space around him. Eyes on him with disgust. Fear. He looked down at the drying blood covering most of clothes. His heart skipped a beat. *Fuck.*

"Hey!" Stone reached to his lower back and dropped into a shooter's stance as his pistol came around to find his other hand. Pointed right at Henry's chest.

The crowd scattered in a screaming panic. Henry threw himself to the side and weaved through the stampede. Stone's voice behind him was joined by the shouted commands of the BCPD. But Henry was gone.

Shadows at the edge of the crowd swallowed him. So he fled into the night, cursing his stupidity.

Chapter Eleven

AFTER THE ALLEY MURDERS, Henry kept the ring on his right hand. It fixed the city's dull throbbing at the edge of his hearing like distant bass booming from a concert and turned gnawing hunger into a nagging heartburn that was easy enough to drown with a bottle.

He had taken up part-time residency at a seedy bar five blocks from Boothe's apartment. Like a snowbird sick of Montana winters, he vacationed at Pub Brothers Bar & Grill. Whiskey and all you can eat chili cheese fries.

He walked through the dark streets, belly sloshing, waiting for a phone call. Or for Mandyel to pop out of a burning bush.

He started watching TV in the mornings. The news was too depressing, so he switched to Telemundo and tried to laugh at the weird ass Spanish variety shows until it was time to go drink. Lonely walks full of alternating boredom and blame.

One morning, after some microwave popcorn for breakfast, he called for an Uber on Mandyel's phone, surprised to find it working. He had sat in the back, avoiding conversation while the rain made trails down the window until the Burg Spires Church of Hope finally crested the horizon.

He ran through the shower to the front door and threw his hood back, stomping water from his shoes. He avoided the eyes of Christ in the window and approached the voice coming from the nave. Pastor Owen held an open bible in front of him, pacing in the chancel, speaking softly to a group of men huddled in the front pews.

Men's Bible Study. Must be Tuesday.

Henry couldn't remember the last time he had known what day it was, his week a blur of drunken self-loathing and *Caso Cerrado*.

The pastor snapped his bible closed and stood bathed in light from the stained glass windows in the south wall. He smiled and swept his arm to the side. A man stepped from each corner with an offering plate. They leaned into the murmur of shifting congregants, passing the plate into their midst.

Someone cleared his throat to Henry's left. He flinched away, spinning his back to the wall. A huge man stuffed into a black basketball jersey stood with an offering plate held in front of him. A bull neck rising to a shaved head with a tribal tattoo crowning his stubble from temple to temple. Eyes hidden behind black shades, he stepped forward like a man who owned the world. Gritty scabs covered his knuckles, the skin along his fingers cracked and angry.

Henry tipped his head toward the man's hand. "You know they got cream for that kind of thing."

The heavy leaned in and put the offering plate right up under Henry's nose with a grunt. He stared at his reflection in the sunglasses and dug for the cash. He pulled a wad from his pocket and peeled off the top bill without looking. He raised it above the plate.

Boothe had money stacked in drawers all over the apartment. In his absence, Henry felt duty bound to spend the shit out of it. He dropped the hundred into the plate then stuffed the wad back into his pocket. He raised his chin and stepped forward until the plate's edge was pressed to his throat. "Don't steal it."

The man snorted laughter, turning with a sneer. He rolled away without a care in the world. Henry watched him waddle away with anger quivering in his chest.

Fat fucker.

Shuffling feet, and he stepped aside as a line of men filed into the rain. Some older men zipping their bibles into their jackets. A few younger men. And a couple of hard hitters that rang alarms in Henry's brain. The kind of guys that would set a hobo on fire. Or kill a comedian. Or at least steal a hundred dollars from the collection plate.

As the last man exited, Henry turned back to see Pastor Owen coming up the center aisle, his face open with questioning welcome. "I'm sorry you missed it. There'll be another session next week, Mr ...?"

"May I please speak with you in private."

Concerned, the pastor nodded. "Certainly. Please, this way." He led Henry to the side, then along the wall under the windows to a door in the front corner. He opened the door and waved Henry inside.

The office hadn't changed since the last time he'd been there. The pastor walked around him to his desk, pointing to one of the oak chairs on his way. "Please, have a seat."

Henry declined, instead changing the ring from his right hand to his left. Pastor Owen slid his own chair out and looked up as he sat. His mouth fell open in shock, and his knees folded, dropping him into his chair all at once.

His teeth clicked together, and he jumped back up, hustling around the corner of his desk. Henry shied away as if the pastor might attack him, but Pastor Owen grabbed his hand, pumping it up and down as a grin split his face.

"My goodness, Henry. I wondered where you'd gone off to." The pastor placed a hand on his shoulder. "I was worried about you."

Henry collapsed against him, overcome with guilt and grief. The pastor led him to the chair, and Henry spilled his guts between hitching sobs, wiping his nose on his sleeve like a snotty child.

There was a knock on the door during Henry's confession. He fumbled the ring onto his right hand before the door opened, then wiped the tears on his cuffs, composing himself while the pastor tended to business. He returned and asked Henry to continue.

This time Henry left the ring on, just in case.

He stopped short of telling the pastor about Mandyel and the auction. It would have led to the murders, and it was bad enough without the pastor hearing that shit.

Pastor Owen lifted a cup of coffee to his lips, looking at Henry over the rim. Before taking a sip, he said, "So this Boothe, he sold you out?"

"Yes."

"But he was able to save his love?"

"I guess."

"What would a man do to save the ones he loves, Henry?"

"What, you're taking *his* side?"

The pastor set his coffee down and shrugged. "I'm not taking sides at all. I'm just asking a question."

"Look, that guy is a piece of shit."

"Henry!" The pastor's voice cut through his anger and made him look up.

He shook his head in confusion, his train of thought interrupted by the pastor's stern tone. "What?"

"What have *you* done for the ones you love?"

The face of the dying kid in the alley. The screams of his victims filling his ears. Shame heated Henry's face. He looked down. "Yeah, I guess."

"For people will be lovers of self rather than lovers of God."

"Don't give me that bible stuff, okay?"

"The word of God is all I have above my faith. If not for that, why did you come here, Henry?"

For some fucking understanding.

"I really wanted to know if you heard anything more about the cult that targeted me." Then, wanting to feel the hate as he said it. "Order From Chaos?"

Pastor Owen sighed.

Henry looked up into his sad eyes, but he refused to let the pastor make it *his* fault. It was the cult's. And Boothe's. Even Randall's, and Henry wouldn't be surprised if Mandyel had something to do with it all, too.

Pastor Owen nodded and lifted his cup for another sip. "Yes, I've been following some recent events. Some scary stuff from the inmates I visit. Before meeting you, I would not have believed it, but there is a spiritual war happening. And not the kind that I wage in front of a congregation. Other cults surfacing. Terrifying acts." He swallowed and looked away, setting his cup down, splashing coffee over the rim to spill onto his fingers. "I am dismayed at the number of people who are turning away from God in such dark times."

"What about Samantha? Has *she* turned away, or does she still come around?"

Owen scrubbed at the spilled coffee with a white handkerchief. He looked up with a smile. "Oh, yes. She comes around every Sunday, and sometimes even through the week."

"With *him*?" Henry asked. "The cop?"

Pastor Owen's face fell, and he sighed. "Yes. I'm sorry Henry. I know she misses you terribly. You and Amélie."

"I just hate him so much. I want to kill the fucker, and I *know* I shouldn't want to, but aside from the guilt and anger, the hate is the only thing I can feel. I want to watch him burn."

Pastor Owen shocked him by laughing.

"What?" Henry said, spreading his hands in confusion.

"You are consumed by it so much that you have named yourself after the very act of revenge you desire."

"Huh?"

"I want to burn him. *Your* words, Henry. *Serafino* means *fiery one*. All the way back to the Latin. Mike Serafino. Burning Michael."

"Yeah well, I just want my daughter out of Hell."

"Be patient, Henry. Trust in God."

"Yup. Old Faithful Himself. Mr. Reliable."

"Henry. He *has* been reliable. He has been patient. He sent message after message asking you not to kill, and you did it anyway. And he has *still* not given up on you. Don't throw that forgiveness away by giving up on yourself, son."

Henry knew it couldn't be that simple, but he nodded. "Thank you."

Owen slid a desk drawer open and reached inside. "I'm almost always here." He handed Henry a business card. Crisp white and perfectly plain. "Call me day or night if there is *anything* I can do for you."

"I really appreciate this. Thanks for listening, too."

Owen came around the desk, and Henry felt uneasy in the man's embrace. Then the pastor led him through his office door, separating from him at the altar. Henry was surprised to see that night had fallen.

On his way out the door, the heavy with the sunglasses cleared his throat from the corner and stepped into the light. He slid his sunglasses off and stared as Henry passed, then he reached into his pocket and pulled out the hundo that Henry had left in the offering plate, stuffed it into his mouth, and chewed it with a smile.

Henry charged with his fists raised, but the door slammed in his face. The lock turned and the light above the door flickered off. Christ stared from the window. Henry ducked his head and turned away.

He felt someone staring at the back of his neck and hoped it wasn't Jesus. *That* poor guy had seen enough.

Chapter Twelve

HENRY LEFT the bedroom after a bone-popping stretch.

He crossed to the kitchen, fiddled with the ring on his right hand, and filled a pitcher with water. He paused with it under his lips. The morning fog cleared from his mind, and he spun to face the open living room.

Mandyel stood at the window with his hands behind his back. A gray wool suit hung in neat lines, and his hair glistened with a pomade shine. Henry slurped on the water, but it sputtered down his chin when his eyes went to the couch. He bent over to cough out the remaining moisture, and stood wiping the water from his chin and the surprise from his face.

A woman Henry had never seen before sat on the couch with her legs crossed and one foot in the air, rocking up and down. Blue high heels with straps around the ankles. Her azure dress a second skin. One hand held a crystal ashtray. The other lifted a cigarette in a silver mouthpiece. Her red lips puckered around it in a smile, and the coal flared as she pulled. Blonde hair piled on her shoulders in heavy curls. Her flawless skin glowed in the morning light.

Mandyel turned from the window, waving smoke away from his frowning face. "Good morning, Henry."

"Yeah, good morning." He tore his eyes from the gorgeous woman and lifted the pitcher. He chugged, feeling more of his energy return with every swallow, then lowered the empty pitcher to the counter. "What's going on?"

"It seems you've been invited to a party, pal."

"Oh, yeah?"

Mandyel pointed to a wrapped garment box on the coffee table. A blue bow hung from the side. "Peterson sends his regards."

Henry glanced at the woman on his way to the table. Her lips twitched with another smile.

He slid the box in front of the chair so he wouldn't have to sit next to her, then tugged on the blue ribbon. The bow fell open and he lifted the lid.

A brown mask of a fox's head. Soft and fuzzy with gold rings dangling from the tufted ears. Nothing below its nose so the wearer's mouth would be free. Underneath the mask, a dark suit with a blue tie and sash. The exact shade as the dress worn by the supermodel at the end of the couch.

Henry lifted the suit from the box to set it beside the mask, and a card fell out. The Viazo Grand dragon spread its wings over a handwritten note.

～

YOU HAVE INTRIGUED US, Mr. Serafino.
   We wish to know how deep you'll go.
   Peterson

HENRY LOOKED UP, but Mandyel's face was as inscrutable as ever. "What is this, some kind of test?"

"I don't think so, pal. Just the next step."

Henry turned the card over, and there was more writing.

ANOTHER AUCTION, but one of dark importance.

Not the standard trinkets of the average collector, but items to nourish the body, mind, and soul.

Bring a date, Mr. Serafino.

She will regret it no less than you.

I promise.

P

"WHAT THE FUCK DOES THIS MEAN?"

"It means, Dear Henry, that this may be the opportunity to learn about or perhaps even obtain, the Horn of the Lamb."

"The Hell is *that*?"

Mandyel stepped around the end of the couch to stand directly across from Henry at the end of the coffee table. His swirling black eyes widened. His fists pressed into his thighs. "It is *very* important that we get the horn, Henry. I need it. *We* need it." He relaxed his hands and raised his eyebrows, tilting his head to the side. "It can save your daughter, Henry."

Henry fell back into the cushion and stared at

Mandyel's face. His mind whirled with all the ways the angel could betray him, like Boothe before him.

Henry opened his mouth to ask the question out loud, but the answer didn't matter. He was losing his ability to care about details. Only the important things mattered. *Amélie* mattered. "Fine, let's do it."

"Even if you have to kill for it, Henry. It's *that* important."

"Yeah, I *get* it. I already said I'd do it, but only cuz you asked so nice and all." Henry turned and pointed at the woman. She regarded his finger with a haughty lift of an eyebrow. "So, who's the dame? She my plus one?"

"She is your date for the day, yes. You may need some help, and I don't want to trust it to some hooker you'd pick up in the phone book."

"So, she's like a *classy* prostitute?"

The woman laughed. Throaty and open, her pink tongue shining behind a flash of perfect white teeth.

"No, Henry. She's a demon who works for me from time to time."

"Like your Goll Friday?"

The music of her laughter filled the apartment, but Mandyel wasn't amused. "I *suppose* that's funny."

Henry waved the angel's scorn away and turned his attention to the creature on the couch. Learning she was a demon set him at ease. Talking to a beautiful woman other than Sam had always caused a flop sweat. A demon in disguise, no matter how fine? Gravy. "You don't really look like the demons I'm used to."

She raised her right hand, the silver ring on her first finger glinting as she rubbed it with her thumb. "I'm Nadia."

"I'm Henry. Or Mike. Or *whatever* you want to call me."

She nodded, and Henry turned back to Mandyel. "So, when's the party?"

"They like to start early at the Viazo. You've got an hour to get ready, so hop to it, pal."

THE MASK's eyeholes blocked some of Henry's peripheral vision. It fit perfectly otherwise, and he had to admit it looked cool. A bit creepy, but still … Nadia walked next to him in a silver wolf's mask. Her ruby lips clamped onto the silver mouthpiece. Smoky eyes challenging every man in the room.

She clung to his arm. Her hips rubbed against his as she walked with a swaying stride that even had a few ladies glancing over in envy or admiration.

"Hey," Henry said, keeping his voice low in her ear. "Are you a boy demon or a girl demon?"

Nadia pulled the cigarette from her mouth and pulled away to look at Henry with that haughty smile he remembered from the apartment. "Does it matter?"

"Not really." Henry shrugged and dropped his hand to her hip, pulling her firmly against him as they followed the crowd up the stairs. "Just curious."

Her laugh brought more stares, and Henry realized some were from men jealous of *him*. "I'm a *girl*," she whispered in his ear.

They neared the entry to the auction room, and the beginning of panic rose in his throat. The men and women were separating before the door. The men continuing inside, while the women moved into a second line flowing toward an open door down the hall.

Nadia pulled apart, and their hands trailed down each other's arms until only their fingertips touched. She flashed a look over her shoulder as she followed the others, a tightness at the corner of her eyes. Her lips pressed into a line. Henry had no choice but to break contact and follow the rest of the men inside.

The crowd pushed him into the line, and he found himself at an empty chair.

Attendees taking their seats, and the doors closing behind them.

Men shuffled and shifted, and soon an eerie quiet blanketed the room.

An occasional cough or sniff, and Henry's nerves rattled. He felt a growing apprehension. Fear rising to the surface. Even with the ring on, he could taste the despair. Like the bean dust floating on the breeze during harvest, it coated his palate as he breathed. Delicious. He wanted to gag.

Anticipation swelled, coming from the men in the masks that no longer seemed cool. Henry wanted to rip his off and run from the room screaming a warning. He sat on his hands and closed his mouth. He needed that fucking horn. *Amélie* needed it.

I can do this.

Footsteps from the aisle behind him. Henry turned with the rest to watch a couple move to the front of the room. The mermaid from the other auction led a thickly-muscled man to the stage. She wore a different dress. Shimmering green like her eyes, red hair pulled into a tail that hung over her shoulder, the tips kissing her cleavage.

Her mask was a horrifying crab head covered in iridescent stones. Its mandibles and antenna bounced as she moved. Loops of chain connecting her wrists to her waist. The man at her side wore black and red. His dark glossy beard fell from the bottom of a devil's mask that was too on the nose.

The mermaid spread her arms. "Gentlemen, for today's offering, your host will be Meyor."

A few good-natured boos, and Meyor waved with a grin shining under his mask. "I know I'm not as pretty as Ariana here, but who is?"

The crowd chuckled, and Henry was struck by how routine it all sounded. Like a cruise-ship comic going through the motions, spouting the same jokes for years on end. Waiting for laughs like ticks on a clock.

"I'm sorry, gentlemen, but I have to attend to the ladies in the other theater." Ariana bowed then moved with crisp strides to the door. Scattered applause and a handful of whistles before she disappeared through the door with a smiling wave over her shoulder.

There was history in this room, and Henry felt his apprehension rise further. Sweat trailed under the mask and down his cheeks like spiders crawling across his skin. He kept his hands under his thighs and his eyes on the stage.

Meyor made hushing motions with his hands, and the crowd settled. He stepped to the edge of the stage and clasped his hands before him. "Ariana may have what you *want*, but gentlemen ... I have what you *need*."

The stirring around him had a frantic heat. A swelling need, giddy and breathless. The taste of pain and fear in the air became cloying. Like sugar-coated maple syrup. Henry's mind screamed, *Get away! While there's still a chance!*

What the fuck is going on?

The door at the edge of the stage opened, and despite the dark opening Henry had fallen through, he wasn't prepared.

His gasp of disgust sounded so much like the appreciation around him that he clamped his hand over his mouth to keep the puke from leaving. To keep himself from screaming. Cursing. Murdering every fucker in this godforsaken place.

Thirteen naked children filed onto the stage. Chained together at the waist, they made no effort to cover themselves, watching the floor as they crossed the stage in a line.

Henry's mind froze in horror. His eyes wider than the openings in his mask, he bit his fist, but felt no pain. He couldn't do it. He couldn't sit and watch this shit.

They were already fucking bidding.

There were already *winners*.

Henry twirled the ring on his finger and tried not to look. To listen. He glanced up after an eternity of occupying his mind with puppies licking his face, and he saw her. A little girl near the end with hair like Amélie's. Eyes like his daughter's. Dark underneath. Glazed with shock or drugs. His heart ached at the pain she was going to endure.

This is one of the mysterious way you work, you fucker? What kind of god lets shit like this happen?

Fuck you!

Something broke inside him. A fundamental belief that he hadn't even known he'd had.

Henry was sure he'd never laugh again.

The girl was the next item, and Henry opened the bidding.

Chapter Thirteen

Some jackass was bidding against him. Henry wasn't listening to the numbers. He was waiting for his turn while staring at the back of the guy's head.

Meyor's eyes gleamed, his lips pulled back in a grin as he guided the men through their bids. Henry stabbed the air with a spiteful finger, his rage hot and showing on his face. The jackass responded with a higher bid, casting an irritated glance over his shoulder, the black feathers of his crow mask swaying.

You sick fucker!

Meyor sent the bid back, and Henry raised his hand.

The price rose through another three rounds. Henry stared at the back of the crow's head. Amélie's face hung in his mind, her smile wilting into grief, her mouth spreading into despair. He tensed to keep bidding, hand frozen in his lap. But Meyor had moved on to the next child.

Henry had won his bid.

He sat gasping for air, his rage a haze over his eyes. He glanced up, and the crow was looking at him over his shoulder, shaking his head. He tipped Henry a salute, and Henry nodded back on instinct, bile rising into his throat.

The auction continued with Henry swallowing vomit. Clinking chains scraped the stage floor. Meyor showing off his wares with the flourish of a seasoned barker, his smooth words like lightning from a grinning face.

Henry pressed his fists into his thighs.

How many can I buy?

He couldn't save them all. He couldn't even save Amélie.

Where is that fucking horn?

He made jokes for a living. Told stories. Made people laugh and cry.

I'm not built for this shit.

Tears sprang into his eyes. He twisted the ring on his finger.

But I'm a monster now.

He wanted to rip the ring off, become monstrous, and tear some fucking heads apart.

A ripple went through the men assembled in front of the stage. Anticipation rolled through the room, and Henry felt the energy change. From polite engagement to a heightened expectation that he remembered feeling from behind the curtain.

He had recorded his third special in Chicago. Coming off a high from his performance and interview with Conan during the promotion of his web series, *Henry Can Wait.* His name was on everyone's lips. It seemed like he couldn't turn the TV on, open a paper, or click onto Twitter without seeing some mention of how he was changing the face of comedy.

Henry Black Isn't Going to Wait. That one was on the cover of *Entertainment Weekly,* right below his pudgy mug. His puzzled expression like a punch in the face.

His interview on the *Hot Cuppa Mo* morning radio show with Mo Diaz and his twat assistant Larry the Mushroom Groom had become legend. Dropping three f-bombs on local FM only increased his demand.

"I'm not a violent man, Mo, but if Larry doesn't shut his fucking suck hole for two goddamn seconds, I'm gonna pick up that fucking phone and hit him in the face so hard that Russell Crow's assistant is gonna send a sympathy card. Fuck!"

YouTube tried to remove the videos, but they kept popping up, and for weeks, excitement for the Chicago show had kept climbing.

Just before the curtains had opened, Henry stood just behind them, peering out, looking at all those faces who'd turned up to watch him walk out and talk for an hour and a half. Sixty-seven bucks a pop. If the show was successful, he could do whatever he wanted on stage. There would be nobody with the balls to tell him *no* anymore.

If it failed, he'd go home, rest his head on Samantha's pregnant belly, and write another joke.

No opener, just a pre-recorded introduction. The voice hit the speakers, and the crowd silenced. As if a switch had killed the sound. Rapt attention. The buzz of excitement washing over Henry as a literal energy. It brought the hair on his arms to life. He waited for the same thing as them, and for a moment, he was in the audience looking up at the stage. Listening to the announcer say his name.

Together, they crested the rise, plunging down the other side, and he walked out on stage in the midst of thunder.

He never remembered doing it, but watching the video afterward showed him stepping out with his wide eyes and a disbelieving smile. He pumped his fist, and his lips formed the words, "Thank you, Samantha." Waving at the crowd and waiting for them to sit back down.

He had looked at Sam to see if she had caught it, and she had leaned back to cover her mouth, tears streaming from her eyes. She leaned over, pulling him into an embrace that he could still feel. "I love you so much."

This woman had supported him and loved him, often when he hadn't deserved it. She was in his arms, heavy with his child, and it had been the absolute best day of his life.

The feeling in the air was so much like the one that had washed over him all those years ago, that he expected Meyor to announce his name. Restless motion and rustling. Shuffling feet and heavy breathing. They were all waiting for something, and Meyor being the showman, was going to make the moment last. Tension screamed. Anticipation screamed louder. Henry longed to bellow.

Just fucking get on with it!

The children were led off stage through the door opposite the one through which they had arrived. Glassy eyes staring at the naked backs of the child in front of them. Mouths hanging open. Shuffling like zombies.

What kind of drugs are they on?

Maybe it's a spell.

Henry turned from the pathetic procession, lowering his head to look down as their little feet slid along the floor in the deep silence. The crowd fell quiet as if someone had thrown a switch. Chains dragging. Henry squeezed his eyes shut, and the silence yawned.

Anticipation became a fever. A pulsing in his temples.

His heart sprinted, heavy beats galloping through his ears.

Come the fuck on already!

"Gentlemen," Meyor whispered, and the men released

some tension in a bump of sound. Gasps and cleared throats.

"Now for the *real* fun."

Fuck this.

But Henry stood with the rest of them. Filed into a line that moved slower than the last time he got his license renewed. Keeping his head down and avoiding the whispered questions. Drilling a hole into the space between the shoulder blades of the guy in front of him. The guy's horse mask nodding as if he felt the rhythm of a song only he could hear.

A horse is a horse, of course.

Through the same door the children had been led. A room so dark, the interior didn't seem to exist. As Henry passed through the threshold, a buzzing charged through his ears and light filled his eyes.

The flash died, and he found himself inside a cavernous stone room. Torches burning in ornate sconces on the wall. A massive table in the center covered with so many candles, it looked like the galaxy in wax. A clear spot in the center of the table. Black with an old stain.

About the size of a human body.

The children stood along the wall behind the table, staring into the flickering shadows. A dirty haze of smoke hung in the air.

Henry followed the men to stand in front of bench bolted into the wall with iron hardware, ornate but ugly, anyway. A door opened across from the one that led Henry into the *Cavern of Doom.*

Explore this unnatural wonder! Bring your family!

A line of masked women came through, looking around with the same wonder as the men. Nadia's wolf fur shined orange in the light. Her eyes were wide and staring. Her hands kneaded the air in front of her.

Meyor and Ariana emerged from a dark corner. Still masked, they were both naked. Ariana's silver chains wrapped around her bare waist. Beautiful people. Even in such circumstances, they were breathtaking. They were followed by four hulking forms in red robes. The rough fabric seemed to swallow the light, but Henry caught his breath when one of them crossed in front of him to stand in the corner. The Order From Chaos symbol stark but proud on the front of his robe.

MotherFUCKER!

He had to get that horn. It *had* to be here. He wouldn't go through this shit with nothing to show for it. His daughter's killers.

Rapist fucks!

He'd get the horn, save Amélie, and then these fuckers were *all* gonna pay.

"Shall we begin?" Ariana's voice bounced from the ceiling and walls in a chorus of echoes.

The men got to it, stripping down without hesitation. The women followed.

Henry raised numb fingers to his tie, loosening it as he watched Nadia reach up to the zipper at the back of her neck. He took his time, folding each item as neatly as he could on the bench behind him.

Two rows of naked men and women in animal masks.

He stood still, the muscles in his shoulders quivering with tension. A shiver ran through him, and he watched Meyor and Ariana walk around the table, their nude forms moving with a practiced grace. Meyor grabbed the mermaid and bent his mouth to her neck. She gasped and pressed her hips into his stiffening erection. Meyor paused to look up, his eyes seeming to lock on Henry's gaze. "What are you waiting for?"

The men and women hopped forward in a breathless

rush. Flesh slapped into flesh like the splashing of a creek. The four robed thugs looked on with bored amusement from the shadows of their hoods.

Nadia squeezed through a group of frantic lovers. Couples dropping to the floor. Leaning against the walls. Standing in the middle of the room. She pressed herself against him, pushing her mouth into his ear. Her eyes behind the circles cut in the wolf mask rolled up to meet his. Her hissing voice was a fierce whisper.

"What the fuck do we *do*?"

"I don't fucking know," Henry gasped. He tasted the salt of his own tears. He looked around, catching the eye of the black crow who had bid against him. The jackass smiled, and Henry returned it. His face was going to split in two.

He dove his head down and smashed his lips into Nadia's, hoping it looked like he was overcome with emotion, and not like he was hiding his terrified panic from the rest of the deviants. "I don't want to do this," he said against her lips, tasting blood but not knowing whose.

"We need to get the *horn.*" Her words muffled against his chin, their masks scratching and catching, pushing his fox ears askew.

From the corner of his eye, Henry saw the jackass still watching, pushing his masked date to her knees in front of him. He grabbed Nadia's breast, turning away from the man's eyes. She grunted in pain, her breath hitching in a sob, and grabbed Henry's flaccid dick. "Oh God," she groaned.

He thought she was playing the part, but she bore down with an iron grip, and Henry grunted in pain. He pulled back and looked at her face, but her horrified eyes were locked on something over his shoulder. He put his right hand on her upper arm and turned to see what was behind him, almost tearing his dick off at the root.

A small boy was on the table, Meyor holding one hand over the child's head. Ariana holding the other. A bidder in a pig mask walked to stand between the child's spread feet. The guy's pig date rubbed her tits on his back as she reached around to stroke his glistening hard-on. The man lifted a knife above his head. A wicked blade the length of his forearm. Ariana and Meyor looked at the hanging knife with frantic glee filling their masked faces.

The pig looked up at the ceiling and closed his eyes. That building anticipation from the auction theater. Just like Chicago. Henry turned back, and Nadia let him go, reaching up to take his hand from her shoulder. She looked at his ring, and lifted her own to send reflected light from its carved surface into his eyes. Henry nodded.

Fuck that horn! Fuck MANDYEL! And FUCK GOD!

They turned to the altar as one, removing the rings from their right hands. Nadia looked up at Henry and smiled.

One of the thugs stepped off the wall. "Hey!"

Henry bent and kissed Nadia on the cheek under the fuzz of her mask. He turned back to see the pig leaning over the splayed child stop and turn, his eyes widening when he saw Henry and Nadia standing in the middle of the disgusting carnality that continued unabated.

Animal noises. Grunting and slapping.

Henry and Nadia slid the rings onto their left hands, and all Hell broke loose.

Chapter Fourteen

THE CHILDREN'S misery crashed into his senses. Henry's human horror drowning in his monster's delight. So much emotion in the air. Pain and pleasure. A menu of too many choices. Dishes dressed in art and pretentious description when all he wanted was a rare steak.

The chick blowing the jackass in the crow mask was oblivious to Henry looming behind her. The crow stared up at the monster that appeared out of nowhere and drew a shuddering breath. But Henry killed his scream with a kick to the chick's head.

Her skull caved in, crushing into the crow's shattering pelvis. He folded over her as Henry's kick sent them into a woman gleefully riding a fat slop in a bulldog mask.

I hope she bit his cock off!

Henry planted his feet and roared at the ceiling. His voice burst into his ears, amplified by the stone, and another voice joined his, screeching and rumbling at his side. Nadia stepped forward in her demonic form. Black scales and onyx claws. Muscles rippling under thick hide, gleaming with cobalt highlights. Her blunt raptor face.

Eyes on fire, heat pluming from a mouth full of serrated teeth.

Henry took another breath, then released it in a scream of fury. He plowed through the orgy, and any sick fuck that escaped his claws met Nadia's in his wake.

His vision narrowed to a pinpoint, bleeding red across his field of view. His victims' screams fell to a hush covered by his rasping breath. Growls swelling from his chest, his anger growing with every touch of his claws to skin. His glee at the destruction smearing his reason to nothing.

The horn was an afterthought. The face of his daughter. The blood spraying up and out, the escaping life force following him in a sparkling cloud. So much energy and power. Absorbing until he thought he would burst. He *flared*, and the sick fucks fell back like he was dynamite and they were caught in his shock wave.

He charged the table and swung, his claws tearing through the pig mask in a cloud of flesh and blood. Horrified eyes gleaming out from an exposed skull. Teeth spun away, trailing blood and gums. The pig flew back, crashing into his bitch pig mistress.

Another swing, and a cat with sagging tits screamed through the bubbling hole in her neck. Her chest collapsed under his kick, and Henry stepped on a furiously copulating couple of deer-masked assholes. Their bodies moved in rhythm despite the murder bearing down. He dug in, pushing off to leap at the next, and the bodies burst beneath his driving weight. Ketchup packets on the sidewalk, his claws slicing them open like water bottles.

He soared across the room, his horns brushing the vaulted ceiling, and landed in the center of a Roman pile, spreading out beneath his approach. Panic and terror drenched his shoulders. Seeped through his nostrils and into his lungs. And then to his blood, where it strengthened his senses further — a shot to his brain like a young man's wad.

Fractal patterns blooming across his eyes, built out of the blood filling the air as he bit and slashed and stomped.

The universe itself opened in the rush of awareness, and he could feel the thoughts of the sick fucks falling under his fury. His twisted monster's face reflected back into his eyes. His blood-soaked mouth wide with a garish, hilarious glee. Henry bellowed with joy, and his imagination filled his ears with applause.

No light from Heaven above. Only darkness below, and Henry sent the souls tumbling down.

He twisted a wrist in his paw, and the arm came loose with a pop. Blood sprayed into his face. Henry swung the arm like a bat. The skull under a spider mask exploded, and the arm splintered into pink mush.

That's gotta be second base, at least!

A swipe of his claws, and intestines erupted from the wound, spilling out to loop over a deflating erection. The man's scream died as he dropped to his knees, and his insides hit the outside. Henry wiped the guy's shit off his fingers, and bit the hand off a tiny woman in a cat mask trimmed with pink pearls.

It felt like a giant spider in his mouth. Henry spit it out with revulsion, and it hit the cat woman's face. The bloody goober covered her horror and muffled her scream. Henry kicked her aside and dropped his knee on her stud's throat. He thrust his hands through the stud's ribs, and snatched it back, full of beating heart. His balls scraped across the guy's mask, and he threw his head back and laughed.

Bonus points for the unintended teabag!

Tears sprang into his eyes, and he lifted the dripping heart over his face, the blood pattering against his lips and into his mouth. So sweet. The energy of the stud's passing spreading through him, and despite the euphoria exploding from every pore, Henry felt a nagging in the back of his mind.

Nadia screamed from across the room. Henry turned, and one of the robed thugs sprang forward with a shotgun held to his shoulder. His face had changed into one of glinting horror. Fangs and spiked eyebrows. Eyes like night. The thug fired before his feet hit the ground, and the slug caught Henry over his right hip.

It spun him to the floor, and in the middle of the ecstasy, Henry felt no pain. He continued his spin from the floor, swinging his left arm wide, and his claws removed the thug's feet, twirling him in a cartwheel, black blood spraying out in a spiral. Henry rose to stand, heaving, his own blood coursing down his leg. He stared at the wound in his side and watched it close. Searing heat shot through his torso, and clarity descended.

What the fuck am I forgetting?

Nadia's scream, and a spear point pushed through his back. The jagged tip burst through his middle, trailing glistening bits, showering his feet with blood. The force rocked him forward, and Henry twisted his head around to see his attacker. Another robed asshole. Gritting his teeth with his slanted eyes wide like a Jack-O-Lantern.

He dropped straight to his ass, and the spear handle jerked from Jack's hands. He scraped in a small circle, raising his hand with a grimace of pain, trying to get the guy to come closer. Jack's smile widened, and he came at Henry in a crouch. He nearly shook his head in disbelief.

What a fucking dumbass.

Jack leaned in with his mouth hanging open, tongue wagging and dripping as he reached for the spear. Henry slammed his fist into the thug's gaping maw, breaking teeth and cutting his knuckles. He drove his fist down like swinging a hammer, and Jack's jaw tore off, trailing a slick smear of greasy blood down the front of his robe.

Jack reeled back, shaking his head like a dog trying to dry itself after walkies in the rain. Blood showered in every direction. Henry grabbed the spear front and back, snapping it in two. He felt it dig through his guts as he pulled the halves apart. He dropped the handle and spun with the smart end, rising up on one knee. Jack charged, his gaping grin a crater of black blood and shredded flesh.

Henry jabbed the spear into Jack's groin, pushing it until the spearhead exploded above Jack's ass crack. The thug folded over it with an eye-popping screech, grabbing the shaft and standing straight as he tried to retreat with sliding steps. The spear jutted out like a splintered wooden erection.

Henry grunted to his feet, his own blood splashing at his feet. He grabbed the spear in one hand and the thug's throat with the other. Then he heaved Jack over his head, kicking and screaming, his blood splashing onto the top of Henry's head.

A deep breath, and Henry roared. Something inside him tore as he pivoted to finish the arc. Jack's head split open on the floor, his body breaking into a jumbled pile of robed goll.

The pressure in his middle intruded into his thoughts as a mounting pain. Energy bled out with every beat of his heart. Weight crashed into him, and he turned with claws raised until seeing a gasping Nadia standing with blood pulsing from a gruesome wound in her chest. Muscle and bone. Gristle shining. Slashes and cuts. Blood and flesh splattering her arms from black claws to broken elbow.

She indicated the room behind him with a toss of her scaled head, and Henry turned with dread. Exhaustion slowed his movements, and his breath sent shivers of pain up into the hollow of his throat. Purpose flooded into his mind, and when he saw the carnage he and Nadia had wrought, the acid of his vomit rolled across the iron of his blood, and he spit it out in disgust.

Twisted bodies in bloody piles. Screams and groans. Dripping blood. Limbs. Heads. Trails of guts and bone. The massacre's rich scent seeping into his mind, sharpening his senses with the pain and despair he tasted with every breath. The wound over his hip knitted with a flash of fire that unhinged his knee. Nadia caught him before he fell to the floor, and he finally raised his eyes to look at what she had wanted him to see.

The children — still glassy-eyed and numb — stood huddled along the wall. The child from the table swaddled in their midst, held in their cowering embrace. Henry's heart ached with a pain and fear that rolled from the children in waves.

Ariana and Meyor backed into the dark corner, their eyes wide and staring. Henry stepped toward them, but Nadia held him back. He twisted in her grasp. "The fuck? We need to stop them. They may know where the ... horn ... is ..."

Nadia's eyes were focused elsewhere. Her jaw set. Her lips in a grim line. The wound in her shoulder closed, and she hissed, exposing her wicked teeth in a sneer. Henry sighed.

Fuck.

He turned to follow her gaze, and his shoulders sagged. A gang of angry survivors rallied at the wall. Humans digging through piled clothing, coming up with weapons. A few pistols. Knives. Another fucking spear, and the shotgun in the hands of another robed thug. Henry couldn't find the fourth in the crowd, but it didn't matter. What he *did* see tightened the skin over his balls, and set him back on his heels.

A trio of demons crouched on the edges of the crowd. Two of them were twisted trolls with spikes and points and glaring hatred in their glowing eyes.

The third demon was a red dragon with a forked tail and swinging breasts. The bunny mask from her human form dangled from a horn, swinging in front of her eyes as she rocked back and forth. She growled, and the rumble of her voice traveled through the stone floor and up into his knees.

Henry felt the damage in his bowels heal with a wrenching spike of heat, and he gasped, standing up straight with a full breath. He dropped a growl of his own, and was surprised at its depth and force. The fractals still at the edge of his vision vibrated, and the blood lust crept back in to color his thoughts with confidence. His concern fell away, and he smiled.

He dropped his hand and reached out to find Nadia seeking with her own hand. He closed his clawed fingers around hers, and he was calm and sure. This had been the right thing. He couldn't remember why he had done it, but he was *positive*. It didn't *matter* why, because he knew it was good.

Righteous.

He suddenly didn't feel monstrous and ugly, or old and useless, because the face of an angelic child spread across his mind. Her upturned face smiling as she reached up to stroke his cheek. The love and forgiveness in her touch brought tears to Henry's eyes.

This beautiful little girl. The ghost of his daughter. Telling him it was okay.

His power came from pain. Fear. The darkness in all things. He pulled it out of the air. Out of the stone. The energy in the blood of the sick fucks who had died under his rage.

It filled him, vibrating in his chest, expanding until he could no longer pull in enough air, his vision spotting with hypoxia, and still it filled him. He *flared* but held the power in check, building into a buzzing current around him. The heat of the unreleased energy boiled the water out of the air in a shimmering haze before him.

The sopping clothes of the victims at his feet sizzled and smoked. The reek of charring flesh made his mouth water even as it filled him with revulsion. He couldn't keep the guilt out of his thoughts. *He never could.* And that's where his comedy had come from.

Amélie's face wavered in his mind. Fading into the depths of his pain. Despair replaced her. He knew where she had gone. Into the very darkness that controlled his life. His decisions. His self-hatred.

The enemy in front of him, the sick bastards who would prey on children, fell back from the blistering heat of Henry's static fury, exchanging confused looks. Fear tightening the corners of their eyes. Turning the corners of their mouths down. The bodies at his feet burst into flames, the heat of the sudden fire cracking the stone beneath them. The air rushed past him, fueling the flames and filling the room with acrid smoke.

The dragon lowered her head, staring into the flickering glow, her mouth dropping open. Her tongue lolled out between the black razors of her teeth. The humans shielded their faces from the light and heat. The other demons smiled.

Ready to rumble.

Henry forced air in his lungs, raising his shoulder and squeezing Nadia's hand one last time. He braced his feet and thrust his head forward in a roaring scream that drove the humans back in terror. Blasting through the curtain of heat, gaining amplitude in its echoes bouncing against the rock walls.

Nadia's demon voice joined his. Defiance and rage. Henry bounced inside his cloud of unvented energy, and his swell of need hit its limit. A warm spot on his cheek where the caressing hand of the girl with the angel's face had touched him. Drying his tears.

Before the last echo of his voice reached his ears, Henry released his *flare*, charging forward in its wake.

Nadia's feet slapped the floor beside him, and they kept pace with each other as they met a wall of discharging weapons and swinging claws.

Henry was about to die, and he had never felt so alive.

Chapter Fifteen

BULLETS TORE INTO HIS CHEST. A shotgun blast shredding the flesh of his shoulder and neck. The spear driving into his thigh. Fire licking across his back. A blow to his forehead splitting the skin, blood bursting across his vision. His *flare* washed into the line, scattering bodies like bowling pins.

Nadia's claws a blur in the haze of blood and smoke, leaving trails through the air, frozen in the time between blinks. Swinging fists and claws, Henry charged into his enemies.

Henry clung to the face of the angel retreating into the depths of his mind, and he forgot her name. Pain twisted his heart, and he flung a human in a giraffe mask into the growing fire.

His voice ragged with his own howls of rage and the heat of the fire, and he stepped into the swing of a knife that laid his chest open, splitting the skin and meat to expose his white ribs. No pain or pressure, just something that happened, as if watching somebody else in the twisted form of a monster rage through a crowd of sick fucks desperate for punishment.

His lungs pumped like a bellows as he looked up at the ceiling, on his back with a troll's gnashing teeth at his throat. The demon's Order From Chaos robes split around his sudden mass as he resumed his monstrous from. It trailed into ribbons around him.

Henry blocked the bite with his forearm, and the troll's teeth sunk to the bone. The troll shook his head like a dog with a snake in its jaws.

Henry's hands went numb, ice spreading through his fingers. He dug into the troll's eyes and drew his knees up.

The troll pulled back to avoid the blinding claws, his wrinkled belly exposed through the tatters of his robe.

Henry drove his feet into the bulbous gut, puncturing the flesh with the claws on his toes.

He kicked, and the troll tumbled away, spilling guts and ichor all over Henry's legs.

The troll's closed teeth pulled a bite out of his arm and sent him flying back. Henry's own blood and gobbets of his flesh glistened with demon saliva as it splashed onto his chest.

The floor trembled with an unseen force. Henry staggered to his feet, twisted arm dangling at his side. The floor heaved, and he almost lost his balance. The ceiling split open, and a light brighter than the noonday sun sent searing shafts through the hanging smoke and mist of blood.

Burning blisters bubbled and burst on his shoulder, then he felt them spreading to the back of his head.

He flung himself to the side, rolling to fetch up against the stone table as a beautiful song filled his ears. A deep voice of melody bloomed in his mind.

Submit and feel the release of the Almighty.

Two Trackers descended through the gash in the vaulted stone.

You will never know pain again.

Beautiful and radiant, their raiment flowing in the wind of their approach. A glowing net held between them shimmered with light like the morning sun running along the strands of a garden spider's web, sparkling off the dew.

Lethargy settled across his shoulders. Pain swelled in his wounds and joints. The face of the little girl flew apart like vapor, and his mind was blank except for the desire to finally surrender.

Step into the light and let the forgiveness burn his sins away.

Henry Black would be no more, but his suffering would be over.

Screams of panic and pain.

Come into the light.

Be not afraid.

Henry rolled to his hands and knees, his mangled left arm collapsing, dropping him to his face, eyes rolling toward the Trackers promising him an end to his struggle.

He tried to rise again, and his gaze fell on the auctioneers in the corner. Staring up into the descending light, Meyor stood frozen with one leg in his trousers, the other lifted to slide inside, hopping for balance. Ariana clung to his back, her slack face turned up to the light cascading from the ceiling.

His dropped his head and closed his eyes. Felt the light and its impossible heat. Heard the music of the Trackers' voices. And with his eyes still closed, Henry saw the face of the little girl. In the haze of his pain, her name jumped to his lips.

"Amélie."

He looked at the faces of the children chained at the

wall, their mouths open with weeping joy. Light reflecting from the tears streaming down their cheeks.

Henry rose to his knees and looked out over the chaos caused by the Trackers' arrival. Humans and demons rolling in the burning of the fire caused by his flare. Trying to avoid the burning of the golden light from the split in the ceiling. Trackers hovering on wings that cracked the air.

Nadia cowered in the corner, her eyes pressed closed, her scaled fists rammed against her ears. She sat half in the shadow cast by the stone bench.

The shadows!

Behind the stone table. At the corner where the wall met the floor. Behind the arches of the pillars holding up this twisted space. Cast by her demon form.

Henry rolled to the dark side of the table and wrapped himself in the energy untouched by light. It cooled his skin like a salve.

Pain and despair hung thick in the room, rising above the demanding call of the Trackers. A glass of water beneath a blistering sun. Henry rose above the fog in his brain, gripped the image of his daughter in a mental hand, and spread himself into the shadows like quicksilver.

Rushing through the dark, just ahead of the holy light tracking his progress across the room, he flowed out of the shadow next to Nadia, and threw his body over her shoulders, clasping his hands behind her back. He lifted her from the floor and plunged backward as though he were falling into a pool.

He sank into the black just before the blistering light removed the shadow from the corner, and Henry was gone.

Carrying her big demon ass through the shadows tore at his muscles and joints. A shattering agony escaped his chest as a gargled scream. Nadia's cry rose into his ears in agonized counterpoint, and Henry burst out of the shadows in front of Ariana and Meyor.

Henry looked over his shoulder, catching his breath. The dragon jumped through the fire to land with her clawed feet tangling in the nearest Tracker's fluttering robe.

His light dimmed, and he fell to the stone. The dragon screamed in triumph as the glittering net sagged.

Except for you!

The Tracker's voice boomed from the walls and split Henry's mind with its volume. Anger tinged with irritation. Indignant. Like Saint George, the Tracker pulled a sword from his back as the dragon thrust her head toward his throat.

Henry didn't want to see what a pissed off Tracker could do to a demon pressing her luck. He stepped forward, blocking Meyor's line of sight. Meyor dropped his pants and stepped back, shaking his head and blinking his eyes clear. Ariana's face twisted with confusion. She looked into Henry's face with her eyebrows raised in question.

Henry jumped forward, grabbing Meyor by the throat.

Ariana jumped around and clutched Henry's wrist.

"Please," she gasped, her face twisting with grief. "Don't hurt him."

Nadia limped over and wrapped Ariana in a hold, pulling her back so that Henry could work.

"Where's the Purveyor?" Henry growled.

Meyor's eyes flitted from the scene over Henry's shoulders and back. The dragon's scream of pain cut through the air, and Meyor ducked in a wince. "I don't know what you're talking about."

Henry bit into Meyor's face. His teeth scraped against

bone, and he pulled back, a glistening strand stretching from the auctioneer's visage.

Henry swallowed, and the strand snapped with a wet sounding POP!

Meyor's scream was drowned out by Ariana's wail, but they were both beaten by the dragon, cracking the stone with her howl, dying in a burst of light and a release of energy that sifted dust from the ceiling into Henry's eyes.

Meyor's head slumped forward, his eyes rolling back in his head. "I don't know where he is."

"How do I find him?"

"I don't know. He always calls me."

"You got a phone from Antioch, too?"

"What?" Meyor shook his head in confusion. "No. On my iPhone."

"Where is it?"

Meyor glanced down at the pants, pooled on the floor at his feet. "I don't know."

Henry looked at Nadia with a nod. She threw Ariana to the floor, and Meyor struggled to keep her in his sight.

Ariana scrabbled back, the thin chains on her wrists jingling as she held her hands up, fending off Nadia's approach. Nadia swung her hand, parting the thin chains with her claws.

"NO!" Meyor screamed.

A blinding flash washed Henry's vision in humming colors. Ariana fell back, her skin suddenly glowing as her face went from terror to dawning realization.

A realization that Henry felt in his gut, that Ariana had once been an angel, made prisoner by Meyor.

Her eyes left Nadia's approaching form, finding Meyor in Henry's grasp. Her brows drew down, and her face twisted into a mask of rage, blood coloring her cheeks. The chains around her wrists and waist crumbled into rust, and she rose from the floor.

Dust and ash rushed around them, swirling and collecting into a tornado at her floating feet.

"At last," she said. Her voice a repellent melody of unspeakable music.

Dread tightened Henry's chest, and he opened his hands and stepped back.

Meyor, who had been cowering against Henry's chest, was forced to face Ariana.

Her light dimmed, and she spread her arms. Henry smelled the ocean. A silence spread to press against him like weight dragging him under a wave.

His own gasping breath.

Meyor's whimpering.

The slow beating of Tracker wings.

"You thought you could hold *me* prisoner?" Her voice crashed into his ears. Ariana's eyes flicked up to the scene over Henry's shoulders. He followed her gaze, and the Trackers hovered toward them. One covered in blood, his robes torn and frayed. The net held out between them. The fire raged from behind.

Henry spun back around, squeezing his eyes closed. He slit one open, peering up into Ariana's face. Her brows drew down further and she shook her head. "Nay, brothers. Your net will not catch this one."

Do not do this, little sister.

Not just an angel, but a Tracker.

Ariana shook her head. The room plunged into darkness as she drew all the light and power to her open hands.

Revenge will draw you away from salvation.

Tears sprang out on her face.

Henry dropped to his knees, ducking under her attention.

Nadia crawled over, pressing into his side.

Meyor stepped on his pants, tangling his other foot on the folds of the fabric. He fell over, his arms flailing, and hit the stone floor, his eyes never leaving her face. He shouted, "I'm sorry!"

Ariana glared, "No, but you will be."

No.

Let us end your pain, sister.

Henry scrabbled forward, and he patted his thick hands against Meyor's pants, pushing the man back down when he tried to rise. Under his palm. *Is that his phone?*

Henry closed his fist and ripped his hand up. The pants split, lifting Meyor from the floor until they tore completely through.

Meyor fell back and Henry crawled away on his ass in a frantic crab walk.

Ariana's energy grew in her palms, spinning whirls of color pulsating and buzzing like electricity. The air whipped into a swirling frenzy. Embers and sparks flooded into the corner, the heat blowing by Henry's face sucking the moisture from his mouth and eyes.

Please.

You must not do this thing.

Ariana looked away from the Trackers, pinning Meyor down with a piercing stare. "The Lord's punishment is meted out in ways unworthy of this one's sins."

You must not assume judgement.

That power lies elsewhere.

"He did things to me … things not even recorded in Hell."

Please.

Let us end your pain.

You will know only joy in His love.

"He made me do things to … others." Her eyes flickered to the children staring at the Trackers in rapt joy.

The bloodied Tracker lowered to the ground and stepped into the alcove in the corner to face Ariana. He sheathed his sword and fell to his knee. The weight of his presence pushed Henry into the corner. He couldn't lift his arms, and the Tracker's glow dug into his eyes, sinking into his brain, washing out Amélie's face.

He clutched the fabric-covered lump that he hoped was Meyer's cell phone against his chest and leaned into Nadia. Her head lowered to his shoulder, and she closed her eyes.

This is it.

Ariana compressed the energy into her fists, the power spitting from between her fingers.

The light from the other Tracker trailed away.

Come children.

You have known enough suffering.

"Thank you," Ariana whispered.

The dragon slayer rose, his beautiful smile radiating through his bloody face.

Then you have seen reason?

"No," Ariana said, raising her head in defiance. "I haven't."

She opened her hands, and the energy released in a burst that could birth a galaxy.

A glowing compression wave roared from her hands, filling Henry's eyes with burning light. His ears with deafening sound.

The floor bucked and split, dropping away to leave his stomach in his throat. He fell as the pillars crumbled. The mounting pressure slammed him into the wall, and above it all, he heard Ariana's wail twining with Meyor's inhuman screams of agony.

Lasting longer than any breath possibly could, the twin voices finally died with a deafening silence.

Henry dropped to his knees, and only realized he could see when he opened his eyes. Black motes of dust floated in front of his face. He blinked at the rubble piled around him.

Meyor was gone. No sign of his body remained. A burned circle on the wall behind where Ariana had floated. No flames burned in the remains of the room, only wafting smoke and swirling ash. Henry turned, but the children were gone.

Did the Tracker get 'em out?

A groan at his feet, and Nadia rose to stand beside him.

She slipped the ring from her left hand to her right, and her nude human form collapsed into his arms. She cried into the chest of a monster, and he fumbled with the scraps of Meyor's pants until he had transferred his own ring, and he held her with human hands. The ring muffled the residual pain floating in the room, cloying remains of grief and despair. He looked up and saw stars through an aperture in the ceiling.

A breath through his nostrils, and he tasted the night air. The shadows outside called to him.

The scrape of stone on stone behind him. He spun, pushing Nadia behind him and dropping into a crouch.

A shaft of light burst through a gap in the destruction. Golden light followed by a sweet song of forgiveness. The bloodied Tracker stood with a cascade of rock and dust. His light spread through the room, showing the bodies and blood and destruction in stark relief. He lifted his sad eyes to look at Henry, and Henry felt it all crash back down.

The Tracker lowered his eyes, and Henry stepped back with a gasp. The Tracker sat on a flat chunk of stone, and lowered his head into his hands.

I have not the will to continue this night.

Henry reached back for Nadia's hand.

Go.

Henry pulled Nadia into the darkness, and they fled into the night sky.

Chapter Sixteen

OUTSIDE, under the stars and in the clear open air, Henry stepped out of the shadow of a family crypt at the edge of the Prince Hill Cemetery. He drew a deep breath and whistled in disbelief when he saw the smoking depression in the ground above the cavern where Ariana had destroyed her captor. "Holy fucking shit."

"Wow." Nadia shivered and rubbed her arms, leaving trails in the drying blood under her hands. Filthy and bruised, she looked like she'd just walked out of a war. They both did.

While their most grievous of wounds had healed, one of the few blessings of their curse, they were still both staggering like drunks walking home.

"We're probably about five miles from my apartment. I think I can make it with both of us." He took a deep breath and held out his arm. "Would you like a ride, Miss?"

Her smile didn't touch her haunted sockets, and Henry wondered what she'd been before falling in with Mandyel.

What deal did she strike?

Who is, or was, she *trying to save?*

She stepped into his arm, holding onto his hand hanging over her shoulder. "My hero."

Henry decided not to ask.

He whisked her into the shadows, and they traveled in a stretching path that flowed to his door like ink. She held him up as they stumbled into the apartment, and he waved toward the kitchen. She filled a pitcher of water, and he drained it, slamming the empty onto the counter. He staggered to the sofa, collapsing into it and dropping his head back into the soft cushion. Exhaustion dragged him under, and the couch rocked beneath him as Nadia dropped onto the seat beside him, curling up under his arm and nuzzling his chest.

He smelled Samantha's jasmine shampoo. Felt her hair tickling the underside of his chin. Then he fell asleep with the fantasy that he was back in his wife's embrace, dreaming of his family before he woke with the sun hitting him in the face.

Cigarette smoke tickled his nostrils.

Samantha doesn't smoke.

He cracked his eyes and squinted through the light. Nadia sat at the kitchen table, a cigarette clamped between her teeth, and a magazine open in front of her. The sun glittered in her hair, and the smooth skin of her legs glowed with a tanned luster that contrasted with one of his gray hoodies draped over her body. The neck hole stretched to fall over one of her bare shoulders.

She glanced up, and her face lit with a smile. "Good morning."

He felt suddenly shy, and wanted to cover his junk with a pillow. Instead he stood up as casually as he could. "Hi."

She went back to her magazine, sparing her scrutiny. "I didn't have a change of clothes. So, I just threw this on."

"Totally fine." Henry stepped into the bathroom and closed the door. His eyes skittered across his reflection in the mirror, and he groaned.

The couch probably needs Stanley Steemer.

He drank a gallon of hot water under the scalding spray, and when he stepped out, wrapping the towel around his waist, there was black sediment in the bottom of the tub. He padded across the apartment, heading to his room to get dressed. Nadia looked up with a sharp intake of breath.

"What is it?" Henry asked, alarm rising into his throat.

The front door flew open, and Mandyel stormed in, his perfect brow creased in anger. The door slammed shut behind the raging angel, and Henry's heart hammered as his escape route disappeared.

Mandyel snarled, and in a blink, his hand was around Henry's throat. Without transition, Henry found himself held against the wall, his head aching from impact, gasping for air in painful sips. Mandyel's face loomed.

"You had *one* job to do, Henry." The angel took a deep breath and roared. "GET THE HORN!"

"Fuck you." Henry wheezed, fighting to pull Mandyel's hand open. He *flared*, and it was like running head first into a wall. He focused his blurring vision on the angel's scowl. "You didn't see that shit."

"You think I don't know what they were doing? What I was sending you into?"

"They wanted us to kill children. To *fuck CHILDREN!*"

"The *horn*, Henry. That was all that mattered. It was the only way to get to the boy."

"What boy? What's going on?"

Mandyel opened his hand, and Henry fell to the floor. He took a whooping breath then coughed, doubling over and filling his lungs with fiery air. "How can I save my daughter and look her in the eye?" Henry's voice was a ragged whisper. "It wouldn't matter if I let them do that shit to those kids."

Henry stood, rubbing his throat. "Besides, the horn wasn't even there."

"Apparently."

Henry's rage boiled over. "But you know what *was* there, you dumb fuck? Tortured children and sick animals. Kids who were gonna be *raped* and *sacrificed*. And you chose to send us into that shit without telling us *anything!*"

Mandyel flipped the collar of his overcoat down his shoulders, shrugging it to the floor. "Don't talk to me about *choice*, you son of a bitch."

"What, did I hit a nerve? You fucking *knew* about what was going on down there and decided not to say anything."

Mandyel dropped his blazer to the floor and loosened his tie. Henry caught Nadia's look over the angel's shoulder. Her eyes were wide, and she shook her head. Her jaw set with a bulge of muscle under her ear. Mandyel rolled his right cuff up past the elbow.

Oh shit.

As if a cloud passed over the sun, the apartment darkened, and Mandyel rolled up his other sleeve. He raised his eyes to meet Henry's, and the darkness filled Henry's sight as if he'd been stricken blind.

Oh fuck.

A spark swelled in front of him, and Mandyel revealed his angelic form in a blaze of holy light that would have made a Tracker don Ray-Bans.

Golden segmented armor over silk. Shimmering wings, their tips stretched to their limits, brushing against either wall. Bare feet rising above the floor. Black hair flowed from his head, suspended as if hanging in the depths of pure sparkling water. His eyes blazed with dark fire.

Henry wept at his beauty even as he gritted his teeth against the heat of the angel's gaze.

You were gifted twice by the Lord.

His voice exploded into Henry's mind, booming down the corridors of every memory.

First was His form. Second was His will.

Henry hadn't seen him move, but the angel's hands pressed into his chest, and a paralyzing cold settled into his bones.

Let me show what the will of Man has wrought.

Henry descended into darkness. Shadows flavored with a millennium of pain and suffering. A tinge of his own scent floating up from the black and into his nostrils. Flames burst into life beneath him, and bodies of the damned in Hell writhed in suffering.

Flesh flayed from bone.

Internal cavities exposed to the light.

Violations of body and mind.

The screams.

Wails from the punished pulsing his ears.

In the center of the flames, a bright spot of white hot light. A girl sitting on the black rocks with her hands folded in her lap. His Amélie. Her attention turned up to the face of a demon with lava flowing from the cracks in his hide. Henry bent, approaching her in a crouch, and she ran to the demon with a smile, her arms spread wide to receive his embrace.

Henry's scream joined the rest. He stood in his old home's foyer, gun pressed to the back of his head. A flash, and the blood and brains arced out to fill his vision. The red cleared, and Boothe stood with his knowing smile curling the corners of his mouth.

You rejected His form for another.

"No, I had no choice!"

There is always choice, child.

Amélie's coffin. Henry's twisted back bent over the shining lid, his tears falling onto its polished surface like tinkling glass.

She was not yet in Hell.

"Boothe *tricked* me."

No, child. You tricked yourself.

"He said he could save her."

He did not.

Memory became reality. Randall and Boothe stepped into the light, one in white and the other in black. Henry raised his finger, stabbing it in Randall's face.

"Like I said, for all I know this is a nightmare or a bad trip, so I don't fucking care. If this is real, fine. He's welcome to trick me after he helps me find my family."

That's what I said?

"Don't mind him." Boothe pointed to the man in white beside him. "He gets fussy because he doesn't know how to get people to play with him."

Henry turned to Boothe. "It's true, right? You *are* trying to trick me."

"Why have me tell you when you can see for yourself? Just say, *I'm ready*, and you can go back."

"Turn away," Randall warned like some doomsayer. "Don't follow him."

Henry ignored Randall, despite the man's intentions, then turned to Boothe and said, "I'm ready."

Boothe smiled like a cat with a mouthful of feathers, but Henry didn't care. He was going home.

He followed Boothe through the mist. It swirled away, and Henry stood in a stone room. A cell.

A beautiful boy sat on a cot, his foot chained by iron

that trailed in to the corner. He looked up, his exotic eyes staring through Henry, his face red and puffy from crying. Henry's heart ached, and he couldn't say why.

Mandyel's voice exploded into his brain. *Adam. The boy that will be drawn when the horn is sounded.*

"Drawn?"

Released from his prison and thrust into a war that will end creation.

"The weapon that can kill God?"

Yes.

Henry's tears fell to the floor and puddled between his hands. He pushed himself up and leaned back. Mandyel buttoned his shirt sleeves and bent to retrieve his blazer and overcoat. He tossed them across the back of a chair and straightened his tie.

"You see, pal. *You* made the choice. You accepted the word of a demon, and now you're unwilling to pay the price. So angry at becoming a monster, and you can't see that the monster *is* your true form. The way you see *yourself*."

"Fuck you."

"No, fuck *you*, Henry. You have always refused to see the truth, even when it punches you in the teeth. Of course, I'm partly to blame. I chose to include you, in spite of my misgivings, and now I must pay the price as well. But unlike you, I am *willing*."

Henry used the wall for support as he stood. "You don't get it, Mandy. You heard me during that fucking Ghost of Christmas Past bullshit. I don't *care*."

"So you've said."

"I just want to save my daughter."

"Doesn't look that way to me, pal. You just want to complain about how everyone's out to get you. Nobody's telling you the truth, when we've all been perfectly square with you."

"I don't give a shit, Mandy! You said if I get the horn, you save Amélie."

Mandyel spread his hands. "Where is it, then? You managed to get your rotten smell up in the noses of every single demon and angel and fairy on this side of eternity. And still, nothing to show for it."

"Oh yeah? I got Meyor's cell phone."

Mandyel slid his hands into his pockets. "Did you, now?"

Henry walked to the couch, giving the angel a wide berth. "I fucking *hope* so. I didn't look at it, yet."

He dug through the remnants of Meyor's pants, and the iPhone slid into his hand. The lock screen flashed on, and Henry's heart scraped the ocean floor. "Fuck. It's locked."

Mandyel grabbed it from Henry's hand, and he flinched from the touch. Screaming souls trapped in Hell swelled in his ears. Mandyel held his thumb to the screen, and the phone chimed as it unlocked.

"Holy shit," Henry cried. "Those things are *unbreakable*."

"*Holy* shit, indeed."

Henry walked around and crowded over his shoulder. Just like anybody's phone, it was filled with numbers and messages and photos. After a few minutes of scrutiny, Mandyel sighed with a shake of his head. "I see nothing of use here."

"He fucking looked right at it when I bit his face off, though."

"Hold on a second."

Mandyel turned the screen to face around. An image

of an inverted cross over a blazing sun painted in blood on a white wall. Trees with reaching limbs on either side.

"What is it?" Henry asked.

"I'm not sure," Mandyel handed the phone over and paced away with his hands in his pocket. "I've seen it before, though."

"I can ask Pastor Owen."

"Who?"

"My pastor. The Burg Spires Church of Hope."

"Henry, old pal. I doubt if a human knows more about these things than an emissary of Heaven. Besides, we shouldn't involve humans in our dealings."

"Well, it's kinda too late. I already told him everything."

Mandyel froze, turning to stare into Henry's eyes.

Henry wanted to hide. "You're not gonna go all *John Wick* on me, are you?"

Mandyel shook his head and rushed to the chair, slinging his coat and jacket over his arm. He paused at the front door. "Did anybody ever tell you that you're a pain in the ass, Henry?"

"Only everyone I've ever met."

Mandyel slammed the door behind him, and Henry turned to look at Nadia. She tapped ash into a crystal bowl, regarding him with a frown through her smoke.

"Why didn't he just disappear like usual? What was all that?"

Nadia shrugged. "That's what you get when you ask the angel of free will to make a choice he doesn't want to make."

Chapter Seventeen

HENRY WALKED MOST of the way to the church, sunshine on his face and a breeze through his hair. The city aroma. Its sights and sounds. He twirled his ring, wondering if he could be like this forever.

He could save Amélie, then watch Samantha live out her life. With the fucking *cop*.

He shivered and shook his head.

No way.

But maybe they could get back together. Even if he couldn't ever have his old body back, perhaps he'd get to keep this ring and live as Mike. He'd take her to all the places they'd gone as Henry. Every place he made her smile.

He took a bus through High Town. Dirt and graffiti. Windows shuttered with plywood. Past Dongles on Eastman. He'd played a bunch of shows there in the salad days. Sleeping on Joey Sosa's filthy couch. Smoking weed on the roof and listening to reggae on a crackling boom box.

He walked to the pier in South Chester. All the way to

the end. He breathed in the salt, thankful he wasn't carrying a sandwich for the seagulls to squawk about. So much bird shit on the rails that only the clueless tourists leaned on them, jumping back in disgust when they realized all that white wasn't just peeling paint.

He stood in front of Creamy Beans — Ice Cream and Coffee on the corner of Patterson and Tinsdale. He shook his head at the specials menu. A mint chocolate chip latte for eleven-fifty. He fucking hated mint chocolate chip.

He and Samantha had stopped there years ago.

"What do you want?"

"Whatever," he'd said. "As long as I'm with you, it doesn't matter."

God, that smile.

She had brought him a cone topped with green ice cream, and he forced himself to eat it with a smile. He had *wanted* to splat it down on the sidewalk, but it was his fault for saying *whatever*.

"What kind of a man eats mint-flavored ice cream?" Henry shrugged, only realizing that he'd spoken aloud when a black kid emptying the trash out front passed him with melted ice cream leaking from the bottom of his bag.

"I heard *that.*"

Henry kept wandering until he found himself at the edge of El Matanso. Copper accents lining the brick walls. Copper fountains and sculptures. The exclusive neighborhood that Samantha had argued against.

It was too much. Too closed off.

"But the security here is fantastic," he'd said.

"They drive around with guns, Henry. I don't want our children seeing that kind of stuff."

"Would you rather them see the kind of people that would run amok without 'em?"

"What kind of people?"

"*Brown* people," he teased, acting like the paranoid racists he sometimes poked at on social media.

"God damn it, Henry! I'm *serious*."

"I'm kidding, for Christ's sake. Look, it's safe and secure, and the city's just right over there." He had grabbed her shoulder, turning her to face the skyline. It twinkled with light from a setting sun.

What a fucking view.

"I don't know, Henry. It's so *expensive*."

"Maybe you haven't noticed, babe, but we're rich now."

She sighed, reaching up to stroke his hand. "The schools *are* good here."

"See? Besides, I heard Brad Pitt has a house just down the street."

"Brad Pitt?" She spun around with her hands clasped in front of her, bouncing on her toes like a teenager about to see a boy band. "Is he *really* here?"

"Well, it's what sold *me*."

Even the Burg Spires Church of Hope looked like money. New world old, it *looked* ancient but had a slick polish that was deeper than veneer. Straight iron fences and sculpted landscaping; fresh paint on the parking lot lines; and a fully staffed daycare that catered to children with gluten intolerance — everything a nouveau riche wife would expect after a two-hundred-dollar visit to the salon.

And the repairs after the shooting were finished faster than a star college quarterback's rape acquittal.

It was a beautiful building, but Henry had never stopped to truly admire it. Not a single mortar line that wasn't perfectly straight. Gutters and downspouts installed with a precision usually reserved for the space shuttle.

And *clean*. Never a stain on the concrete outside. No dust collecting in the corners. Every bible and hymnal in its place, lined neatly enough for the barracks. There wasn't even any dust in the air, sparkling in the rainbow of light beaming through the new stained glass windows.

Stepping onto the church property was like entering a germless world free of entropy.

Even though the church seemed empty, Henry kept his hood up as he walked along the wall to Pastor Owen's office. He knocked like a whisper, but it echoed off the high ceilings like a hammer, then looked over his shoulder, waiting for the door to open. But the pastor didn't answer. He felt exposed. Watched.

Henry tried the handle. The door swung in so he ducked inside with a sigh, and eased the door shut behind him.

The office was full of Pastor Owen's work, but for some reason it reminded Henry of his attic. Not the high-tech nonsense on the first floor, but the cozy space at the top of the house where he felt the most comfortable and creative.

Papers and books scattered the pastor's desk. Shelves lined with innumerable volumes of who knew what. The room was full, but it didn't seem cluttered. It had an order that Henry couldn't discern, but he knew if Pastor Owen reached for something, he would find it right there in his hand.

Uneasiness settled into his chest. He was looking into the life of a man without his permission.

But that man is a pastor. He won't mind, right?

Henry read the spines on the shelf to the left of the door. Standard academic stuff. Even a couple of books that Henry owned himself.

Between that shelf and the next was a mirror. An old piece of glass with a black frame trimmed in gold. Some of the silver had been scraped away, but the reflection was still clear. Henry squared himself in front of it, threw his hood back, and stared into Mike Serafino's eyes.

That's not me.

Thinner and better looking. A full head of hair. No dark bags under his eyes. Henry twisted the ring.

Mandyel was right.

He switched the ring from his right hand to his left, and met the eyes of a monster.

Howdy.

His horns were longer than they had been. Smoother. Sharper. His black eyes swirled with red sparks. A lantern jaw with a mouth full of gleaming fangs. Hair as dark as Samantha's fell across his forehead. The neck of a line-backer, swollen into shoulders that could hold the weight of Atlas.

The real me.

Henry snarled and snatched the ring off, jamming it onto his right hand. Serafino's face twisted in rage and disgust. He took a deep breath, relaxing his face. He forced a smile, and it almost looked genuine.

The door opened, bathing him in light. Henry spun around, raising his hands into claws in front of him. But his human hands were ill-prepared for anything more than a slap fight.

Pastor Owen froze, his face slack with surprise. His hand fell from the knob. He squinted into Henry's face then sighed in relief, his shoulders collapsing with his breath. "Henry, you scared the devil out of me."

"You're welcome."

Pastor Owen entered his office. The door clicked shut, and he extended his hand. They shook, and the pastor edged past Henry then gestured at his chair. "Please. You're always welcome here. Sit."

"How's Samantha?"

"She'll be here tonight, actually."

"Really?"

The pastor lowered his eyes. "There's a survivor group that meets here on the last Thursday of every month." He looked back up, sorrow creasing his brow. "For *rape* survivors."

"Oh, man, I wish I hadn't heard that."

"I'm so sorry, Henry."

"I know."

Pastor Owen nodded and watched his fingers twine around each other on his desk calendar. Fidgeting his nerves away. "But I am."

"Hey," Henry said, his voice too loud. "I'm looking for the Purveyor. You ever hear of him?"

The pastor shook his head. "Purveyor of what?"

"Very bad things. I can't get any information on him, but I might've found a clue."

Henry dug into his pocket and pulled out Meyor's iPhone. He opened the picture gallery and flipped it around so the pastor could see it. "Look familiar?"

The pastor reached for the phone but snatched his hand back before touching it as if he could sense the evil permeating within it. His forehead creased in thought. "You know, I *have* seen that."

He leaned out of his chair and reached into the bottom shelf of the bookcase beside him. His hand came up full, and Henry smiled to himself.

See?

Pastor Owen opened the book, its spine cracking with age, and leafed through a few pages before stopping with his finger on a picture. He spun the book around so Henry could examine it.

An old drawing, like an ancient handwritten bible, the symbol rich with details that could never come from a bloody splash on the wall. Trees with meticulously rendered leaves reaching for the inverted cross hovering above a shining sun, its rays spreading in sharp lines to the top of the drawing.

"This talks about old earth magic," Pastor Owen said. "Some ancient European paganism that was supposed to bring about the downfall of Christ before there even *was* a son of God."

"What's it doing in Burg City."

"I don't know. Where did you get it?"

Henry slid the phone back in his pocket. "From some sick fu ... *people* who wanted to hurt children."

"My Lord. And did they?"

"No, I stopped them.

"Did you kill anybody, Henry?"

"Maybe."

"Henry, God can't help you if you won't let him."

"If God was doing His job, then those kids would've never been there. God had nothing to do with it. *Nothing!*"

Pastor Owen closed his eyes and clasped his hands in front of him. He breathed through his nose for several seconds. His lips moved as if in prayer, and Henry opened his mouth to explain.

The pastor forestalled him with a raised finger. "I have someone who may be able to help you. Come back tomorrow night."

"I'm sorry."

"I know, Henry. You're *always* sorry."

Pastor Owen opened his eyes with a worn expression that made Henry want to shrink away and punch himself in the face. "It's bingo night, and I'm the featured caller, but my friend will talk to you. Is that all right?"

"Yeah, of *course.*"

"Well, then. I'd like to be alone, please. God may be

nothing to you, Henry." He clasped his hands back in front of him and closed his eyes. "To me, He's *everything*."

Henry watched the pastor's lips move in silent prayer. He wanted to tell him more about the children and the demons, but he knew the pastor wouldn't understand.

Nobody fucking understands.

He left Pastor Owen's office, barely resisting the urge to slam the door.

Chapter Eighteen

THE NEXT EVENING, Pastor Owen met him at the front door. His smile sent a thrill of relief into Henry's chest. Henry had spent last night trying to sleep past the memories of the pastor's sad eyes. Ignoring the cries of pain damped by the ring. So many souls in need.

He drank pitcher after pitcher of water. Visiting the bathroom enough times to make an old man with a swollen prostate sob with sympathy.

He had made it until morning, getting dressed and wandering the city again. This time, hitting the bars.

I didn't kill anyone, either.

"Come inside, Henry. My friend is waiting in my office."

Henry followed the pastor past the empty pews. "Where is everybody? I thought you said it was bingo night."

The pastor laughed. The kind that Henry had heard from the stage. It annoyed him that he hadn't been trying.

"Do you think I just shout the numbers from the pulpit, Henry?"

"Kind of, yeah."

"No, we do that in the rec room next door."

"Oh."

Duh.

He opened his office door and ushered Henry inside. A small man with thin hair jumped up from Henry's chair. Jeans and canvas sneakers. A *Vote for Pedro* T-shirt under a gray sport coat. Small round glasses, and a sparse goatee.

"Hi," he said in a booming voice much deeper than his thin chest suggested.

"Henry, this is Ezekiel Crown."

The little guy took Henry's hand in a crushing grip, pumping like a campaigning senator. "Call me Zeke."

"You got it." Henry retrieved his hand. "Unless you break my hand."

"Sorry about that. I'm a climber."

"Well, I'm a sitter."

Zeke grinned and moved to the next chair. He sat on the edge of the seat and looked at Henry over the top of his lenses. "Hey, before we get going, can I see it?"

"See what?"

Pastor Owen laid his hand on Henry's shoulder. "I told him a little about you, Henry. He'd like to see you in your other ... state. Only if you feel comfortable."

Henry was charmed by Zeke's childlike anticipation. His tiny frame.

Henry shrugged. "What the Hell? *Heck!* What the heck?"

He slid the ring from his right to left hand as Pastor Owen stepped back.

Zeke's face filled with wonder. He sat back in the chair with his jaw hanging open.

Henry raised his claws up in front of him like a T-Rex. "Rawr."

"Magnificent." Zeke pushed his glasses up with a middle finger. *"Lasciate ogne speranza, voi ch'intrate."*

"Huh?"

"Dante," Zeke said.

Pastor Owen nodded. "You see the horned beast from the fifteenth and sixteenth centuries?"

"Some Cornelis Galle. Perhaps Tmi Venomary?"

"Yes," the pastor nodded. "You can see the inspiration. Even if only subliminal."

"Usually so much stronger than the ego."

"Even leaning into pop culture depictions …"

Henry cut the air with his hand. "What are you two talking about?"

Zeke looked at him with confusion. "Why, the form you have chosen for yourself."

"I didn't *choose* this shit!"

The pastor put his hand on Henry's shoulder again. "Are you *sure* about that?"

Henry shrugged the hand away. "Oh, Mandyel would just *love* to hear you say *that*."

"The angel of free will?" the pastor asked.

"See?" Zeke said. "He's been exposed to images and descriptions at *some* point."

Henry clamped his mouth shut.

God damn it!

"I didn't know you were a religious scholar, Henry." Pastor Owen looked at Henry with piercing scrutiny.

"I did a bit about God in my act. Maybe I over-prepared a little. In between the dick jokes, there was a bunch of stuff about angels and shit."

The pastor shook his head and stepped toward the door with a sigh. "I really have to get next door. Thanks for coming by, Zeke. Henry."

Zeke jumped up with a wave, but the pastor had

already closed the door behind him. Henry swapped the ring to his right hand and plopped into the empty chair beside the waving nerd. "So, now what?"

"Oh." Zeke sat, pulling the bottom of his coat from under his legs. "Owen said you had an image for me."

Henry reached into his pocket and had to stop himself. He almost pulled out Mandyel's phone instead of Meyor's. *Idiot.*

He fished out the right phone and unlocked it with an angry swipe. "I had to recharge this bitch at one of those Apple stores. Had one of those genius asshats up my dick-hole the entire time."

"I'm a Linux man, myself."

"Yeah, I bet you are. Here you go."

Zeke leaned forward to look at the glowing image of the inverted cross. He nodded. "Yeah, that looks like what Owen showed me. I think they're the same thing."

"And what would that *thing* be?"

"Well, Saint Simon Peter begged to be crucified upside down. He wanted to show his humility. He wasn't worthy of being killed in the same manner as the Savior."

"Uh-huh."

"He was one of the apostles of Jesus Christ, but a Roman centurion, Marcus Lucilius, fought to deny Saint Simon's request. He was unwilling to allow this new Hebrew order to supplant his traditional faith."

"Okay?"

"He sought the support of his fellow Romans but felt they had succumbed to the hypnotic fervor of the martyr Christ."

"Hypnotic fervor, huh?"

"He enlisted the help of a pagan priest, sort of a precursor to theistic Satanism."

"Obviously."

"Essentially, he swore to ally himself with the only power that would possibly provide support against the Usurper. Or the Oppressor of Man."

Henry wished he had a watch to look at. "And who was that?"

"The only one who would parlay was a demon named Anameloch. A female spirit of the moon. Her symbol was the branches of a tree bending in to block the light of the sun."

"It's always a woman, amirite?"

Zeke shook his head in confusion. "I'm sorry?"

"Never mind."

"Anyway, Lucilius's family adopted that symbol on your phone and in Owen's *Signa Diabolicum*. A mash-up of Saint Simon and Anameloch. Over time, the name eventually became Lucius."

"Lucius, huh? Sounds familiar." Henry felt a wave of nausea track through his gut. *"Lucius*? Malcolm Lucius? The fucking mayor of Burg City?"

"I believe so. They have a family crypt with that very symbol on the doors."

"Motherfucker!"

"What?"

"It's in the Prince Hill Cemetery, isn't it?"

"Yes. How'd you know?"

Henry sat back and covered his face with his hands. "You didn't happen to hear anything about an explosion there recently, did you?"

"No. Should I have?"

"Of course not. You can cover up *anything* when you got a whole city behind you."

The fucking mayor of Burg City.

Perfect.

Chapter Nineteen

HENRY WAS GETTING sick of hoodies and jeans.

The hood blocked his peripheral vision and filled his ears with his breath, covering the sounds of anybody approaching. He dropped the hood with a rustle of fabric and strained his ears into the silence. Nothing but his heartbeat and dry swallowing.

He was also starving. Water kept his energy up, but the gnawing in his gut kept him reaching for the ring. Owen's disapproval would hang in his mind, and Henry would drop his hand and close his mind to the sweet suffering in the city around him. He could do it. Save Amélie without killing, and maybe rescue himself in the process. *Somebody* would be proud of him then.

Believe it or not, I'm still coming, sweetie.

He crouched in the shadow of a dump truck in the center of Prince Hill. Burg City Works had wasted no time in starting repairs on the *sinkhole*. Apparently, a recent reduction in the water table had left a void beneath the cemetery.

Fucking global warming.

Nothing to see here. Just a fleet of trucks and bull-dozers and city workers getting over time. But not double time. The work area was clear and dark. Still, like it was frozen.

Henry shivered and moved deeper into the property, skirting the treads of a backhoe and squinting at the map Zeke scribbled on the back of his business card. The stars made the paper glow.

The front was covered in religious symbols. *Ezekiel Crown ~ Occult Consultant ~ When you need to know.*

"When you need to know what?" Henry muttered. "How to get a ghost out of your Kindle?"

The closely-packed headstones and monuments gave way to broad paths and crypts. Ornate mausoleums and carved slabs. Edged grass and tended flowers. Just like El Matanso, this part of the cemetery was covered in money. But unlike Henry's private neighborhood, Prince Hill Cemetery was old.

Here before the settlers, it was started with the burial of a Choctaw prince who converted to Christianity. Some believe it was a myth of history. Some thought Panther Grissom was some kind of saint. Burg City started as a tourist attraction where believers flocked to the unmarked grave for a mystical blessing. In the twenties, city founders installed a hand-carved monument in the prince's honor and set the surrounding twenty acres as a preserve and cemetery.

It wasn't long before they needed to erect a fence to keep folks from boning up against his headstone and on the grass and the graves to either side and in the trees and … everywhere, really. Dark rituals in the dead of night left the grass scorched, and enough animal offerings to make the place smell like a dog food factory.

To subsidize the cemetery's reclamation, the city sold

exclusive plots for rich industrialists making scratch on the backs of immigrants. Soon, the oldest part of the cemetery was the richest, and the immigrants were laid to rest at the bottom of the hill in plain pine coffins.

Henry's shoes squeaked on the wet grass. He froze, waiting for any sound that might alert him to a follower. He imagined the light of a black helicopter snapping on to surround him in blinding bright light as he shit his pants in surprise.

As long as it's not a Tracker.

He pressed his back against the smooth granite wall of a massive crypt. Roman carvings and columns. Bas-relief horses dragging a banner with a Latin phrase etched into it. *Quae Descendum Volo Videre.*

Scraping from around the corner sent Henry's heart into palpitations. He bit back an exclamation and eased to the edge of the wall, waiting for a demon or even a fucking raccoon to shoot out of the dark.

Orange light flared, and with another scraping, the light died. He peeked around the corner. In the space between a fluted column and the crypt wall, Henry could see a sliver of flickering light in the gap between the doors of the Lucius Family's burial vault. The rayed sun behind the inverted cross. The reaching trees. The carving sparkled with reflected light like Gandalf had spoken *friend* and entered.

Henry crept around the column on his tiptoes, his shoes scuffing against the stone steps. He pressed his eye to the split in the doors.

What the actual fuck?

A naked old man sat in the center of a pentagram drawn on the floor in blood. Two headless chickens dribbled the last of their lives in a widening puddle of sticky crimson. There had to be forty candles pouring black smoke into the crypt entry, and their combined light flashed and danced on a giant oval frame that looked like pewter. A Victorian mirror with no glass, the frame held up by iron worked into an ornate filigree of twisting serpents.

The old man's hair stuck out in wispy spikes that fluttered as he bent to press his forehead into a spot of blood before his knees.

Now, that's flexibility.

The old man rose with his arms crossed over his chest, and he tipped his face to the ceiling. "*Sestama fendo anamo enGAR!*"

What is that? Span-Latin?

"*Sestama fendo aNAmo enGAR!*"

Portugeezer?

"*Enla farn ALto SEN! SesTAma fendo aNAmo enGAR!*"

Red sparks exploded from the air in the center of the frame, showering the old man with arcing pinpoints of fire. Red light split with gold like flowing lava filled the oval, and a thrumming vibration crashed through the vault.

"Holy shit," Henry whispered.

He eased the stone door open, its scraping across the top step lost in the mirror's growing hum. Henry turned to make sure the door was closed completely, wincing with a squealing hinge.

"Yes," the old man shouted in breathless joy.

Henry closed his eyes and shook his head.

I don't want to turn around.

"Yes!"

I don't want to look.

Henry turned and cracked his eyelids open to slits. A cloven hoof stepped through the rippling fire in the mirror's center. Liquid flames dripped from the leg as it extended to the floor. A clawed hand gripped the top edge, and a horned head slid through.

Henry's eyes sprang open, and his jaw fell to his chest.

The demon pressed through the opening like he was squeezing through a window to get ahead of an apartment fire. His face reminded Henry of the grotesqueries carved into a Samurai helmet. The old man stood, blocking the view, and Henry stepped to the side to see what came next.

The demon's glowing eyes flicked to his movement, his eyebrows falling in a snarl. He halted his progress through the frame and drew his arm back inside.

"No!" the old man shouted.

The demon bared his fangs and ducked back through the fire. Lava dripped to the floor, sizzling into the stone.

"NO!"

The cloven hoof returned to Hell, and the light disappeared. The mirror became an empty oval, scorched by the fire of another world, and the old man dropped his head. The candles' guttering flames made shadows dance in the corners. The old man's shoulders twitched with his sobs, and Henry threw his hands up in frustration.

"Suck it up, for Christ's sake!"

The old man turned with his eyes wide and his mouth open in shock. He fell to his knees, leaning back and extending his hand to the dead chickens.

"What? You're gonna cluck me to death?"

The old man sprang to his feet with a spryness that Henry didn't think even *he* could muster. A bloody dagger trembled in the old man's fist, aimed at Henry's chest. The old man took a firm step out of the pentagram, his face clouding with anger.

Nope.

Henry switched the ring to his monster hand and stepped forward with a growl.

The old man fell back, his face filling with awe. The knife fell from his fingers, clattering and bouncing out of reach. He smiled and clasped his hands under his chin. "You're … one of *them.*"

"That's right," Henry snarled.

The old man's smile became a grin of perfect dentures. He squared his shoulders and stuck out his hand. He marched forward with his sagging balls bouncing off his withered thighs, and Henry found himself shaking the hand of a naked old man covered in chicken blood.

"I'm Hennessy Lucious. Pleased to meet you." He tipped his head, waiting with a polite smile.

"Um … Henry."

"Henry?" Hennessy dropped his hand and stepped back, looking up into Henry's eyes in disbelief. "That's it?"

"Well, yeah. I mean, what did you expect?"

"I don't know. A more demonic name than *fucking Henry?*" Hennessy cocked his thumb at the mirror. *"His* name was Thamuz."

Henry sighed and put the ring back on his right hand.

"Look, I'm sorry for interrupting … whatever the fuck that was, but I'm looking for something."

Hennessy walked to the corner and picked up a pile of folded clothes. "Aren't we all."

Henry looked everywhere but at the old man as he wiped the blood with lemon-scented baby wipes.

"I didn't really expect anybody to be here. I was just kinda looking for clues. I need to find the Purveyor."

Hennessy spun around with his shirt half-on. A blue silk number with white buttons that gleamed in the light. "The Purveyor?"

"Yeah, you know him?"

"Of course. That's where I got the mirror."

"Well, I need to find the Horn of the Lamb."

Hennessy whistled. "Now, *that's* an item of some interest."

"You know about it?"

"I should say. I sold it to that very gentleman last week." He ran a white silk tie under his collar and busied himself with tying it while Henry winced in mental pain.

"Why?"

"I needed the money."

"Did you blow it?"

"The money or the horn?"

Henry sighed. "The *horn*."

Hennessy dropped his hands and leaned forward to fix Henry with a look reserved for the insane. "Of course not, and I told *him* not to, either. Doubt if either of us could, anyway. It's an angelic instrument. It would probably kill him to try."

"And he still wanted it?"

"*I* still wanted it." Hennessy tucked the tails of his shirt into tailored gray slacks then slid a glossy leather belt through the loops at his waist.

"You don't really look like you're hurting for money, though."

"Not the kind of money *you're* thinking of. I'm not just a seller. I'm a buyer, too." He squatted down, showing off those flexible joints and tying the laces on a pair of black wingtips that shone like a calm pond.

"So what are *you* looking for?" Henry asked.

Hennessy stood and shrugged into a tailored jacket that matched the slacks, looking at Henry from the side of his eyes. "Something that will let me live forever."

"Can I talk the Purveyor? The man you sold the horn to?"

Hennessy shook his head. "He is a very private man. He usually doesn't accept calls, but if you have a phone of your own? Perhaps one like this?" He lifted a brass brick out of his pocket that looked like Henry's own hotline to heaven.

"You have a Holy Phone of Antioch, too?"

"That's very funny, yes." Hennessy latched a heavy gold watch to his wrist and slid a sparkling gold ring onto his pinky finger.

"Let me see yours," he said.

Henry reluctantly fished his magic phone to the man. He opened it, running his fingers along the outside edges and closed his eyes.

Henry wasn't sure what the hell the man was doing, maybe this was some method for figuring out the phone's number. The man handed the phone back to Henry. "Okay. He'll call you after I speak with him, I'm sure. You'll need to offer him something in trade."

"Like what?"

Hennessy slapped his thighs in exasperation. "I don't know. *You're* the demon. *Think* of something."

"All right, all right. Tell him to ask for Mike Serafino."

"Not Henry?"

"No. Henry is … my *demon* name."

Hennessy drew a comb slick with pomade out of his inside pocket. He pulled it through his hair with practiced strokes then replaced the comb and patted his goatee flat. He shook his head. "Henry."

He shot his cuffs and straightened his tie, and when he turned to present himself, Henry caught his breath.

"Holy shit, I know you!" Henry shouted.

The door scraped open, and Henry jumped to the side, his fingers on the ring. A man in a dark suit leaned into the crypt. His eyes roamed the corners, flickering over Henry and immediately dismissing him. They landed on Hennessy, and he lifted his wrist, tapping his watch with a gloved knuckle. "It's time, sir. Were you successful?"

Hennessy Lucius, the mayor's brother, squinted his eyes in thought. He smiled and shrugged with his hands at his waist. "Yes and no."

The man in black tipped his head and held the door wide. "Very good, sir."

Hennessy nodded to Henry on his way by and stepped out into the night. The security stiff shut the door behind him, leaving Henry in the Lucius family vault, his eyes burning from the acrid candle smoke.

"Hey! I'm not cleaning this shit up!"

Chapter Twenty

HENRY SAT on the edge of his bed, staring at the sky between buildings. The sun was rising, and he'd been awake all night. The city's victims called to him, begging for help, begging for him to feed on the evildoers. Every angry shout. Babies crying. Like a migraine's point pounding into every splintered crack in his resolve.

A whole pizza and some smothered nachos hadn't touched the gnawing in his belly, because that was a hole that couldn't be filled. A twelve-pack of Pabst Blue Ribbon, and then dessert couldn't either.

Every time he closed his gritty eyes, he saw Samantha curled up next to Stone, a smile on her face and blood in her hair; Amélie smiling up at her tormentors; and then the hollowed-out terror on the faces of the children at the Viazo Grand auction.

He let himself fall back into the mess of blankets and fixed his eyes on the ceiling. He didn't have the energy to kick off his shoes. His eyes drooped, and he was sinking. His eyes closed, and he was under water. Fire roared across the surface, but he was safe in a current that let him drift like the breeze.

A ringing phone splashed him with ice and shattered his dream.

Henry bolted upright, shielding his eyes from the blazing morning that beat against them. He leaned over to dig the phone out of his pocket. He slid his thumb across the screen, but it continued to ring.

He shook it. Slapped it against his palm, and still it filled the room with its scream.

What the Hell?

The sleep sat on his brain like the chunky fat in the top of a can of beef stew. He growled and slung Meyor's phone across the room. It spun like a disc, hit the floor, and skipped under the dresser.

A ringing phone, and Henry realized it was coming from his other pocket.

"God DAMN IT!"

He leaned the other way and fished in his other pocket, jerking the phone out with a snarl. It stuck in the lining, and he screamed in frustration, snatching it up and tearing his pocket to shreds.

He flipped it open and jammed it to the side of his head. A flap of fabric poked into his eye. He batted it away and took a deep breath. "*What?*"

"Hold for your party, please."

Henry dropped the phone in his lap and pressed his fists into his eyes. Another calming breath, and he lifted the gently against his ear.

A baptist choir singing *Victory in Jesus*.

Click. "Good morning, pal."

Henry rolled his eyes and fell back with a *whump* of the mattress. "Good morning, Mr. El. To what do I owe this pleasure?"

Mandyel took a deep breath and exhaled in a huff, making the speaker crackle. Henry knitted his brow with suspicious thought. "Are you smoking?"

"Yeah, I am. What of it?"

"Whoa, calm down. I was just asking a question. So, the toothpicks didn't work, huh?" Henry smiled and settled in.

"No, it wasn't the toothpicks, Henry. It was my *choice* to give in."

"Free will and all, right?"

"That's right, pal."

Henry giggled. "Keep telling yourself that if it makes you feel better. It's what *all* the junkies do."

"You know, I was actually calling to apologize, but I don't think I will now."

He pictured Mandyel hanging in the air in front of him. The terrible, beautiful rage on his face. Henry's own panty-pissing fear.

Maybe I've pushed him far enough.

"Nah," Henry said with a joviality he didn't feel. "That was *weeks* ago. All is forgiven."

"Thank you, Henry." The angel's sober tone wiped the smile from Henry's lips. "That means a lot to me."

"Come on, nobody got hurt. Don't mention it, buddy."

Mandyel snorted laughter. "He said you were funny, but he never said you were smart. You surprise me sometimes, pal."

"Hey, thanks. So who we talking about?"

"Boothe."

The phone fell onto Henry's face. He jumbled it back into his numb fingers and sat up. "Come again."

"He feels bad, Henry. He really does."

"How do you know how he feels?"

"Who do you think gave me this idea?"

"The fuck what?" Henry rocked his head to the side like he was shaking water from his ear.

"That's right. *Boothe* came up with this deal to get your daughter out of Hell."

"Fucking *Boothe* sent you? I thought you were an angel?"

"I am, and Boothe didn't *send* me."

"Oh, you came here on a whim? Using my daughter's suffering against me … like … by *choice?*"

"Henry!"

Mandyel's sharp voice brought Henry to a freezing stop. "What?"

"You are a *terrible* person. *That's* why you are in this mess. Stop blaming everyone around you for your own bullshit. I cut you break after break, and you won't stop *bitching.*"

"No. This isn't *my* fault. It's *Boothe's* fault. And *Randall*. They tricked me, and now my daughter is *in Hell*, and my wife is fucking another man." Henry swiped his tears with the back of his free hand. "How is any of this on *me?*"

"Your wife is in bed with another man. So what?"

"The fuck you mean, *so what?*"

"Her husband was murdered in front of her."

"I know. I was kinda *there.*"

"Her daughter killed at the same time."

"I *know.*"

"She was raped in her own home."

"I fucking *know* what happened to her, goddammit, I don't need a 'Last Time on *Henry's Shitty Life*' recap! I was there."

"No Henry, you weren't. You were dead."

Henry leaped from the bed and charged to the dresser. He lifted the phone over his head and smashed it down on the gleaming wood.

I know I was fucking dead!

Over and over, chunking away like a lumberjack. Spit and wood flying.

They took them away from me!

He screamed wordless fury. Ragged breaths, gasping through his torn throat.

The only thing!

He kicked the face of the bottom drawer, his foot sinking into an explosion of lacquered wood.

That ever meant ANYTHING!

The next drawer up disintegrated under a wild punch. The ring dug into his finger, and he pulled it off, holding it in a tight fist.

His mind filled with a red haze, molten and dripping with rage. Henry *flared*, and the dresser crumpled into splinters. The bed crashed to the floor on broken legs, sliding back to smash against the wall. The bedroom door blew off the jam, flying into the apartment to knife through the coffee table glass.

He stood in the calm of the center. Scorched tendrils extended away from his feet like sun rays on the Lucius vault.

His chest heaved. Snot dripped from his nose. His eyes blurred with tears.

And she had to go on without me.

He turned in a daze to survey the damage.

She had to go on without our baby girl.

The small modern entertainment center dropped from the wall. The fifty-inch Mitsubishi sat at angle, its screen a crazy web of cracks. Henry heard Mandyel blowing another mouthful of smoke into the receiver. He lifted the phone back to his ear.

"I broke the TV."

"Do you feel better?"

"No, Mandy. I *don't.*"

"What happened to you was heinous and *wrong.* But what happened to her was much worse, Henry."

"I know," Henry whispered.

"Have you cried yourself to sleep most nights these many months?"

"No."

"Spilled your guts to a dozen shrinks?"

"No."

"Relived the moment over and over in testimony to the cops."

"You know I haven't."

"Every time some mundane task rears its head. The normal things that nobody ever thinks about. Calls from the insurance company. Lawyers. Production partners. Magazines asking for an interview. And a man comes along who also lost something. Same as her."

Mike Stone.

"A good man, Henry. Maybe even a *better* man, and you never once thought about her. Not *really.*"

"That's *all* I've done is think about her. Her and Amélie."

"Your wife and daughter weren't taken from *you.* Samantha's husband and daughter were taken from *her.*"

"Ah, fuck."

"You, Henry, are a selfish bastard." The angel's voice was so tired. Sick of trying to pound a point home into the thick skull of a dumbass who refused to listen.

Henry's knees unhinged, and he fell to the floor, his ass planting in the middle of the scattered dresser. The ring slid from his hand and fell to the floor. It rolled away, flashing sunlight off the scales of the snake carving. It tipped like a spinning coin, ringing into the silence. Swirling and slowing like water flowing down the drain.

Henry sniffed and wiped his eyes. "She was the only reason I woke up in the morning." He looked up at the ceiling. Cracks spread out from where he had been standing, radiating from a point above his head toward the walls.

"She saw something in me ... that I still can't figure out. Never could. And you know what? I lived every day like I was waiting for the joke to climax. That fatal punchline where she would scream laughter in my face. *Just kidding! Ha!*

"But it never came, and the harder I listened, the louder the fear. God, that terror that she would see me for the fucked-up piece of shit that I really was? It was all I could hear."

Henry trailed a finger through the dust in front of his knees. He saw her face. Amélie's, just like hers. The sound of their laughter together. A weird genetic harmony.

"It was enough just to be in the room with her. Or just in the *house* with her. I knew I could look over and there she'd be. Catch me looking at her and smile. Or sometimes, she'd chatter non-stop. Knowing I was only pretending to listen, but still. Just talking away. Amélie did the same thing. I was pushing for TV. Writing instead of performing because the road had been getting ... like I resented it. Every minute away from them was like a knife in my stomach. I fucking hated everything that took me away from them. They were the best of me. Why would I leave *that*?"

His throat closed. He cleared it with a loud cough, but it tightened again. He sniffed and swallowed, shaking his head, and the sobs burst out of him like vomit. Doubling him over and taking control of his muscles in waves of shaking cramps.

"Ah, fuck. That's what I did. I left them." Henry

lowered his head into his hand, and an angel listened to him cry.

Henry shook his head and sat up. He took a calming breath, sighing it out in a yawn.

"Shit, I'm sorry. I didn't mean for you to have to sit and listen to my bullshit like that." His nervous chuckle trailed away. "What were we talking about, anyway?"

"Boothe."

"That's right. Where is old Boothe, anyway?"

"In Nowhere. With his love. Thanks to you."

Henry smiled with false cheer. "Good for him. You get what you pay for, huh?"

"He followed the rules, Henry."

"Yeah, yeah. I get it. I still hope he gets lost in The Forgotten and rots there, but I get it. What's next?"

"You tell *me*."

"I gotta wait for the Purveyor to call me. Should be today some time."

"That's great, Henry," Mandyel said, not sounding like he meant it.

"Yeah, I know a guy now. A couple in fact. Amazing who you meet at church. Or the cemetery."

"And this guy has the horn?"

"Probably, but he'll only take something in trade. Maybe you can make yourself useful and get me something shiny for him." Exhaustion yawned through his body. A swelling tide crashing against him.

"I think I can come up with something."

"That's just great, Mandy." His eyes sagged, and his head nodded forward.

"Henry?"

"Yeah. What's up?"

"We are the choices we make, pal. You understand that now?"

"Sure. And I'm choosing to tell you to go fuck yourself."

"Come on, pal."

"Nope. I've already chosen, buddy. Go fuck yourself."

Henry snapped the phone shut and tossed it away. His head dragged his shoulders down, and he spread out in the mess he had made with his hissy fit.

He fell into a dream where he stood on a dark stage, shouting the same dumb joke on repeat.

The crowd was there, but nobody laughed.

Chapter Twenty-One

THE RINGING PHONE jolted Henry awake.

He lifted his head and focused on the dented brass brick. His tongue felt like burlap. A paste of dust and spit clung to his cheek.

The emotional weight of the city pressed on his shoulders as he rose to all fours on quivering muscles. Fear and pain drizzled a glaze on his brain. The phone was a spike in his ears. He had reverted to his demon form while sleeping.

At least there's no crazy rebound bitch screaming at me.

He scraped through the rubble and slapped his hand over Mandyel's ring. It lowered the city's incessant roar. He slid it on, becoming Mike Serafino, and the psychic noise dropped like he had slammed the door on a screaming argument. He could hear the tone but not the words, and he sighed as the weight floated away.

I'll take it.

He flipped the Holy Hotline open and mashed the button. "Yo."

"Hold for your caller, please."

No music, just a click, and a raspy voice filled his ear. "I understand you are looking for something, Mr. Serafino."

"A couple of things, actually. Are you the Purveyor?"

"I am."

"Then I found *one* of 'em, already."

Breathless laughter. "I admit, I am difficult to reach at times. I am… medically fragile, shall we say. It has slowed me down, but I do so love to trade. What about you?"

"Oh, yeah. Super fun. Look, did Hennessy tell you what I was looking for?"

"He did."

"And?"

"Your offer?"

"Let's just say I have an angel on my shoulder for guidance."

Silence filled with the Purveyor's rough breath. Henry couldn't tell if he was waiting for more or thinking or scratching his balls. He cleared his throat with a soft cough. "Very good. 829 Watershed. Shall we say ten this evening?"

"That'll work."

"Then, good day, Mr. Serafino."

"Sure."

Henry snapped the phone shut and tossed it over his shoulder and onto the bed. A few hours of sleep made his eyelids gummy. He was still surrounded by a wall of mist. Henry sighed.

Might as well get going.

The pitchers of cold water and a hot shower didn't touch his exhaustion. His sour stomach and black mood escalated in equal measure.

He stood in Boothe's walk-in closet, staring at another gray hoodie and another pair of jeans. Magical clothes that would make the Hulk jealous.

Fuck this.

He snapped on the light and stepped deeper into another man's wardrobe.

"Jesus Christ, Boothe."

He had never looked into the depths of the closet. At all the suits. Shirts and ties in every color. A wall of watches. Shoes that could put an eye out with their shine. Henry dropped his towel and opened one drawer after another. Silk underwear. Patterned socks. Garters and cuff links.

Henry's deepest shame had been his body. He never understood people who hated things about them that they couldn't change. Or being proud of their blue eyes. The genetic lottery was exactly that. A roll of the evolutionary dice. Being a fat slop? That was all him.

His struggles lasted *years.* Every pound lost was another victory celebrated with Little Debbie. Staring at himself in the mirror and pointing at all of his flaws, sinking into despair with each bullet on the list. Demon Henry was powerful and hideous. Mike Serafino was slim and confident and *not fat.* Might as well dress the part.

A slick black three-button suit. Gray shirt with a tie the same color. Standard black shoes with a high polish and a stainless-steel diver's watch. Some smellum in his hair combed through with a stiff bristled brush that looked like animal hair. He stepped back and admired what Mandyel's ring had given him.

Instead of hating himself and feeling even fatter in nice clothes, he nodded.

So, this is what pride feels like.

Watershed was above Northpointe in the hills. Posh and fake. Just like him. The Halcyon Tavern was a pretentious and expensive restaurant a few blocks down. When courting the networks, he and Samantha had eaten there several times, always gawking at the bill with an incredulous laugh.

Not this time. Filling his pockets with Boothe's money, a monster in a demon's clothes left the magic of his borrowed apartment to catch a ride to a luxurious lunch. Then, off to find the weapon that can save God. Or kill Him. Whatever.

Now, that's a full day.

The Halcyon was an exclusive place that tried to look fresh but couldn't quite keep the wear from showing. He slid a fifty into the hand of the brute watching the front door, then stepped into a movie set. Perfect faces and bodies glossing over the dirt with a manufactured sheen. The coy slant of a bare shoulder. Capped teeth in a predator's smile.

Deals being made. Hearts being broken.

He headed to the bar to wait for a table to open. It looked out over the dining room with a glimpse of the expensive tables up in the balcony. Even as high as he'd made it, Henry had never sat at the top. Always at the bottom with the other writers. Mid-level agents and people with talent but no looks, moving up the ladder.

The regular type of drinkers were leaning against the bar. Suits and dresses. Everyone pretty. For once, Henry felt like he belonged. A woman in a tight black number caught his eye. Hair as black as Samantha's. Glossy and shimmering when she tipped her head for a glass of red. There was space to either side of her.

Maybe she's alone?

Nah, her old man is probably in the shitter.

Henry headed away from her to belly up at the end of the bar, and she turned to look at the door.

It was Samantha.

He froze. She turned back to her wine and glanced at

her watch. Henry's feet moved without feeling or thought. His hand rose to brush the hair from her shoulder. He fought it like Peter Sellers in the War Room. He was close enough to smell her perfume. Arcana Rosa.

"Excuse me," Henry said.

She turned further away, glancing over her shoulder in a look that didn't even touch him. "I'm waiting for someone."

"I knew Henry."

She spun with a gasping inhale, her eyes wide. Even after knowing her for so long, Henry couldn't tell what emotion was playing across her face. He panicked, flapping his hand in embarrassment and shaking his head. "I'm sorry," he muttered, the muscle in his legs contracting to run.

She reached out and held him there with a hand on his forearm, looking into his eyes. "You really knew Henry?"

Henry looked out over the diners. Most faces he didn't recognize, but many that were familiar. "Jesus, you probably hear that all the time."

She chuckled with a bitter twist of her face that he'd never seen. "Not anymore." She indicated the space beside her with a nod. "How did you know him?"

Henry covered his nerves with an awkward shrug and leaned against the bar. "We used to roll together back in the day. Name's Mike Serafino."

She took his offered hand and constricted his heart. Her brow drew down in concentration, making the line appear between her eyes. He had called it her *thinking line*. "I'm sorry, but I don't recall that name."

"Well, we had a falling out a long time ago. Never spoke since."

"A falling out?"

Thoughts flooded his brain. "Oh, yeah. I've kind of regretted it ever since."

A thousand answers flashed by. What to say that would have made him stop talking to someone but still keep a little sympathy for Mike Serafino. "There was a guy used to roll with us." Henry dug for a name, and it popped out of his mouth unbidden. "Curly Sanders."

Samantha's face twisted with disgust. Curly had been a piece of shit. Hitting on teenagers and getting sloppy drunk. Running on the same circuit as Henry for a summer during his *What Happened to Me?* CD release.

"Yeah," Henry said. "He stole one of Henry's jokes."

Samantha hissed with a wince. She knew what that would have meant to him.*

"I know. And he was *wrong*, but I tried to defend him."

"Oh, no."

"Yeah. Curly and I had history, and I owed him a lot. Probably even my career *now*. Anyway, I defended him, and Henry and I never spoke again."

"Oh, I'm sure if you had called after the tour and talked, he would have forgiven you."

That's bullshit, and you know it Samantha. If that had really happened, I would have gone to my grave telling the guy to go fuck himself.

"You think?"

She squeezed his hand. "I *know* it."

The bartender came up, and she slid her hand off of Henry's, leaving a cold spot behind. Henry moved his attention from her beautiful face. "Margarita, no salt."

He looked back, and her face was slack. "What?"

"That's what Henry always drank when we came here."

"Oh, shit." *Stupid, stupid asshole.* "I'm sorry. I can order something else."

Her eyebrows rose in surprise, and she laughed. Free and without self-consciousness. "No, that's fine. It just caught me off guard."

"He talked about you all the time, you know?" Henry blurted it like it had been growing in the back of his throat for days.

"Really?"

"Yeah, he said the thing that used to keep him going was the crowd. Their laugh, you know? But after he met you, *you're* what drove him."

His drink arrived, and he took a sip. The citrus and tang mixing with the floral cloud of Samantha's scent, and he was back at Halcyon's a decade ago, with the only woman that ever mattered. Like none of the insanity had ever happened, and they were sharing a drink before dinner. The silver ring on his right hand sparkled, and he stared at it.

The fuck am I even doing here?

He swirled the margarita and watched the spinning ice.

"He used to write letters, you know? These *long* letters. Page after page, sitting by the window or in a diner booth or something. Personal, you know? And sometimes, he'd read 'em to me. Before we stopped talking."

The road was so lonely. Just miles under the wheels, slowly grinding the funny right out of the routine. Pounding out words on his shitty Dell laptop that he had to balance atop a stand of Coke cans to keep it from overheating.

Just one more call to that guy he'd met out front of the club that said he knew a guy that was friends with a guy at ABC. Coffee and weed. Transferring money from his credit card to his phone card to call Sam every other Friday. She'd tell him *enough*. She couldn't keep waiting for him. Then he'd come home, and there'd she'd be.

"He wrote this one letter. The end of May just outside of Arizona, and it was *hot*. I think they broke a record, like a hundred and ten or something. Even though he hated taking his shirt off, he'd taken it off *that* day because the air conditioner in the room wasn't working.

"We were sitting outside under the awning to catch a little breeze. I was writing a bit I was gonna try out in Scottsdale, and he was writing a letter to *you*. He was being morbid all morning, and I remember he wanted to make a list of things to tell your children if he died on the road.

"I know you guys had been talking about having kids, but he didn't think he was ready. Not enough stability. At least, that's what he *claimed*. It was mostly because he thought he'd make a bad father. That, and the money."

One of the ice cubes cracked with a pop that spit margarita on his hand. Light refracting through split as the two halves of the cube floated to either side of the glass.

"The part that had taken him the longest was the part about dating and relationships. He'd write a few words and wipe the sweat off his chest with his balled-up shirt. And the letter said, *being alone hurts. Almost more than anything. Even more than a broken heart.*

"I spent so much time by myself, that I didn't know how empty my heart was until your mother came along and filled it up. And that's what hearts are for. Not for moving blood like they'll tell you in school. Nope. They're made to pump love. Love that will fill it to the top, spilling out like when your Mommy leaves the water running in the sink. But instead of spreading across the kitchen floor and getting Daddy's shoes wet, it will spread through your body, all the way out to your fingers. Then, you can give it back to the one who loves you. That way ..."

"Your heart will always have room for more," Samantha said.

Henry snapped out of the memory and looked into her

eyes. Shining from the tears that rolled down her cheeks. And then, tears of his own. "Ah, shit. I'm sorry … I just regret … you know, falling out with him."

"No. Thank you so much. I still have that letter, you know?" Her face twisted into grief, her bottom lip quivering. His throat ached, and he longed to pull her into his arms. To feel her pressed against him, wiping her tears on his shoulder. She grabbed his upper arm and drew him into a hug.

He took her against his chest, laying his cheek against the crown of her head.

"Thank you," she said.

"What's going on here?"

The voice at his back raised Henry's flank. He let go of Samantha, and they jumped back at once, spinning to confront the person who had interrupted such a private moment.

Mike Stone stood with his arms crossed and his eyebrow cocked. Calm, but with an energy brewing in his stance. Henry smoothed the rage from his face and forced an innocent smile. He thought he might bite the fillings right out of his mouth.

Samantha put her hand on the cop's arm, joining him to look at Henry. "Mike," she said, wiping the tears away with her fingertips. "This is … *Mike*. He knew Henry."

The tension fell from Mike Stone's frame, and a guilty twitch ruined an otherwise friendly smile. He nodded and extended his hand. "Good to know you."

Henry took the hand, fighting the urge to bear down with all his strength. He held his smile, wiping his own tears away with the back of his hand. "Same here, Mike."

Stone peered into Henry's eyes, his expression confused. "Have I seen you before?"

"Probably. I'm on TV."

Stone shook his head and opened his mouth, then stepped back when a hand fell on Henry's shoulder.

Henry turned, and the Halcyon hostess stood by with a menu in her hand, and an empty grin on her face. "Mr. Serafino, your dinner companion is waiting at your table."

"My dinner companion?" Henry followed her finger to Mandyel. He raised his whiskey glass in a silent salute, and Henry rolled his eyes. "That's right, my angel. *Agent.*" He shook his head and took the menu. "I'll be right there."

"Enjoy, sir."

He turned back to Samantha with a rueful shrug, but it was wasted. She was looking up into the cop's eyes. A look Henry remembered all too well.

Motherfucker. She's not YOURS!

"Hey, it was good meeting you, Mike. And seeing you, Samantha. Sorry for coming at you like that."

"What? No, no. Thank you for that memory of Henry." She dug into her clutch, the one Henry bought her for Mother's Day two years ago. She scribbled on a scrap of paper and held it out. "This is my number. Call me sometime. I would love to hear more. Please."

He took the paper with a small bow. "I will. Promise."

The smile felt more natural as he turned away, but the ache in his clenched jaw had spread down his neck. He wanted to look back, but was terrified to see her looking up at the cop with eyes that should have been for him.

Chapter Twenty-Two

HENRY SAT across from Mandyel and blocked the angel's face with the open menu. The Halcyon Tavern had started putting their prices next to the lovingly crafted descriptions.

Holy shit.

Mandyel cleared his throat. "How is she?"

Henry dropped the menu and took a deep breath. "She's really good."

"Does that bother you?"

"What are you, my shrink? Yeah, it fucking bothers me."

"That she's doing well?"

"No, God damn it! That she's doing so well with *him.*"

"I know it hurts, pal."

"Do you?"

The angel's tired eyes and drawn mouth. The weary hang of his shoulders. "Yes, Henry. I do."

"I'm sorry." Henry put a fist to his mouth and looked around, but nobody seemed to be paying attention.

Maybe they think I'm auditioning.

"Are you able to feel happy for her at all?"

"Of course, I am … I just … is there any way I can keep this ring forever? You know, maybe come back and be with her?"

"You can keep the ring, but know there's a price for wearing it."

"I don't give a fuck about the price. If it means I can be with her, I don't care."

"Well, as to that …"

"What do you mean?"

Mandyel sighed and leaned forward. The dark fire in his eyes swirled, and Henry fought the urge to lean away. "What would she wake up to in the morning. Have you learned *anything?*"

"Fine. What's the price?"

"You don't care, remember?"

"Fuck you," Henry said in a fierce whisper.

"*Fine*. You don't want to be square with me Henry? As soon as our deal is done, you can be *Mike Serafino* to your heart's content, but don't come crying to me when the price becomes too dear."

"You still haven't said what the price *is*. Wait a minute … does that mean you're still going to save Amélie?"

"Of course, Henry. As soon as we get the horn."

I'm crying again for fuck's sake.

Henry wiped his face with a linen napkin. The monogram thread scratched his forehead. He took a calming breath. "Then I'm not changing my mind. I'll pay anything."

"It's your choice."

"Yeah, yeah. Let me use the gifts God gave as I see fit."

"And that's the beauty of free will, Henry."

Henry threw his hands up. He took a drink of ice

water, crunching on some ice to clear his head. "So, did you bring something for the Purveyor?"

"I did." Mandyel set his glass down and reached into his breast pocket. Henry thought the angel was going to pull out a check, but instead he saw a small leather bag drawn with a piece of copper wire. Mandyel set it on the table then slid the bag into Henry's hand. He reached into his pocket again and pulled out a similar bag. He opened it and spread out a line of tobacco into a flat paper square.

"What is this? God's stash?"

"That is the Zechariah's Whistle."

Henry worked it open and poured a small copper whistle from the bag into his palm. "What's the whistle for?"

Mandyel licked the edge of the paper and rolled it over into a cigarette. He lit it with a match that appeared in his fingers out of thin air.

"That's a neat trick. But there's no smoking in here."

Mandyel stuffed the bag into his pocket, blowing smoke from the side of his mouth. "Nobody'll even notice, pal."

Henry looked around again, but the diners were as oblivious as before. "Fair enough."

"It's a shepherd's whistle, made to call back one's flock. It represents God's promise to gather the Jews back to Israel. He sowed them like seeds all across the globe, Henry. Planting them in the ground in every nation. How a farmer doesn't forget those seeds, the same way God won't forget about His people. But see, He plants his seeds in difficult climates sometimes. Testing them against the unfavorable conditions of a life set against them, one that might in fact *kill* them. That way, they will not trust in themselves, but rather in God."

"That's … great? It still doesn't tell me what it does."

"You blow the whistle, and help will arrive, just like God's delivery of the Jews from slavery."

"What kind of help?"

"Whatever kind of help is nearby."

"Like you?"

"If I'm nearby, yes."

"That is oddly *not* reassuring."

Mandyel smiled through the smoke and leaned to the side. He dug back into the pocket of his overcoat, hanging on the back of his chair. He slung a length of rolled fabric across the table. Henry fumbled the catch, the roll spinning like a baton in front of his face before dropping into his lap.

"Fuck, you're being kind of casual with this stuff aren't you?"

The angel smiled and lifted his glass. He drained the whiskey, smiling with the cigarette hanging from the corner of his mouth.

Henry lifted the roll. It was tied with golden twine. A rich blue, the fabric glinted with a sheen of unbroken wax. It flattened into a bag with a wide opening at the top. "Okay, what's with all the bags?"

"You ever hear of the Horn of Plenty? Well, that's like the bag of *enough*. It is actually called the *Gratia Lapides Sacculi*. A satchel full of grace."

Henry held it upside down. "It's empty."

"It allows the bearer to pull whatever food he desires from the bag, three times a day."

"Holy shit."

"As we've already established."

A waiter came by and took Mandyel's empty glass, replacing it with a fresh one, a single ice cube floating at the surface. The waiter sat a margarita with no salt in front of Henry, and spun away, carrying his tray above his head.

Mandyel lifted his glass, stretching across the table. Henry shook his head in confusion before realizing the angel wanted to toast. He tipped his margarita glass against Mandyel's whiskey.

The angel nodded with a smile and knocked back half the glass before taking another puff. He blew the smoke from his nose in twin jets. Henry thought of a dragon.

"Are you drunk?"

"I'm trying, pal."

"Why?"

"Because I will have to make a choice this night, and unlike you, I *know* the price that will be asked."

"Yeah? And what is it?"

"In their hearts, humans plan their lives, but the Lord establishes their steps. He calls the Heaven and the Earth as witnesses against them, setting before them life and death. Blessings and curses. And they must choose life, so that their children may live. But death is *also* a decision."

Mandyel drained the glass, lowering it with its rattling ice cube spinning the light into Henry's eyes like a star. The angel's eyes watered. Henry couldn't tell if the tears were from his words or the alcohol's burn. The angel took a final pull from the cigarette before stubbing it out on the ice, halting its spin. A tiny swirl of black smoke sizzled up, and he waved it away.

"Henry, if we say we are without sin, even if it's only in our minds, then we are lying. We sin through choice. Not admitting fault or blame. *Responsibility.* Sin is always by *choice.* Maybe even *design.* Just like yours, my choices will lead me to stand for judgement at the seat of God, and I will have to give an account of myself to Him."

"But, you're an *angel.*"

"In a way, pal." He nodded his head toward Henry's glass. "Drink up, and then we'll go get the horn."

"You're coming with me?"

"I already have plenty to answer for, Henry. I'm not going to let you go off alone and have to add *that* to the list."

"Because then you'd have to stand in front of God some day and tell Him all about how you fucked up?"

"That's exactly right, Henry. And it scares the shit out of me."

Chapter Twenty-Three

THE PURVEYOR'S house was a massive Gothic block of angles and peaks. The darkening sky turned all the shadows into purple streaks, and the windows reflected the orange burning just above the horizon. Heavy iron gates swung wide at their approach, and Francesco pulled the limo through the turnaround to park parallel to the front door.

Francesco waddled to the back, but Henry didn't wait. He opened the door and stepped out, buttoning his jacket over the bulging bags in his pocket.

Francesco held the door for Mandyel. "I'll be honest, gents. I don't like this one bit, and if *any* shit goes down whatsoever, you ain't gonna find me and my car anywhere near here. You got me?"

Mandyel laid his hand on the driver's shoulder. "I will bear with you and remember no more."

Francesco nodded in relief. "Thanks, Mandy. Appreciate that."

Mandyel smoothed his overcoat and adjusted his hat. Francesco shut the door and slid back behind the wheel.

Henry watched him drive off. "Wait a minute. The fuck is he going?"

"I told him to leave."

"That's not what *I* heard."

"That's some of the cost of wearing the ring, pal. You are numb to the turning wheel."

"What are you *talking* about?"

"You can't feel it, but something is in the air. Your senses have been dulled. Your demonic powers muted. All for my benefit."

"Why can't you people just say what you mean?"

"Ah, but that's the point, Henry. We *have.*"

A light sprang on in the mansion's front window. Next to the ornate entry still lit by the remains of the sun. Mandyel slung his arm over Henry's shoulder. Alcohol rolled from his breath and Henry flinched away. "You ready, pal?"

"I don't even know what the fuck I'm doing?"

"You want to know a secret?" Mandyel ascended the grand steps to the front door, dragging Henry with him. He raised his fist to knock. "I don't know what the fuck I'm doing, either."

"Wait, what?"

His knuckles fell on the front door, and instead of signaling their arrival, they slid down the door as it opened on a squeal of hinges.

A grand hallway stretched out in front of them to the rear of the house. Impenetrable shadows in contrast with the light from the open room to the light washing the parquet floor. A sprawling staircase disappeared into the gloom to the left. Mandyel dropped his arm from Henry's shoulders and entered.

"Peace be to this house," the angel whispered.

Henry pushed on the opening door to keep it swinging, then he and Mandyel turned to face the light.

Peterson sat in an easy chair with his legs crossed. Canary yellow suit and bow tie over a black shirt. Black shoes with yellow laces. His round lenses opaque with reflected light. He held a tea cup and saucer perched on his knee. He lifted the cup and took a sip, his mouth curling into a smile over the rim.

A small table with a Tiffany lamp sat at his side, between the easy chair and a hospice bed. An array of prescription bottles circled the lamp like supplicants of an incandescent god. A withered man in a red satin robe was stretched on the bed. His hands held with Velcro cuffs. A hissing oxygen line clipped to his nose.

Peterson set the saucer on the table, pushing the vials and bottles aside to make room. He placed the cup on the saucer and turned back, smoothing his pant leg before looking into Henry's eyes. "Mr. Serafino. Thanks so much for accepting the Purveyor's invitation."

"Don't mention it," Henry said, relieved that what with the Trackers coming and interrupting the child sex murder orgy that Peterson hadn't figured out that Henry went and murdered a bunch of his shady friends.

"Who's your detective friend?"

"Mandy? He's actually from the Fashion Division."

Mandyel stepped around from behind Henry to stand at his shoulder. "That's right, pal. And I see a lot of violations."

"Mr. Serafino, please." Peterson leaned back and tipped his head back to look down his nose. "You made a right mess at Prince Hill. Shut the portal down to the Grand. But bringing a Tracker? That was not nice."

So much for not being blamed.

The door clicked shut behind them, and Henry twisted

his neck to look. A brute with a spider web tattoo on his face moved his hand from the door knob as a sawed-off shotgun in his other hand centered on Henry.

The steps creaked, and a line of hardcore biker types filed into the hallway from upstairs, spreading out and brandishing an array of weapons. All leather, beards, and attitude.

"But I forgive you, Mr. Serafino. After all, you brought us to the Purveyor. And to the horn."

"Well, that's nice of you."

"*I* thought so." Peterson removed his black pocket square. He leaned over the rail of the hospital bed and snatched the oxygen tube off the wrinkled face with a look of disgust twisting his lips. He stuffed the silk into the old man's mouth, and pressed his hand over the wad of cloth, covering the Purveyor's nose.

The old man's wasted frame strained against the restraints. Pushed into Peterson's hand. His eyes rolled to every corner of the room, heels beating into the sheets beneath him.

"Motherfucker!" Henry stepped forward with his fists balled at his side, and Peterson's horde stepped forward to meet him.

Mandyel grabbed Henry's shoulder and dragged him back in line.

The old man bucked. His eyes squeezed shut, tears running into the folds and creases of his cheeks. Peterson grinned with a lion's mouth, and the Purveyor died with a feeble kick.

"Henry, old pal," Mandyel said. "Could you put your ring on the other hand, please?"

"Fuck yeah." Henry transferred the ring and burst out of Boothe's suit in a tornado of luxury fabric. Tatters stretched across his heaving chest and hung in strips at his calves. The line of thugs seemed unimpressed, even when Henry split the entry with his most bestial roar.

The air cracked with the lightning of Mandyel's spreading wings, and the goons took a terrified step back as righteous light smeared across their faces.

That'll do it.

Henry squinted into the dazzle revealing the true forms of Petersons' demons. The man himself sat with shocked awe hanging from his slack face, shielding his eyes from Mandyel's fire.

Why wait for an invitation?

Henry jumped forward and took the face off a man transformed into a slavering beast.

Mandyel whirled, and shafts of light speared out from his gleaming armor. Henry moved to the next guy up for a beating, and his world narrowed to a blur of movement and pain.

Claws dug a chunk of meat from his thigh. His leg collapsed and dumped him to the floor. On his way down, Henry dug his claws into the guts of a bear aiming a shotgun. Covered in filth and blood, Henry continued his fall. The gun roared, and most of the right side of Henry's face disappeared in a haze of agony and noise.

His vision went dark, a flap of skin hung over his remaining eye. A fresh spike of agony dug into his guts when a knife pierced his side above his hip, twisting and grating against bone.

The horrified screams of Mandyel's victims barely covered his own pain-soaked bellow, and Henry reached up to rip the skin out of his eyes. He *flared*, and Mandyel's light dimmed as an omni-directional wave of demonic energy spread from Henry's center.

It laid the survivors flat, blowing into Mandyel, who

flapped his wings in a thundering answer to keep himself stable against it.

Henry's pain dulled to a deep heat. In the wake of his *flare*, he tasted the remains of the Purveyor's life force swirling away in wispy flutters. He sent a silent apology to the old man and pulled the energy into himself, breathing the sorrow deep into his chest. The sweet pain of the old man's passing lit his palate like a rare liquor, and he rose to his knees.

A searing heat spiked into his cheek as his eye regenerated. The wound in his side knitted itself closed.

Fresh light registered in his healed vision, and Henry rose to stand under Mandyel's buffeting wings.

A demon in a leather jacket pushed to his feet with a snarl. He lifted a club studded with nails over his head, and Henry let him charge.

They collided under the angel's feet, and Henry ducked under the demon's swing to grab him in a rib-cracking hug.

Henry sunk his teeth into the demon's thrashing neck, and the flesh under its chin tore free in a torrent of black blood, filling Henry's mouth and eyes with stinging salt.

He let the demon's gurgling body slide to the floor, and Mandyel struck with a fist that split its head open in a blinding flash.

Blood pattered to the floor like the end of a spring rain, and Henry and Mandyel turned to Peterson as the final two demons cowered in the hallway.

"Where's the fucking horn, Peterson?" Henry growled.

"I did not expect that, truth be told." Peterson swallowed, his pale eyes round behind his glasses. He cast his eyes aside to avoid the angel's holy light. "But I'm not going to tell you where the horn is."

Henry stood straight, confusion etched into his face. "What? But why not? We *won*."

He looked up at Mandyel for support, but the angel was looking down the hall with narrowed eyes.

Henry turned back to Peterson. "We won, right?"

Peterson stood and buttoned his jacket. Straightened his tie. "I said I didn't expect it, old son. That doesn't mean I wasn't *prepared*."

Music flooded Henry's ears. Beautiful. Terrible and sad, it filled his mind with a desire to sit. To give up with a knife to his throat, watching his life bleed out onto his chest.

A Tracker's song, twisted with bitterness and hate.

Light swelled from the back of the house. Gold glittering through the staircase balusters, spreading the shadows in a twinkling haze.

The Tracker from under Prince Hill floated around the corner into the hallway, his wings folded to clear the walls. His wrists were chained to his waist with silver links as thick as Henry's ankle. His hollow eyes blazed with sparkling light. He lifted a black sword in both hands, veins tracked up his forearms like pulsing tree roots made of shadow.

Who will release me?

His voice exploded in Henry's mind, the query's weight driving him down to his knees.

Mandyel rose to the Tracker's level, his arms out in cruciform.

I will, little brother.

The Tracker slid into the grand foyer, and their combined light filled every corner with a dazzling that pierced into Henry's brain. The skin on his face tightened as it burned, but he couldn't look away.

The Tracker spread his arms to match Mandyel's, his sword digging into the ceiling.

Then come.

They flew at each other, and their clash filled Henry's body with electricity. His jaw clenched, his body jittering as he fell.

He looked up at the angels in holy combat and found that they'd all somehow moved from inside the house to outside in the dark. He was on a flat plain of stone. Wind rushed by, carrying the sound of their struggle under storm clouds, roiling with their effort.

Peterson stepped forward with his hand inside his jacket, his jaw slack with terror and wonder. Dirt swirled at his ankles.

A leather-clad demon hid behind an outcropping of rock. The remaining thug hunkered in the shadow cast by his buddy. Both faces were turned to the sky, light playing in their wide eyes.

Henry staggered to his feet, the remains of his suit flapping around him in the cold wind.

How the fuck did we get here?

Not just this plateau of stone, but also the this situation. This true comedy of misfortune.

Light blossomed as the clouds parted, and Mandyel rode the Tracker's plummeting body to the ground. One hand held the Tracker's throat, and the other held the wrist to keep the black sword at bay.

Mandyel's face flinched away from the dark power emanating from the blade. The Tracker's teeth were bared, his eyes squeezed shut.

They crashed into the stone like a fallen star. Dirt and rock flew from their crater in a hanging cloud that rolled into Henry's eyes and nose.

The Tracker's light dimmed beneath the radiant glow

of Mandyel's glory. The angel stood with his foot planted on the Tracker's wrist.

Henry stepped away from the raw emotion etched across the angel's face and bumped into Peterson behind him. Agony laced through his chest from a white-hot point over his left shoulder. He twisted away with a scream, and Peterson stood with a blood-stained hand held up in front of him, red spots making a warped smiley face on his yellow suit.

He pawed at the pain in his shoulder, drawing in another breath to scream into the wind. A black blade jutted from the muscle at the base of Henry's neck. It burned when he touched it, and his knees folded.

He crumbled to the ground, tumbling out of his demonic form to land on his side as plain old Henry. Fat and pale, bleeding to death on an angelic battlefield far above the earth. The boiling agony of the onyx knife in his shoulder radiated into his body, and with every wave of pain, Henry split his lungs with another scream.

HENRY!

Mandyel's voice rippled through Henry's mind, images of golden clouds played across his sight with every echo.

Amélie reached for him from the end of a dark hallway in his mind, her eyes filled with fear, her mouth open in a silent wail.

Samantha looking into the eyes of Mike Stone as he climbed on top of her in Henry's bed.

Nadia smirking at him through her smoke.

Mandyel turned and stretched out his hand. His beautiful face filled with panic and loss. Stepping from the Tracker, he kicked the blade buried in Henry.

It tore free, flipping through the air, humming as it flew.

Henry gasped and the demon rose back up within him, twisting his bones, stretching his skin to fit his true form.

Blood pouring from the ragged wound slowed, and Henry pressed his hand to the cold stone to lift himself up.

He noticed that in helping Henry, Mandyel had lost track of the Tracker, who had slipped behind him.

Henry tried to shout a warning, but he was too late.

The black sword burst through Mandyel's breast, squealing against the golden armor as it passed through. The angel's wings wilted, and a geyser of black blood shot from Mandyel's mouth in a scream that dwarfed Henry's pain in both volume and length.

The clouds disappeared, and Henry slid through his own blood on the slick wood floor, back in the Purveyor's foyer, as the outside and inside became a single knot of surreal architecture and chaos of swirling debris and rain.

Mandyel's face twisted as he dragged another breath past the smoking sword in his chest.

Henry dug into the floor, and charged through the angel's waning light. He launched into a drop kick that hit the Tracker in the face, slinging him to his back and slashing blood from his torn cheeks.

The blade slid from Mandyel's body, and the angel collapsed in a gurgling heap, blood gushing from the split in his armor.

Henry fetched up against the bottom of the stairs, spinning to right himself as a wave of dizziness rocked his brain, spinning the house all around him.

The Tracker gasped in pain, and his light dimmed. Mandyel's light winked out. *NO!*

The Tiffany lamp next to the dead man in the front room was the only light to banish shadows from the scene. Henry froze. *Shadows.*

The Tracker groaned, and Henry shook his head. His thoughts cleared.

Peterson stood from the corner with the black knife sizzling in his hand, and Henry launched himself into Mandyel's back. He dragged the angel into the darkness, and the swirling shadows that glowed in Henry's mind like a darkened theater's EXIT sign.

Pulling Mandyel into the escape tore the power out of Henry in a crippling wave of agony, nearly as sharp as Peterson's blade. But he held on. Without Mandyel, he'd never see Amélie again.

He somehow found the door in the swirling clash of interior and exterior structures. The door flickered in and out of existence, sometimes a crop of rocks, and other times the solid door that would — with any luck — lead them back to the real world outside.

He timed his leap from one shadow to the door to coincide with the exact moment the rocks became the door, and he rushed at it, carrying the dying angel back out into the night, and out of the house of whatever the hell was going on.

It was the perfect time to pray, but he'd be damned if he asked for God's help now.

He'd leave it to the professionals, and Henry happened to know just the guy.

Chapter Twenty-Four

HENRY BURST out of the shadows in front of the Burg Spires Church of Hope. All the windows were dark, but the front door opened under his hand.

He fell into the entry with Mandyel tangled in his arms, landing on top of him and driving the breath from his lungs. He struggled out from under the angel's flopping weight and stood with Mandyel's arm slung over his shoulder. Back in his Sam Spade costume, bright blood spread across his white dress shirt, dripping onto the floor.

The wound in Henry's shoulder had torn open during his flight to the church. Blood dripped from his fingers to mix with the angel's. When they met, there was a sizzling and a puff of smoke.

Where the fuck is everybody?

Henry dragged the wheezing detective down the side of the pews toward Pastor Owen's office, sliding in blood, fighting against Mandyel's dragging weight.

It was nearly pitch black inside the church.

That's right. Fucking bingo night.

He hitched Mandyel higher on his shoulder and

reached for the door handle, freezing in confusion. *No wait. Bingo night was yesterday, right?*

"Henry?"

He spun, heart in his chest.

Mandyel slid to the floor with a wet thud. Pastor Owen stood in the front door, silhouetted by the street lights outside.

"You're not supposed to be *here.*"

Henry sagged in relief. A passing car sent a shaft of light through the stained glass, and colored reflections across the opposite wall. Henry dropped to his ass next to Mandyel, chin to his chest. "Yeah, sorry about that. How was bingo?"

Another set of headlights splashed through the window, and the colors bloomed into a sparkling kaleidoscope caroming across the room.

The Tracker's song filled Henry's ears. He fought his exhaustion to look up at the religious images of redemption depicted in colored glass, and the window exploded in a shower of twinkling shards and blazing golden light.

The Tracker burst through the shattered glass, black sword extended in his right hand and a glowing net fluttering from his left. Peterson dangled from the chain at the Tracker's waist.

Pastor Owen rose to his knees, his dazed eyes filling with blood from a gash on his forehead.

You will know peace this night.

Henry fell back, barely able to throw his hand out to keep his head from bouncing off the floor. He welcomed the Tracker's message. He was exhausted. An end to his suffering seemed like just the thing right about now.

The Tracker's net spread above him and fell to cover him in rippling waves, like a sheet fresh off the line.

Peterson jumped down and walked over to Mandyel's

crumpled body. Kicked him over and lowered into a squat. Pulled the angel's shirt, jacket, and overcoat open, exposing his chest wound. Then he lifted the black blade over his head and plunged it into the split in the angel's breastbone.

Mandyel's eyes sprang open, and they lit on Henry's gaze.

He reached for him, but Henry lacked the energy to reach back. Mandyel's hand fell, and his eyes rose to fix on something overhead.

Henry forced his gaze toward the angel's attention. Christ. Hanging from the cross, His carved face spoke of forgiveness through pain.

Sacrifice.

Mandyel's final breath returned Henry's attention to the floor. The angel was dead, and Henry felt only mild curiosity. The heat from the net settled over him, and his pain fell away. His troubles were a thing of the past. He no longer needed to worry, and he almost wept with relief beneath the net.

Peterson stood with his wild eyes on the bleeding angel's heart in his palm.

He lifted it to his mouth and took a squelching bite, blood squirting onto his cheeks and dripping onto his chin. He *swelled*, his form filling his yellow suit to a ripped stitch from bursting.

"The power!" He exclaimed.

The back of his suit split with a rasping tear. Dark leathery wings spread from his shoulders. Black horns at the tips, and pulsing veins running the length of his translucent skin. The Tracker's light reflected off of bristling hairs.

The remains of the heart blackened in his hand, and Peterson let it tumble through his fingers to the floor. He bent down and gathered a handful of the net, smirking at the sizzle in his hands. He slung the net containing Henry over his shoulder with nary a strain of effort, and Henry curled into its comforting heat.

"We'll be leaving now, padre," Peterson said, his voice now deep and beastly.

"You have much to answer for," Pastor Owen shouted, sounding *pissed*.

Henry nodded.

You're fuckin' A right, Peterson.

Peterson shrugged. "Maybe. But not *this* night, guvnor."

"Begone!" the pastor shouted, and Henry rose, carried into the night by the beast and its beating black wings.

HENRY WOKE in a stone room lit by candles set into the walls. On a wooden chair with the Tracker's light warming his face. His mouth watered from the roasting meat.

Peterson walked in to block the forgiving light, his black wings folded along his back. He wore only the yellow pants, and the Order From Chaos tattoo glistened with the sweat on his chest.

He strode up to Henry and flicked the black knife through the net at his throat. Burning strands fell away, and the searing pain crashed into Henry's senses in a blinding wall of agony, crashing harder by the heartbeat.

Peterson smiled and jabbed a thumb at the Tracker standing in the corner with his eyes at his feet. "Yeah, them cunts know how to hurt a guy, don't they?"

Henry moaned as the pain wracked his body, burning wherever the net sunk into his steaming flesh. He rolled his eyes up and fixed Peterson with a desperate glare. "You're one of them, you fucker."

Peterson wiped a finger across his tattoo. "What, this? Of *course* I am, Mr. Serafino. Or is it Henry?"

"You killed my daughter. MotherFUCKER!"

"Your daughter?" Peterson's face fell in thought, only to brighten with memory. "Henry *Black?* The *comedian?*" He laughed and slapped his knee. "Mr. Punchline, his very self? Sorry, that wasn't me. But I *did* show up to join the boys soon after and put my cock in your wife's bum while you bled out at her feet."

Henry lunged forward, but the net held him in check, his boiling flesh sending ripples of heat and smoke in front of his eyes. He fell back, gasping for breath, tears making cool paths down his face. "I'll kill you, you son of a bitch! You're fucking dead, and you don't even know it."

"Come now, Henry."

"You don't even fucking know." Henry's voice was a wheezing whisper, choked by pain and the smoke of his own burning skin.

"I was told to keep you alive, Henry. And alive you'll be. But first …" Peterson stabbed the black knife through the netting, piercing Henry's hand, staking it to his burning thigh. His red skin turned pale. His black claws thinning into dirty fingernails. Pain jolted through him in a galvanizing flood, seizing his muscles and cracking his thoughts into a thousand points of light.

Peterson reached through the net, slid the ring off of Henry's finger, then stepped back and slid it onto his hand.

Henry fought for breath. For sanity against what he saw standing before him: Mike Serafino looking at his hands in confusion.

"What's this?" Serafino's voice and accent. Only his hairdresser would know. "*This* will come in handy the next time I see your wife."

Henry vented his rage and pain in a howl that made Peterson fall back in alarm. The Tracker raised his head and stepped from the wall.

"That was impressive, Henry. But too little, too late, I'm afraid. I *would* like to thank you for this ring, though. And for finding the horn. Adam will love being a part of The Order."

"*Adam?*"

"What, your angel friend never told you? Adam is a very powerful child, but he will be the most powerful *man* in the history of the world." Peterson looked up at the ceiling with Mike Serafino's eyes slitted in rapture. "*He* is the one destined to bring order from chaos. Not just the opposition to the identity of Christ, but a reigning king of Earth. A conqueror. A *true* savior."

He looked back at Henry, and tears streamed down his face. He transferred the ring, and Peterson's feline grin split his dark face. He spun and walked out. As he passed through the Tracker's waning light, he said, "Put him in the hole."

The Tracker stepped forward with weary shoulders, his growing song seeping into Henry's brain. Bone glistened beneath the rips in his face, and still the Tracker's eyes shone with sympathy.

Will you take my offer now?

And an end to your suffering?

"No fucking way."

The Tracker held his open hand above Henry's head, and the pain dimmed to a dull throbbing. His face and throat healing, knitting in the light spreading from the Tracker's fingers.

I will defy them, end your misery, even at great risk to me — only because of your efforts to save those innocent souls.

"You want to help, then set me free."

That I cannot do. I can only offer you death. Child, I can only make the offer this once.

"I'll take my chances."

The Tracker nodded, his face crumpling with sorrow.

So be it.

He grabbed Henry in a rough embrace and lifted him from the chair. Henry's moan of pain was lost in the folds of fabric covering the Tracker's shoulder above his armor. Vertigo bubbled the acid in his stomach, and he fell.

To the bottom of a shaft, with his stomach rising into his throat, and the circle of the Tracker's light shrinking above him. He crashed down into wet rocks. Ribs splintering and stabbing. A bright lance of pain as his skull cracked on a jagged stone. Warm blood mixing with the cold water that swirled around his head.

Light dimmed, and an object filled the shaft, growing as it fell. Mandyel's body, his overcoat flapping behind him like the frantic wings of some giant tan bird. It landed in a jumbled heap across Henry's legs.

Blood and water splashed up into Henry's eyes. The angel's felt fedora floated down like an autumn leaf.

The grinding of the cover stone vibrated through the walls as the Tracker sealed Henry off from the light.

Panic burst through his mind, and the searing pain swelled as the net bit into his burning skin.

The walls reflected the red glow of his burning wounds, and Henry screamed his daughter's name.

Chapter Twenty-Five

I'M GOING to kill them all.

Henry was blinded by thoughts of murder. But also of being stuck here, dying. Maybe he would just waste away in the dark while the net ate through his body, leaving little chunks of his old self in the steaming water on the well floor.

No.

I will get out of here. I don't know how, but I will. And then ...

First, I'll kill that fucker Peterson.

Drink his blood while he watches me tear his dick off.

Then, I'll find the rest of the fuckers. Every last one of those Order from Chaos cunts, and kill them all for what they've done.

He thrashed his hips until Mandyel's body rolled off his legs. His broken ribs dug into his chest, and he licked blood from his lips. He looked up to where he remembered the stone lid dropping over the hole and strained to slide his hands up under the net. If he could only get his hands free.

"If anybody's listening," he croaked, "I sure could use some fucking help right now!"

Maybe he could bang some rocks together. Get out of the net and scale the walls. Burn the rest of his suit and send a fucking smoke signal.

A signal.

He halted his efforts to loosen the net. He took a calming breath and crawled his hand up his body like a blind spider. The net sizzled into his knuckles, smoke rising from his claws. He dug his hand under the flap of his shredded lapel and felt a lump in his interior pocket. His mouth watered with the thought of the bag with the food, but he could tell it wasn't the Sack of Three Squares. It was the whistle.

He got the edge of the leather sack between two fingers, then slid his hand out with the slow patience of a beekeeper gathering honey with a case of the shakes. Laying the bag flat on his chest, he worked his burning fingers past the copper wire holding the neck closed.

He poked his fingers into the bag, his claws clinking against the copper whistle. Skin on the back of his hand blistered and puckered under the net. He fished the whistle out, pulled it into his fist, then paused for another breath and rolled off the rocks with the pain in his ribs knifing through his chest.

He ended up face down in the brackish water. He held his breath and submerged his burning hand into the cool soaking his front. Soothing relief, but his back started burning where the net touched skin. He held himself still for a slow count of ten, and he jerked his head out of the water, rolling back for the rocks to stab into him, his ribs screaming in agony that took his breath away.

He worked his hand up into the crook of his neck, the net burning the water away. With a final push, his fist burst free and he punched himself in the chin. Henry bit his tongue and blood filled his mouth.

"Gawldamma muttafucka thit!"

He spit the blood, working the rest of it to the back of his mouth. He swallowed and licked his lips, smearing the blood in a frothy swirl. He raised the whistle and took a breath.

Thank God I didn't keister this fucker.

He blew as hard as he could but heard only a sputtering whisper. He drew another breath around it and then blew harder. The whistle shot from his mouth and his lips farted with bloody spit spraying his shoulder.

The whistle splashed into the water next to his head, and Henry did an impression of a panicked salmon, flopping to get his face lined up with where the whistle had fallen.

He took a breath to plunge his face down and froze in a painful arch when the stone grated above him. He spun to his back, and the well opening filled with a writhing shape that dropped to land with a splash next to his head.

A shadowed hand reached out to grab the net, jerking back with a hiss of pain. The hand came out again, and a clawed fist grabbed Henry by one of his horns. His savior climbed the algae covered walls, dragging Henry behind. He thought his head would tear off, the bones in his neck grinding and popping. Or the horn would yank the skeleton out of his meat sack where it would rattle against the stone.

At least I'll be out of this fucking net.

He slid over the lip of the well like a fat paralyzed snake, then looked up into a pair of glowing eyes set into a gray smiling face.

"Hello, Master Henry."

"Ezra!"

The goll nodded, his tongue wagging out of his wide jaw like a dog waiting for a stick to chase. The last time

Henry had seen Boothe's servant creature, he'd been guarding Samantha's hospital room after her overdose. He always thought Ezra had broken some kind of rule by bringing him to her room, but he'd never gotten the chance to ask. He sure wasn't gonna ask *now*.

"How's it hangin', Ezra?"

"With great difficulty, Master Henry."

Burning pain rolled up Henry's body in shivering waves. "Tell me about it."

"I would like to Master Henry, but we should flee first."

"Fuck, Ezra. I want nothing more than to flee, but I'm kinda stuck here."

Ezra leaned forward to scrutinize the web holding Henry in its holy cocoon. The goll looked at his hand, singed from contacting the Tracker's net, and his eyebrows shot up in understanding. He bent over and pulled a bag around to the front of his waist.

Henry hissed in fresh pain. "Rocking a fanny pack, huh?"

Ezra ignored him. He pulled his hand from the bag and held it over Henry's body. He rubbed his fingers together like a chef seasoning his dinner, and a sparkling purple powder cascaded down. The threads sparked and shattered.

The pain stopped bit by bit, until the net fell away, its magic broken. Henry stared at the ceiling with tears streaming from his eyes. Tried catching his breath against the sobs that jerked pain through his broken ribs.

He turned to Ezra, and the goll looked back with a sweet smile that Henry wanted to kiss.

"Oh, that fucking sucked." He sat up, holding his arm pressed into his side. "I'm gonna kill that rat bastard piece of shit motherfucker with my own goddamn hands, Ezra."

"Of course, Master Henry."

Henry struggled to his feet. Black dots swirled in his vision, and he felt the maw of the well open behind him. Ezra reached out and steadied him with a hand on his forearm. "Can we flee now, Master Henry?"

"They killed my daughter, Ezra. Raped my wife. And now they have the horn."

Ezra leaned forward, his eyes fierce in the dim light. "What horn, Master Henry?"

"The Horn of the Lamb."

Ezra's jaw hung open and his eyes widened to their limits. Terror filled his face. The goll trembled in his grip. "We need help, Master Henry."

"Tell me about it." Henry swayed, fighting to keep his feet.

Ezra tightened his hold, claws digging into Henry's burned skin.

"Come!" The goll shouted in a hissing whisper.

Henry's guts folded in on themselves as they vanished. He didn't have the energy to scream this time.

Chapter Twenty-Six

HENRY HEARD a baby crying in the darkness. As if from a great distance. In an alley. Its lonely voice bouncing off the featureless walls of the building looming above it.

He opened his eyes. Henry was in Nowhere on his side, curled into a ball. His head hung over his shoulder, scraping the dirt with his horn.

Mist clung to the base of a crumbling city. Thick, swirling, like unseen objects pushing blindly along, afraid to step into the clear air. The baby's cry rose again, and Henry thought of San Diego.

After Samantha's second miscarriage, after little Avery had failed to enter the world, he took her on a trip. A little ocean and a lot of sun. They could sit and talk and try to come to terms with a world that wouldn't even *let* them bring a new life into it.

Fog had rolled in so thick on the second morning, he hadn't even been able to see past the railing of their shitty little balcony. It had lasted for three days, only breaking during the early dawn just before the sun. By the time the light was bright enough to see a path to the beach, the fog was back to slapping the window. They spent the entire time watching South Park reruns and eating delivered pizza.

Henry pushed off the ground to a sitting position, raising his arms and stretching with a jaw popping yawn. Scraping footsteps, and Henry looked over to find Ezra sitting on his haunches, watching him with a smile. "Good morning, Master Henry. How do you feel?"

Henry cocked his head and considered the question. He looked himself over, and had to admit it. "I feel pretty damn good, little buddy."

Ezra clasped his hands in front of him, and his smile became a grin.

The memories of the last couple of days pushed to the front of his thoughts, trying to harsh Henry's mellow. But he wasn't ready. He shook his head and forced a smile. "Thanks, Ezra. You really saved my ass."

The goll's cheeks darkened in a blush, and Ezra looked aside. "It was nothing, Master Henry. I heard your whistle and came. Happy to be of use to you again."

The pitiful wails of the baby floated out of the mist. Henry wanted to get away from it. Put it far behind him. He stood and stretched again, turning to leave the Forgotten, and its many ghosts, at his back.

Thick roots pushed through the ground a few feet in front of him. He ran his eyes along their twisted length, following them to the gnarled trunk of the massive Tree.

Under the swaying branches was a small stone table littered with chess pieces. Instead of the long table Henry remembered, it barely held room for two. A man with his back to Henry leaned with his elbow on his knees. A shining white suit hung perfectly from his shoulders. His black hair smoothed back in styled waves.

Henry felt his heart swell with confused joy.

Mandyel?

The man on the other side of the table leaned over his side of the chessboard, flowing white robes sweeping the ground at his feet.

Randall.

Henry's good mood soured, and his face twisted with disgust.

Great, I thought maybe somebody else would be on the night shift.

He looked at Ezra with a shrug.

"Well, let's go say *hi.*"

Ezra bounded off like a puppy ready to run for miles. He stopped next to the table, dancing from foot to foot. He pointed to Henry's approach, and Randall looked up, his mouth twitching in a smile. The other man stood, smoothing his slacks before turning around with his hand extended in greeting.

Boothe.

Henry's rage flashed like a grease fire. His vision clouded over with a red haze, and he charged the remaining steps in a blur, swinging his fist up with all his hate to fuel it. Boothe's face snapped back from the impact, and his body followed the recoil, sailing over the table and scattering the game with his shiny white loafers.

He crashed into the ground flat on his back, but bounced immediately to his feet, eyes blazing with red fire and lips drawn back over bloodied teeth.

Henry charged in and swung again.

His hand was met by Boothe's raised arm in a block that jolted through his bones like he'd hit a steel pillar.

"Motherfucker!" Henry drew back his hand, baring his claws.

Boothe vanished with a rush of air.

Henry sensed him reappear from behind. He spun with

his hands raised in defense, but Boothe stood on the other side of the table, smoothing his hair with a silver comb.

"I'll allow that one, Henry. I may even deserve it, but I won't ask for your forgiveness."

"Fuck you, you son of a bitch! You don't *deserve* my forgiveness."

The skin around the demon's eyes tightened. He sucked his teeth with a nod. "That is probably true, as most things go. Still, I will continue to make amends as best I can."

"*Make amends?*" Henry stared, his shoulders dropping and hands flopping on his thighs. "What can you possibly do to make amends?"

"Why, save your daughter, of course."

Henry's knees wobbled, and he stumbled to the lump of stone Boothe had been using as a chair. "The only one who can do that is gone."

"And who is that, Henry?"

"Mandyel. He died last night. Or whatever fucking night it was."

"Mandyel died, did he?" Boothe exchanged a look with Randall.

"I *saw* him die."

Randall stood and put his hands behind his back. "Did you?"

"Yes, Goddamn it. I saw Peterson eat his fucking heart."

"Peterson?" Boothe frowned. "That sot from the Viazo Grand?"

Henry put his head in his hands and his elbows on the stone table. "He's the head of the Order From Chaos cult."

Boothe laughed. A breathless guffaw that startled Henry out of his self-pity. The demon held his stomach and shook his head. "I hardly think *Peterson* is the head of anything more complicated than the hotel kitchen."

Henry jumped to his feet and leveled a clawed finger at Boothe's face. "Maybe not. But he raped my wife and helped kill my daughter, and I'm gonna *fuck* his *ass*."

Boothe sobered. He wiped his eyes with a square of silk then returned it to his pocket. "And I'm sorry about that, Henry. Truly, I am."

Henry dropped his finger with a shrug. "What difference does it make, anyway? He has the Horn of the Lamb now."

Randall's knees unhinged, and he grabbed the table to ease himself back into his seat. Color drained from his face, and he looked into the distance past Henry with eyes wide with shock.

"Henry?" Boothe's voice was quiet, without the mocking lilt that made Henry feel so inferior. "Are you certain?"

Henry nodded. "Mandyel came with me to the Purveyor's place. We were gonna trade some stuff for the horn, but Peterson was there. He had a Tracker chained up like a dog. Stabbed Mandyel through the back with a black sword. Peterson was pissed because me and Nadia tore his kiddie carnival a new asshole."

"I heard about that. Very well done."

"Mandyel was *pissed*. I thought he was gonna kill me."

"Oh, no," Randall said. "That one is *thousands* of moves ahead. You probably did exactly what he wanted."

"I don't know. I seemed to be fucking up all the time, and the ring was making me walk through life like I was asleep, kinda. I don't know anymore."

Boothe mimed putting a ring on his first finger. "Was it silver? A frog eating a snake which was then eating the frog in turn?"

"Yeah, how'd you know?"

"And where is this ring now?"

"Peterson's wearing it."

Randall and Boothe shared another look.

Henry bristled. "Stop doing that shit. Come on, what?"

Randall bent over with a grunt. He picked up the white king and placed it on the table where the board had been, then flicked it with his finger. The king fell over, and he leaned back with his arms crossed.

"The fuck does that mean?" Henry demanded.

Boothe whistled. "It means, Dear Henry, that Mandyel is a master, and we are but pawns in a game he plays with a skill earned over a day stretching into eternity."

Henry threw his hands in the air. "You fucking people. Or whatever you are. Just answer one question with a straight fucking answer. Just once."

"And what is your question, Henry?"

"Is God gonna honor Mandyel's deal?"

"Of course."

"How?"

"Once He receives the thing He was promised in return, Henry."

"Why would the devil give up my daughter?"

"I've tried to tell you so many times. There are rules. And we must all abide by them. Even Lucifer, though he does bend them to their utmost limits."

"Will he trade her for Adam?"

Boothe blanched. "He would trade the universe itself for that boy."

"Does he even know about him?"

"Calm down, Henry. It is quite possible that he *doesn't* know about him. Order From Chaos is powerful. And as they are consolidating that power further, they may be keeping secrets even from Hell."

Power.

A thought tickled at Henry's mind. Some detail that flitted like a moth. "Power."

Boothe tipped his head to listen. "Go on, Henry. You have something, I can tell."

"I know who the leader of the cult is. It's the mayor. Fucking Malcolm Lucius and his wackadoodle brother."

Boothe leaned back, and he slowly nodded. "That makes sense, actually. His family is very well known in the shadows."

"Yeah, but his brother sold the horn for money when he could have just given it up. They could have blown it and drawn the kid to their cause, and we'd all be in Bonesville."

"That's not so troubling when you know about Hennessy's obsession with immortality. He's even tried summoning *me* before. *His* cause is not necessarily his family's. Or the Order's."

"What do you want me to do?" Henry asked.

"Still asking questions to which you already know the answers? I thought you had learned that lesson at least, Dear Henry."

He looked down at the tattered remains of the suit he had taken from Boothe's closet. Blood stained and charred. Busting the seams of the silk boxers that barely covered his balls. "I guess I should probably get some clothes, huh?"

"That is certainly a start."

"I had plenty of sleep, so maybe some water?"

"Very good, Henry."

"I guess the last thing is to see when the Viazo Grand starts check-ins."

Boothe smiled and turned to Randall. "Tell Maria that I'll be back soon… God willing."

"After this ..." His voiced cracked and he cleared his throat. "You'll help me get my daughter?"

"Henry, have I *ever* lied to you?"

He bit on his seething hatred and pictured Mandyel's burning gaze. The paths opened by his choices. His lack of trust. His self-loathing. "You know, I'm beginning to think the answer to that question is *no*. But what you said just now was not an answer. Please, Boothe. Will you help me get her back?"

The demon's face softened. Regret flashed by, almost quicker than Henry could detect. Boothe covered it with a smile, and placed a hand over his heart. "Dear Henry, I swear it."

I'm not gonna fucking cry. Not anymore.

"Thank you."

Boothe nodded. "Now then. Let's go kill the good Mr. Peterson!"

Chapter Twenty-Seven

HENRY FILLED another pitcher at the kitchen sink. He tilted his head back and drank, the cool water spilling from the corners of his mouth. He set the pitcher down and caught his breath. Utter silence in his mind. He could feel the weight of the city's sorrow — a low hum of pain that left his thoughts mostly alone.

He closed his eyes and sent his mind out, questing beyond the walls of Boothe's apartment. The screams of the damaged and damned crashed into Henry's senses, and he drew his mind back, snapping into his body with enough force to send him staggering into the counter.

I'm getting control of this shit. Hot damn.

"What have you *done* to my place, Henry?" Boothe's voice floated to his ears, and he winced at the memory of his tantrum.

"It was like that when I got here," he shouted.

Boothe stomped out wearing a fresh suit. Dark blue with a crisp red tie. Starched white shirt, polished black shoes, and his hair was perfect. "I think we *both* know that isn't true."

"Look, I had a meltdown, okay. You got your old lady back, you know. Not me, so fucking save it."

Boothe pressed his lips into a line and nodded. "Get dressed, Henry."

"The old hoodie and jeans. Yay me."

"Learn to inhabit the form of your choosing, and you can dress with style and class." Boothe spun in an elegant circle. "Like me."

"What do you mean, the *form of my choosing?*" Henry shouted over his shoulder while stepping into the closet to pick between the gray one and the gray one.

"Mandyel told you nothing of choice?"

"That's all the guy fucking talked about."

"He *is* the angel of free will, after all."

Henry slid the hoodie over his horns, grown longer since the last time he'd worn one. "Yeah, but he said *this* was my true form. Like I hate myself so much, that I subconsciously picked this form for me or something."

"And that's true. An unconscious decision is still a decision, Henry."

Henry stepped out in his demon uniform stretched tight across muscles that had grown thicker and denser in the last few days. "I can't concentrate on all this shit right now. Let's just take care of Peterson, and if I'm still alive tomorrow, we'll chat about free will versus predestination over some waffles."

"Whatever you say, Henry."

That was way too easy.

Ezra poofed into existence in front of the refrigerator, jumping up and down with glee. "I went to the Purveyor's house Master Henry."

"What in the world for?"

Ezra's face fell, and his dance broke into an embarrassed shuffle. "To bring back your things." The goll held up his brass phone and the Buffet Bag over his head. Both were stained with blood but none the worse for wear.

"Holy shit. That's awesome, but that stuff's not worth you getting caught or hurt."

Ezra looked up from under his brow. "Truly?"

"Fuck yeah." Henry slid the phone into his front pocket and opened the leather bag. "I'd way rather have *you* around than just this crap, no matter how cool it is."

Boothe wrinkled his forehead in curiosity at the bag. "What does that do?"

"Check it out." Henry snatched his hand out in triumph, holding a thick slice of sizzling pepper bacon. He took half in one bite, and closed his eyes as he chewed. "Oh man, that's so fucking good."

"It … *makes bacon?*"

"Yup. Three times a day if you want it."

"The *Gratia Lapides Sacculi?* You use it for … *bacon?*"

"You got that right." Henry tossed the other half of the bacon to Ezra. The goll caught it and stuffed it into his mouth. He closed his eyes like Henry. The corners of his mouth glistened with drool. He swallowed and looked up with a smile.

"Thank you, Master Henry. It was delicious."

Henry rolled the bag up and stuffed it into his back pocket.

Boothe raised his eyebrows. "You're just going to walk around with the *Gratia Lapides Sacculi* in your jeans?"

"Where else am I gonna get my bacon?"

"I have no idea."

"Then, there you go." Acid roiled in his stomach. Henry swallowed it down and took a calming breath. The effort to keep from thinking was making him sweat. "We gonna do this shit, or what?"

Boothe held out his hand, and Henry took it. Between

blinks, the light from the apartment faded into the illumination from a vintage chandelier hanging in Peterson's office, deep in the Viazo Grand.

Four cultists in flowing robes stood in front of his desk with their hoods drawn. Three in brown, and the fourth in red.

Peterson paused at Henry and Boothe's entrance, a steaming cup of tea frozen under his nose. Ezra poofed into the office facing the corner behind his back. Peterson spun with a look of chagrin, and the cultists stepped back in shock.

"Gentlemen," Boothe said. "I'm terribly sorry to interrupt, but we need to speak with this man." A black spear appeared in his hands. The cultists turned at the sound of his voice, and Boothe spun the spear with a flourish, planting the butt at his feet and leaning on it with an enviable nonchalance.

The man in the red robe stepped away from his fellows and clapped his hands in front of his chest. A blinding flash accompanied a booming crash, and he was gone. The remaining three eyed the empty space, then their heads rose to face Boothe as one.

The one on the left snapped his hands up and two gleaming blades dropped into his palms, the metal gleaming with dark energy.

The cultist in the middle threw his hood back to expose a face completely blue with tattoos. He reached between his open hood and his neck and drew a sword, ringing into his hand like a tuning fork.

Peterson set his tea on the desk and stood with a smile. His wings opened behind him, snapping out like the billowing sails of a pirate ship. "You were saying?"

The third cultist shrugged and raised his fists in a boxer's stance.

Henry stepped forward and roared. It filled the office with a screeching rumble.

Not bad.

The swordsman leaped forward with a thrust that met Boothe's spear, and Henry launched into the heavyweight champ with his claws extended. The boxer slid aside like water and rocked Henry with an overhand right that dislocated his jaw.

Holy fuck!

Mr. Knife stepped under Mr. Sword's lunge, and Boothe's spear sparked when it blocked the blades, driving the slices toward the swordsman who danced back with a parry.

The boxer peppered Henry's face with jabs, splitting his eyebrow and squashing his nose with a *CRUNCH!*

Blows so quick, that his blurring eyes couldn't see them coming. Henry backpedaled, driving his claws up in a blind swing that caught the champ in the ribs, digging through muscle and bone.

The champ squealed, and Henry closed his fist over the thick flesh under the champ's armpit. He jerked a handful of meat free with a wet ripping, louder than the shredding fabric of the robe.

Boothe spun under another swing of the sword, and sent the tip of the spear into the soft spot under the cultist's chin. Blood shot from the swordsman's mouth, followed by his flopping tongue. It hit the floor like a steak on a butcher's block. His scream matched the boxer's, and Boothe dropped to spin on his knees as knives flashed overhead.

Henry swung twice more, each blow tearing through skin and bone.

The boxer spun away, and Henry caught him by the hair. He yanked his head back and dragged a claw across his throat. Blood sprayed across the office, painting the wall in a rainbow of crimson.

Boothe finished his spin by pulling the spear from the swordsman's jaw and planting the butt on the floor. He leveraged against the shaft, and whipped a foot up to kick Mr. Knife in the balls hard enough to lift his feet out of his boots.

Mr. Knife wheezed a scream, like a steam kettle boiling over, and Boothe silenced his voice with a strike to the throat. Mr. Knife gurgled out his final breath through the gaping wound in his neck, then crumpled to the floor.

Henry wiped the blood from his claws on the front of his hoodie.

Boothe stepped up with every hair still in place, and not a single drop of blood to mar his outfit.

God damn it.

Boothe and Henry joined each other at the center of the room in front of the desk. Peterson stood stock still with Ezra hanging on his neck, the goll's fanged mouth pressed into his skin just hard enough to draw a trickle of blood.

Henry wiped snotty blood from his nose, flinging it from his fingers to splat on the floor. "Now, *you* were saying?"

"I wasn't saying anything."

Ezra gnawed and Peterson sucked in a wincing hiss.

"Ezra," Henry shouted. "Down!"

The goll dropped like a stone, and Henry leaped across the desk.

He grabbed Peterson's bloody throat with one hand, and dug his claws into the dickhead's crotch with the other. His weight drove Peterson back against the wall. The Ben Franklin specs flew from his face, and he snarled in fury.

Henry felt Peterson *flare*, but his power hit a wall only to echo back into him with the rumble of distant thunder.

I know just what that feels like.

"You see, Henry?" Boothe stepped around the side of the desk to regard Peterson's predicament. "The ring dulls a demon's power. Like the snake eating the frog, only to be eaten by its prey, the power doubles back on itself, rendered useless without an outlet. It also acts as a teleport beacon. That's how Mandyel always knew where you were. An infinite loop that told you where you were going because it always knew where you'd been."

"I always wondered if I was the frog or the snake."

"But that's the trick, Henry. You were always *both*."

Peterson rolled his eyes. "Can we get on with it?"

Henry squeezed a handful of balls, and Peterson groaned.

"Fine," Henry growled. "Have it your way. Where's Adam?"

"I thought you wanted the horn?"

Henry released his hold and spun Peterson around. Two vicious swipes of his claws, and bone broke like twigs, skin parting like bloody paper.

Peterson screamed as his wings dropped to the floor in gory lumps.

Henry spun him back around and reset both grips. He leaned into Peterson's face and roared, "WHERE IS HE?"

Peterson slumped in Henry's grip, tears welling in his eyes. "He's in the cells beneath the dry pantry."

Henry looked at Ezra over his shoulder. "You know where that is?"

Ezra stilled and closed his eyes. He nodded, his eyes springing open. "Yes, Master Henry."

"Good." Henry leaned in and dropped his voice to a whisper. "Now that we have that out of the way. You said you raped my wife, and I don't know if you were telling the truth or if you were only trying to hurt me, but I did make myself a promise." He leaned in until his lips were touching Peterson's ear. "And I keep my promises."

Henry dug his claws in then tore Peterson's cock and balls off with a wet snap of his wrist.

Peterson crumpled against him with a strangled wail, and Henry held him up to watch the light leave his eyes as he bled to death.

He opened his hand, and Peterson's body slid down the wall. His life force rose up to tickle Henry's nose, and he waved it away in disgust, flinging the mangled genitals into the corner.

He turned to find Boothe inspecting him with his hands behind his back, his eyes gleaming. The demon bowed.

"Bravo, Henry. Bravo."

Henry looked at Ezra, and swept his hand toward the door. "Lead the way."

Chapter Twenty-Eight

Ezra BOUNDED into the hallway outside Peterson's office. A service corridor bustling with activity. Porters and wait staff pushing carts covered in white linen. They kept to their side of the hall, avoiding Henry with down-turned eyes.

Ezra didn't receive a single glance.

Just another Friday night.

They followed the goll into a busy kitchen full of noise and the heavy aroma of a gourmet preparation. A few sighs of annoyance and the rolling eyes of exasperation.

Boothe moved through the place like its architect. Henry walked like he'd entered a different world.

Past the massive refrigerators, they made a left through a stone arch. Much older parts of the building, missing the modern touches covering the ancient stones and plaster. Through another arch and into a larder stacked with barrels and crates. Sacks piled in a corner.

The door at the end was a thick, dark wood. Iron hardware with a giant rod pushed into a rusting hasp. A ring of keys hung on a peg driven into the joints of the stacked stone wall. Ezra stopped at the door, turning around to look up at Henry with an expectant expression on his gray face.

Henry looked over his shoulder, listening for anyone following through the oddly regular activity. "I don't get it. Nobody gave a shit that a winged goll was leading a demon and a salesman through the kitchens?"

"It is, after all, just a *hotel* at its heart, Henry."

"I guess." Henry shook his head and grabbed the keys from the peg, iron tingling through his fingers like a nine-volt battery to the tongue. "We going through there, huh?"

Ezra nodded. "Yes, Master Henry."

"What are we gonna find down there?"

"I'm sorry, Master Henry. I can't see through all the rock."

"Quite all right," Boothe said. "And to Henry's point, why don't you go back and watch for anybody who might want to cause us harm. Like that red-robed fellow with the tricks."

"Yes, Master Boothe."

Ezra took off like a cat that just heard the can opener. He cut around the corner before turning to the door.

Henry turned back to Boothe. "You think there are any guards?"

"This deep inside the hotel? I doubt it, but let's be cautious."

"Fair enough."

The third key clicked over with a grinding jolt, and the door swung open. An uneven set of stairs descended into the dark. Bright light spilled between the floor and the bottom of the door.

"What, are they growing weed down there?"

Henry ducked then dug his claws into the damp stone of the steps. On the slick landing, he paused and sorted the keys. A scent filled his nose, like the char on a burnt cookie — smoky and hearty with a sweetness underneath that had his mouth watering.

The Christmas after her first miscarriage, Samantha decided there would be no holiday baking. Henry hadn't blamed her, but after two days, he cracked. How hard could it be to make brownies from a box? After the smoke cleared, Samantha tried not to laugh while mixing a new batch. For the next two weeks, every time they heated the oven, burnt chocolate would rise into the air and he would smack his lips in anticipation.

"What is that smell?"

Boothe's voice was husky, and unnaturally loud in the close quarters of the stairs. "Virgin blood."

"Wow. And you know this *why?* Wait, never mind."

"Just find the key, Henry."

Even though the third key had opened the door at the top of the stairs, he tried it again. Just in case. The same grinding click, and the door swung in on a rusty grumble of ancient hinges to flood the stairs with light.

A long corridor lined with doors. Six and six with one at the end. The burned brownie scent washed over him, and he breathed deep. Sugar and spice. That char. Something floral.

Boothe squeezed past, sending a disgusted look over his shoulder.

"What?" Henry asked.

Boothe shook his head and pressed his fingertips to the first door. He closed his eyes. "They've collected the blood, but she's dead."

"Shit."

Boothe looked at him with a sad earnest expression that Henry couldn't interpret. "Yes, it is. With her passing, the blood now loses power the longer it remains unused."

Henry smiled and slapped Boothe on the shoulder. He tipped the demon a theatrical wink. "What, you want to drink it?"

"I'm half-tempted, yes."

Henry sighed.

Just when I think I'm learning something.

He pointed to the next door. "What's in that one?"

Boothe blinked as if waking from a daydream. "Nothing."

And nothing in the rest of the cells until they reached halfway to the end, and a breeze rippled the fabric of Henry's hoodie, washing the floral brownie char away with a blast of hay and dry leaves. They rustled underfoot. The sun beamed through the limbs of the trees above the path, and colorful bugs danced to the song of a bubbling spring.

Boothe stepped up next to Henry and looked around in appreciation. His forehead wrinkled.

"Don't trust your eyes," Boothe said. "It's a glamour."

He then called out, "Charlie? Is that you?"

The bugs froze, their wings beating in place, and a rough voice floated out of the trees. "No …"

Whistling intruded on the glamour.

Is that 'Always Look on the Bright Side'?

The whistled tune further broke the illusion with its jaunty immediacy. Rushed and shrill. The bubbling water sputtered to a halt, and the bugs fell to the ground in fluttering spirals. The whistling grew louder. More desperate.

Henry winced away, and the peaceful glen broke apart like burning mist. A demon roared from behind the fifth door, chains rattling with rage. The demon caught his breath, and the whistling from the end of the corridor continued unabated.

"That you, Boothe?"

"Yes, Charlie. It's me." Boothe flapped his hand, stepping toward the door, and Henry handed him the keys. The demon didn't fumble through them like Henry had. The door squealed open.

A red demon hung from the ceiling. Wrapped in iron chains from ankles to neck, the only things free were his smooth head and clawed feet.

Boothe stepped forward, but Charlie thrashed like a fat butterfly trying to leave its chrysalis. "No! Don't try to save me. Just go down there and shut up that God *damn* WHISTLING!"

The spear appeared in Boothe's hands, and he raised it overhead. Charlie closed his eyes and jerked his head back as Boothe sliced through the chains. They parted with a crackling sizzle, and the naked demon tumbled to the floor.

The spear drooped and melted in Boothe's hands. He tossed it into the corner, wiping his palms on the front of his jacket. Charlie pushed himself to his feet. Thick muscle covered every inch of his body. His squat legs like kegs. His hanging gorilla arms bulging and roping up to his cannon-ball shoulders. A neck as wide as his head.

He looked up at Boothe with a beaming smile. "Thank you."

He transitioned into movement in a heartbeat, blurring through the door, veering up the corridor with a whoop of joy. At the last door on the right, he went from full speed to stationary, sinking his claws into the iron door and planting his feet. His face stretched into a grimace, and the muscles in his back rippled.

The skin on his fingers peeled back as it burned, and he shook his head with a growl. Every time he heaved against the door, it bulged out, warping like taffy. One last pull, and the door tore free of the stone with a clang that shook the floor. Charlie dropped the door behind him and blew on his fingers.

The whistling finally stopped, but a weak voice floated through the open door as Charlie rushed inside with wide and gleeful eyes.

A British man's voice asked, "I wonder if you would be so good as to … *hurrk*—"

A squat man stepped out of the cell brushing his hands off in front of him. Built like a bricklayer, he had Buddha's face and a shiny black ponytail. His oiled goatee extended to a point under his chin. Jeans and a black mechanic's shirt, he sighed with a grin and turned to face Henry, dropping his hands to rest them behind his back. "Much better."

Boothe indicated Henry at his side with a wave. "Charlie, this is Henry."

Henry stepped forward with his hand out. An instinct that he didn't bother fighting.

This is all too fucking much.

Charlie looked at Henry's hand with his eyebrows riding up into his widow's peak. "Why not?" He grabbed Henry's hand in greeting. "Charlie Mara."

"Henry Black. You're standing where I think I need to be."

Charlie snatched his hand back, and the mirth drained from his face. "You don't wanna go in there. You don't need *that* shit."

"I'm afraid we must," Boothe said.

Charlie looked from Boothe to Henry and back. He raised his hands. "Fine, but do me a favor and put me back in the chains first."

Charlie moved to the side, walking on the bent door with echoing steps. Henry stepped forward, and the right key fell into his hand. He knew with more certainty he'd ever felt. It slid in and unlocked the door as if turning on its own.

The door swung open and Henry looked directly into the eyes of a beautiful boy sitting on the edge of a cot with his hands in his lap. Small and dirty, his face puffy from crying. He smiled, and Henry fell in love.

Don't look into his eyes, Henry!

Words without meaning. A warning he couldn't possibly heed. He looked into Amélie's eyes for the first time, his breath hitching, swallowing tears that threatened to pour from the deepest part of his soul.

"Are you here to free me?" His voice in Henry's head and ears. Hesitant. Expectant. Strained with a short life full of pain.

Amélie's tiny squirming face had been red from the cloth used to clean the birth from the folds in her skin. She was a wondrous beauty, and he felt hideous standing there with her in his arms. He knew she couldn't really see yet, but the feeling that she was looking into his heart, and his darkest thoughts, made him shrink deeper into his hate and self-loathing.

Henry, don't look!

He *had* to look. He saw the same thing in the boy's eyes now. And just like staring at his daughter, knowing she would forgive him anything, he felt it from Adam. His promise to Amélie on the day she entered the world, echoed through him with the weight of crushing responsibility.

I'll never let anyone hurt you, baby. Daddy will always be here.

Henry tumbled into the boy's gaze, but he knew which way was up. It was the direction of her love. Her understanding and forgiveness. Things he didn't deserve, and yet he clung to them with all his might.

The boy's power washed over him, but it didn't touch his resolve. He already knew what a monster he was. He'd shown the world his demon face his whole life. If he couldn't save one child, he'd save the other, and maybe that would be good enough.

Tears filled his eyes, and Adam's face became Amélie's. Henry nodded, and the child rocked back as if struck by an unseen hand, his power bounding back into him. "Yes, I'm here to free you."

Adam blinked, fresh tears tracking through the dirt on his cheeks. "But you are champion to another."

"Doesn't matter." Henry marched in and swung his claws, striking the chain from Adam's leg in a flash of sparks. Thunder in the distance. The blast of trumpets heralding the child's release, and Adam flung himself into Henry's arms.

I'll never let anyone hurt you again.

I'm here.

Adam bawled into his chest, and Henry stroked the boy's pale hair with a twisted hand tipped with black knives. Boothe walked in, and his face was unsure and questioning. "Henry?"

Adam pulled back with a gasp. He looked up at Boothe, and his face twisted with rage and terror. He beat on Henry's chest with tiny fists and screamed, "Kill him!"

The compelling power dug into him, but Henry brushed it aside. "Suck shit, kid."

Adam froze with a hand drawn back for another strike. "What?"

"What?" Boothe echoed.

"Boothe's an asshole, for sure. Don't get me wrong. There's nothing I'd like to see more than that fucker get eaten by a pack of syphilitic rats, but I had to admit earlier that I maybe kinda owed him, so … fuck that shit."

"Henry!"

He looked up at Boothe's scolding tone. "What? Don't

just tell a kid that it's bad to say *fuck*. Let 'em hear it first so they know why you're smacking them when *they* say it."

"You disobeyed me," Adam whispered.

"Yeah, I guess *I'm* an asshole, too."

He squeezed Henry in another hug.

What he wouldn't give to feel Amélie's arms around him again. He buried his nose in Adam's hair and rocked him until the child stopped crying.

Adam leaned back, wiping his nose on the back of his hand. "You saved me because you wanted to?"

"That's right."

Adam looked up at Boothe from under his brows, his eyelids flashing as he blinked. "I'm sorry I commanded Henry to kill you, Mr. Boothe."

"It's quite all right, Adam. Henry?"

"Yeah, yeah. Let's get this little guy out of here."

"That kid ain't going *nowhere*," Charlie said from the doorway.

Henry spun with a growl, setting Adam behind him on the floor.

"Whoa!" Charlie raised his hands, his round face an *O* of shock. "I didn't mean it that way, *mòmíngqímiào*!"

"Then what *did* you mean, Charlie?" Boothe stood calmly, but Henry saw the tension in his shoulders.

"Until that kid is called, he has the weight of destiny on him."

Boothe pursed his lips. "Henry, will you pick up the child, please? We're going to my place."

Henry slung Adam up on his hip. Boothe grabbed his shoulder and looked at Charlie. "Would you like to join us?"

"Not really." Charlie walked in shaking his head. He took Boothe's hand with a rueful shrug.

Boothe reached through time and space to take them back to his apartment, but nothing happened.

A blip of power hit Henry in his chest. A flicker like a movie reel with a missing frame.

Charlie walked around to sit on the cot. "Maybe I'll just put *myself* back in the chains."

Boothe scratched his head, looking at Henry with his forehead wrinkled in apology. "This may have been an error on my part."

Ezra burst into existence in the doorway. "Master Henry! Oh, hello, Master Charlie."

Charlie waved without looking up.

"Master Henry!"

"Yeah, I hear you Ezra."

"They're coming, Master Henry!"

"*Who* is?"

The goll lowered his eyes to the floor, rubbing the top of his head with rough passes of his gray claws. "Trackers, Master Henry."

Chapter Twenty-Nine

"What's a Tracker?" Adam asked.

Henry hitched the boy higher on his hip. "They're kinda like God's fishermen."

Boothe shook his head. "More like fishers *of* men."

"Nah, my man," Charlie said. "Fishermen of *demons.*"

Adam's brow wrinkled. He lifted his hand and pressed his fingertips against Henry's cheek.

Henry's memories shuffled across his mind until the Trackers swelled in his imagination, growing with his pain and terror and panic. Adam pulled his hand away. "Oh, *that's* a Tracker."

"You just did the Vulcan mind meld. You're like a little Spock."

Adam rolled his eyes and raised his face to the ceiling. He opened his mouth, and the Trackers' song issued into the silence. Demanding. Commanding. Echoing with distant horns and thunder.

Henry stared in awe at Adam's face as a golden glow filled the cell. Shimmering like the sun streaming through rippling water. Heat at his back, and Henry turned, squinting into the holy glare.

The Tracker that had thrown Henry into the well floated down the corridor, his wings brushing into the upper corners and his hands clutching the black sword that was stained with another angel's blood. The chains that held him to the service of the Order dragged across the floor, jangling in chiming counterpoint to Adam's song.

The yellow fire in his eyes reflected off the scars streaking across his face. Puckered skin where Henry's claws had slashed. He hovered in front of the door, his light tightening Henry's skin across his forehead.

Charlie hid in Henry's shadow, while Boothe backed up out of the Tracker's view.

"Put me down, Henry."

Henry lowered Adam to the floor, and the child walked out of the cell, his silhouette burned into Henry's retinas.

Your song has beckoned me forth.

Who here can free me of this torment?

Henry looked at Boothe with his hands spread in a question, but Boothe shook his head. "Don't look at me. Those chains are under an enchantment far beyond *me.*"

Adam stood on his tiptoes and laid his hand against the angel's thigh.

The Tracker's light dimmed, flowing into the small hand in pulsing flashes. He lowered to the floor, staring into Adam's eyes. His wings folded in, and he lowered his sword.

Henry blinked the spots out of his eyes. Adam turned with a smile, and Henry smiled back. "Break his chains, Henry," the boy said.

The Tracker jerked his head up, his eyes narrowed and his jaw clenched, the muscles under his ears bulging.

"Um, I can't."

"You *can*. It's easy."

"How do *you* know, kid?" Boothe asked.

"You are a paladin, Henry. You have sworn to free those who can't free themselves. There are no chains that can hold against you."

"Oh." Henry nodded. "Sure."

Adam stepped aside, and the Tracker lifted his hands. Henry charged forward with a roar and swung his claws at the chains with all his might.

They shattered like ice.

The Tracker reeled back, and the sword dropped from his hands. He caught his balance and dropped to his knee. One fist over his heart, the other pressed into the ground in front of his feet.

I swear fealty to you.

The booming voice in Henry's mind held a finality he didn't care for you. "Oh, fuck no." Henry pointed to Adam. "Swear to *him.*"

He is already served by another.

"God damn it! Boothe, tell him. I'm just some fuck-up comedian who you suckered into all this nonsense."

Boothe spread his hands in genuine confusion. "Henry, I have no idea how to proceed. I believe I was suckered, as well."

Ezra hopped back into view. "We must go, Master Henry and Master Boothe."

"Fuck, why is everybody looking at me?"

No answers. Just looks.

"Fine." He pointed at the kneeling tracker. "What's your name?"

Ramiel.

"And stop talking in my head for fuck's sake. It hurts."

A smile played at the edges of the Tracker's mouth, and he spoke with his mouth. "I am Ramiel."

"All right, Remmy. Your brothers and sisters are coming to … do whatever you guys do. They're probably busy laying the smack down on the Viazo riffraff, but we should heretofore … as to … you know, fuck off."

"That was poetry, Henry." Boothe pressed through the door, leaning away from Ramiel as he passed.

Henry shrugged. "We need to get out of here. It's as simple as that."

A booming concussion above their heads sent dust cascading down like sifted flour. The fluorescents flickered, blinking back on at half intensity, angry hornets buzzing from their ballasts.

Charlie jumped from the cot. "I got no weapon or nothing."

"Peterson's office," Henry shouted. He spun to find Ezra hopping from foot to foot. "You remember how to get back there?"

"Yes, Master Henry."

Henry crowded into the hallway and scooped Adam up, slinging the boy onto his back.

Adam held onto his savior's neck, fingers laced under his throat, weighing nothing.

He charged past Ramiel, giving him a sharp slap on the ass that stung his palm as he passed. "Let's go."

They compressed into the stairwell and burst out into the pantry. Henry couldn't wait to see the expression on the first busboy to see them coming down the hall. Ramiel's light flared behind them, and Charlie passed in a humming blur of pumping arms and flashing teeth.

Retracing their steps, Ezra led them through empty hallways to Peterson's office.

The floor shook as Henry crossed the threshold, bucking him off balance. He recovered in time to see Charlie stand with the cultist's daggers held up in front of him. A swirling mass of entropic energy flowed from the blades to surround his forearms in swirling tendrils. He smiled in appreciation. "Oh yeah."

Boothe scooped the sword from the floor, and it rang, black wisps of energy radiating from its tip like sound waves.

"There's nothing for *you*, Henry," Adam said in his ear.

"Don't worry about me, kid. Even the champ couldn't take me down."

The floor heaved, and Henry braced himself against Ramiel's solid shoulder. The lights died, and only the Tracker's glow kept Henry from losing his direction. The noise of war swelled in the distance. Explosions and gunfire. Shouted curses.

A porter sprinted by pushing a luggage cart on squealing wheels.

Henry cocked his head to listen. "It sounds like fucking *Apocalypse Now* out there."

"Great movie," Charlie said. "Why I started surfing."

Boothe stepped to the door with the sword out in front of him and peered around the jamb. "Well, Henry. Front or back?"

"Shit, it sounds like it doesn't matter."

"The lobby is wide open. Room to swing a weapon. Time enough to see the enemy coming."

"Or to hide behind this thick slab of angel, here." Henry turned to look at Adam from the corner of his eye. "What do you think?"

"I think this is the most fun I've ever had!"

"All right, then. The front door it is."

Ezra scampered out in front of them, leading the way. Boothe and Charlie walked in a hurried crouch behind him. Henry followed, and Ramiel brought up the rear with his light making their shadows dance along the walls as they ran toward the battlefield thunder.

They left the hallway, stepping out onto the balcony overlooking the lobby. When they passed the spot where Ariana had announced the auction, Henry convulsed with a shiver.

They pounded down the stairs, and a group of four gun-toting cultists popped out of the darkness at the base of the statues at either side of the lobby.

The two at the front held AR-15s pressed into their shoulders.

Looks like somebody's been going to the range.

They opened fire, and Ramiel's light exploded into blinding brilliance. Bullets sparked into the disintegrating fire, and Boothe charged with his sword a blur.

Flames gouted like blood wherever the dark blade touched flesh, and screaming cultists collapsed to ash.

Charlie was a whirling dervish of color. Unable to track him with his eyes, Henry only knew where he'd been by the howls of the cultists as he rendered them into dog food.

A demon rushed in with his panicked eyes and saw Ramiel rise over Henry and Adam, his feet coming out from under him as he backpedaled. Ramiel dropped in an arc that took him to the demon scampering back on his ass. The Tracker plunged the sword down, driving it through the demon and into the floor.

A clap of thunder, and deep cracks spread out from the impact. The demon erupted in a slurry of black blood that washed across the lobby from wall to wall.

"I'll be honest," Henry whispered over his shoulder. "That seemed excessive."

Adam snickered, and Henry grinned.

First this boy, and then Amélie.

They gathered at the front door, and Boothe still didn't

have a speck of blood on him. Charlie was soaked to the elbows. Ramiel's entire body was awash with gore.

"Fuck it," Henry said, and he pushed through the glass door into the sudden quiet in front of the Viazo Grand. Wet air slapped him in the face. Drizzle blew in under the overhang protecting the guests as they exited their vehicles.

They gathered under the roof's edge. A flash of lightning illuminated a group of cultists and demons standing at the top of a rise twenty yards away.

Henry's group turned as one to run the other way, and the sky filled with the blended light from a dozen Trackers flying over the hotel to meet them. They froze, and the Trackers dropped to the ground to spread out.

Ramiel dimmed his own light, and they all crouched into a tight group.

The Trackers advanced, and their song spread through the rain. They were covered in blood, both black and red, and their nets were empty. Their song sounded like a lie.

"Back inside?" Henry asked. Golden light descended the staircase. "Motherfucker!"

"Henry," Boothe said. "You must get the boy away from here."

"What, just run away?"

Ezra took Henry's hand in his. "Yes, Master Henry. Take the lamb far away."

"I can't take him into the shadows with me. His *destiny* is too Goddamned heavy."

Charlie leaned over. "Then use your fucking feet, shithead."

Ramiel nodded. "They have served you well thus far, Master Henry."

"This is bullshit." They were right. Until he could free Amélie, Adam was all that mattered. He reached back and pressed a steadying hand against the boy's backside, then ran in a crouch to the wall, facing the cultists and demons on the hill.

He turned back to his companions, "If any of you fuckers die on me, I'll find you. And you'll be sorry."

"I'm already sorry," Charlie muttered.

The Trackers drew their weapons. Henry squinted into the darkness at the cultists. "They don't have a fucking chance."

A red glow spread across the hill — maybe he'd spoken too soon.

In the center of the glow was the cultist who disappeared from Peterson's office. Swirling fire flickered from his hands. Hellish light sparkled off the rain. The ground shook, and the Trackers slowed.

The red-robed leader threw his hands into the air, and fire rolled down the hill, arcing from his fingers in sizzling waves.

Shadow demons erupted from the ground in every direction. Screaming with the voices of those they had tortured in hell, they threw themselves at the trackers. Their feet left burning spots of lava as they passed.

They swarmed over the angels like hyenas on a carcass, and the cries from the hill drowned out the screams of the Trackers as they fought.

The demons and cultists charged down the hill to end the battle in a rout, but the glass wall of the entry exploded in a shower of sparkling shards as the Trackers inside the hotel burst into the night to defend their brothers and sisters.

Shadows shooting from the ground, trailing dripping fire. Slobbering demons running with weapons raised. Robed cultists firing semi-automatic rifles. The horizon glowing red with evil light. Trackers wasting hoards of the enemy with mighty strokes of righteous intent.

Henry's group crouched in the chaos, their backs to each other and their weapons raised. Boothe turned, slinging rain from his eyes. "RUN!"

Henry dug in and sprinted with his head down. The explosion behind him when the armies met under the Viazo Grand's carriage porch seemed to shake the world. It knocked him to his knees to skid in the mud, but he held onto Adam and pushed back to his feet.

He heard Ezra's scream of pain, and he ran.

Boothe's bellow of rage, and he pumped his legs as Adam bounced wildly on his back.

Ramiel's song turned from comfort to vengeance. And still, Henry ran.

First this boy, and then Amélie. I'm coming, baby!

The fighting receded into the distance behind him, and the ground flattened out before him. He ran faster than he could imagine, the wind deafening as it whipped past his ears.

The rain soaked through his clothes in seconds, and Henry only knew he was crying when he tasted the salt of his tears.

Chapter Thirty

At the edge of the Viazo Vineyards, Henry slowed and turned around, walking backwards into the trees that lined the hotel property. Flashes of light at the top of the hill. Muted thunder. Swells of color. It looked like fireworks, or a Phish concert.

"I'm sorry about your friends, Henry."

"Don't be sorry yet, kid."

Henry pulled Adam off his back and cradled the boy in his arms, holding him against his chest and blocking as much of the rain as he could. He tried stretching into the shadows, but Adam became an albatross. He couldn't keep them in the trees for much longer. They were on the edge of a huge city. The trees would end, and everyone would see the monster. He reached for the darkness again, but instead of pouring himself into it, Henry pulled it up like a blanket across his shoulders.

The mental weight of Adam's presence in the shadows dragged his shoulders toward the ground, but Henry gritted his teeth and kept planting his feet.

He couldn't tell how old the kid was. He was so small,

but he'd spoken with an odd assurance that made him think of Amélie. She was a negotiator, wielding logic like a rapier. He learned to prepare for situations of discipline like a lawyer trying a case. It didn't matter if he won, so long as he didn't end up looking like a dumbass.

More often than not, she would end up with a snackie cake instead of punishment, and Henry would sit at the table with a shell-shocked sort of pride, wondering how the Hell she'd gotten so smart so fast.

She became obsessed with Giggly Girls, a line of knock-off Barbies that laughed when shaken. He thought they all sounded like cackling harpies, but Amélie loved them, swiping through the website on Henry's iPad for hours. Her collection was soon obnoxious, and it had been a constant struggle for him to get her to clean them up.

It may have been *her* toy room, but Henry paid the bills, so one day he put his foot down. Five minutes later, he was sitting on the floor with a tiny pink brush, gently removing the tangles from Precious Paula's red hair.

Samantha had stuck her head in. "Clean your toys up, please."

Without argument, Amélie put everything away in record time. Henry looked up to realize he was alone, and the room was spotless. Her little voice floated in from the kitchen, chattering away about how she and Daddy had played with her dolls all day.

He stood with a grimace, his hips popping like twin shots from a cap gun. Then he hobbled over to Amélie's toy box and spiked that Paula bitch into the pile.

Her hair had looked incredible.

The rain tapered to a thin mist that seemed to appear rather than fall, and the trees thinned to an occasional weed-choked clump. In the tall grass next to the

Thompson Turnpike, Henry followed the traffic south-west, cutting through Sheldon and Harbor Square.

His feet knew where to take him, and the boy was asleep in his arms, so Henry kept his head down and the shadows pulled tight against the reflected glare of head-lights and streetlamps. He pushed the sound of Ezra's scream way down, covering it with a memory of Amélie's smile.

He looked up, and his vision cleared his daydream in a haze of reality. The Burg Spires Church of Hope. The shadow fell from his shoulders, and Henry gasped in relief. Standing under the dripping leaves of a maple tree, he looked both ways like a child readying to cross the street.

The church rose out of the gloom, dark except for a single light at the side door. Only familiar with a few of the rooms inside, Henry couldn't tell how they translated to the building's exterior.

A final check to make sure the coast was clear, and he carried Adam to the front door.

Heavy plastic covered the hole where the stained-glass window had been, fluttering and snapping with the swirling mist. Adam stirred and lifted his head to look over Henry's shoulder.

Ready to draw the shadows around them again, Henry rounded the corner and mounted the front door steps.

The handle turned, and the door swung in on silent hinges. Henry carried Adam inside, half expecting to be heralded by trumpets or light, but nothing happened. He closed the door behind him with a soft click then passed out of the entry and down the center aisle toward the altar.

He sat Adam in the first pew and turned to look at the damage from Peterson's entry. It was even worse than the day of the massacre, but at least there wasn't any blood. Pastor Owen's tired face sprang into his mind, and Henry burned with guilt. "I've brought so much pain to that man."

"Who? To *him?*"

Henry turned, and Adam was pointing at the statue of Jesus hanging above the empty baptismal pool. "No, that's Jesus."

"Oh." Adam nodded, a line appearing between his eyebrows. "I'm supposed to *be* him."

"Huh?"

"Well, maybe not be *him,* but be *like* him?"

"I guess, kid. That's why God wants you."

Adam jerked his head up in surprise. "God? Wants *me?*"

Henry shook his head and sat in the pew across the aisle. "It depends on who you ask."

Adam nodded. "Some people say I *am* him, already."

"Or the Antichrist."

Adam nodded again. "That, too."

"Yeah, well, people are dumb."

Adam giggled, and then his face grew serious. "Can I trust you?"

"I think so, yeah."

Adam pushed off the pew and walked over to Henry. He stood peering up at him, gold and blue light flickering in his eyes like sparks. He reached up and touched Henry's face.

Memories from the last few months flooded into his senses. Every moment relived with Henry at the center. The awful things he said. The terrible things he had done. Samantha and Amélie. Their pain doubling against his own.

He gasped and pulled his head back, breaking contact. Tears streamed from his eyes, and he heard Amélie's voice screaming for him. Begging for his help.

Adam cried with him, his lower lip quivering. "You love her, don't you?"

"More than anything in the whole world."

"You've been through so much, trying to save her."

Henry nodded.

"And you don't know what to do now, do you?"

Henry shook his head. Wiped the tears away with the back of his hand. Drew his sleeve under his nose. "Hey, you hungry?"

Adam wiped his own tears away as he nodded.

Henry dug into his back pocket and pulled out the Bacon Bag. "Here. Think of the food you want most of all, and stick your hand in here."

The child's eyes lit with expectant joy, and he thrust his hand into the bag. Then he drew it back out holding a huge slice of thin crust pizza. The kind they sold on every corner in town. Floppy and soaked with grease.

Adam folded it in half lengthwise like you're supposed to, then drew it toward his mouth in anticipation. He paused. "Do you want some?"

Holy shit. This kid.

"No, you go ahead."

Adam took a bite, and the cheese stretched, steam rising into the air. He chewed with his mouth open, sucking in a breath to cool it before swallowing. He spun in a joyous circle then took another bite and marched to the bottom step leading up to the altar.

He jumped onto it, holding the pizza over his head as he walked down the step's length like a balance beam. He took another bite, grease dribbling down his chin. "I have an idea."

Henry leaned back and crossed his arms. The kid's mindless fun on the carpeted stair made him smile. He wanted to have fun, too.

"My father was a demon named Baelzor."

Fuck.

"He's a con-artist. Always called himself a *low-level guy*. He got caught trying to steal something from a church in Spain. He never told me what it was, but his eyes always got far away when he talked about it."

He took another bite of pizza and spun, balancing his way back toward Henry. "They tried to exorcise him, not realizing that the man they saw wasn't possessed but just looked like that when he was working. So, it didn't work. They locked him up and asked him where the others like him were. A nun who was supposed to feed him and keep his wounds dressed felt bad for him, and tried to help him escape."

Adam dropped off the step and offered Henry the last bit of pizza with a half-sneer of disgust. "You want this? I don't like the crust."

"Sure, kid." Henry popped the warm dough into his mouth. Soft and salty, covered with Romano. The best part.

Adam went back to balancing. "They killed her."

Of course they did.

"Or they thought they did. She was an angel."

At first, he thought the kid was just describing his mother like *any* kid would, but realizing the boy was speaking literally made Henry sit forward.

"My dad didn't know it, though. He came back and killed every last person in that church. And with her gone, he didn't have anything else to live for, so he tried to kill *himself.*

"That's when my mother revealed herself to him. Like a vision. They fell in love, got married in secret, and I was born."

Such a dry way to put something so monumental.

And then a child was born.

"Some angels found out, and they came to put an end to the blasphemy. That was before they even found out about *me*, Elioud. Descendant of the sons of God. Higher than the offspring of Seth and the daughters of man. So, they ran away to New Mexico. I never really saw anybody else. Only them, and even though they loved each other, they were always fighting. He was angry all the time, and she was crazy. At least, that's what they said about each other."

Adam dropped back to the floor and stood still, looking down at his feet. "Then, a man came. A hunter for the cult."

"Order From Chaos?"

Adam nodded. "Petrev Obisev."

"You remember his name?"

He looked at Henry, one eyebrow cocked in question. "Would you remember the name of the man that killed your daughter?"

Patrick Harrison.

"I think so, yeah."

Adam shrugged with only one shoulder.

So there.

"He's the man who killed my parents, and I remember *everything* about him."

The church was filling with light. Henry's balls crept up when he thought it was a Tracker, but his heart slowed when he realized it was only dawn burning through clouds.

Henry swallowed the lump of fear clogging his throat. "All right, kid. You win. What's your idea?" A useless question. Henry already knew.

"I'll help you save your daughter if you help me find and then kill him."

Henry sighed. *What's one more deal?*

"Sure thing, kid."

Adam flung himself into Henry's arm with a wordless cry of relief. Henry rocked back from the impact and held the boy to his chest.

Now I just need to figure out how to do it.

Henry froze. He pried Adam loose and planted him on his feet. The boy looked up in confusion. Henry rammed his hand into his front pocket and withdrew Mandyel's phone. "Holy shit! The Holy Hotline."

He flipped it open and mashed the gold button. He slapped his head and waited for the operator.

"What number, please?"

"Uh, yeah. I need to talk to Nadia. Big lizard, looks like Garbo."

"One moment, please."

Click. Hank Williams singing *I'll Fly Away*.

Henry chuckled. "They *do* like the classics."

Click. "Mandy's Export Emporium."

"Nadia?"

"Henry?"

"Yeah, it's me. Look …"

"Where are you? Where's Mandy? I've been worried *sick*. And I've heard things, Henry."

"Yeah, and I'll tell you everything, but I need a ride. Can you send Oddjob to the Burg Spires Church of Hope?"

"Oddjob? Oh." She laughed like music. "That's funny, he *does* kind of look like him. As soon as I hang up, I'll call him. Should only be a couple of minutes, but Henry. You better have a good reason for leaving me in the dark."

"You bet." Henry slapped the phone closed and slid it into his pocket. He scooped Adam up and spun, jogging to the front door. Just as he reached for the knob, it swung in and Pastor Owen rushed inside, flinging water from his dripping hair.

He bounced off of Henry's shoulder with a gasp and dropped a bundle that had been clutched under his arm. Brown or red fabric, but Henry couldn't tell which in the dim light of morning.

"Henry!" The pastor gripped the coat over his chest, panting as he backpedaled. His eyes found the boy, and they widened to their limits, his brow wrinkling up in shock.

"Whoa, whoa. It's okay," Henry said.

"Henry, what is this?"

"Sorry, it was the only place I could think of to come."

Adam pushed off Henry's shoulder for a better look. His small face lit with a shining smile. "But then he had a *better* idea!"

Pastor Owen returned the smile. Nervous and hesitant.

Jesus, I put this guy through a ton, already. He deserves a fucking break.

A long black car slowed to a stop at the bottom of the steps with a whine of its brakes. Francesco honked, and Pastor Owen jumped with a yelp. Adam giggled, and Henry covered his own laugh with a polite cough.

"I'd love to stay and chat, but I have a man to kill."

"Henry," the pastor groaned, his pale face pinched and reproachful.

"Sorry, but I promised."

"What about your promise to God? Who is this man?"

"I didn't make any promises to God." Henry felt the heat rising into his cheeks. *"You* made those promises for me. Petrov Obisev *deserves* to die."

"Yeah," Adam chimed.

Pastor Owen covered his eyes and stepped aside. "Then, go."

"What?"

The pastor bent to retrieve his bundle. "Please leave, Henry. And don't ever come back."

The rejection hurt more than Henry imagined, but this man deserved more from him, and Henry knew he couldn't provide it.

Francesco honked again and sent an angry wave through the door. He turned to watch the pastor walk into his church with his shoulders slumped and head down. "Look after Samantha, will ya?"

Pastor Owen flapped his free hand in dismissal. "I always have, Henry. May God have mercy on you, my son."

Henry turned with his eyes burning, pulled the door shut behind him, and carried the child into the rain.

Chapter Thirty-One

MANDY'S EXPORT Emporium was a strip mall storefront between Los Mariachis and Brandy's Hard As Nails beauty salon. Even in the rain, the morning was bright enough to banish the shadows. Henry would be exposed if he got out now.

The window between the driver and passengers whined down, and Francesco looked at Henry in his rearview. "How 'bout I go around back?"

"Sounds like a good idea."

The window slid back up, and the limo pulled away, making a ponderous turn around the end of the squat building.

Adam had bounced on the leather seat during the ride, the light from the little TV making his gold eye glitter. His damp hair bounced around, falling to the side as if styled that way.

Henry wanted to peel his wet balls off the insides of his thighs, but something about reaching into his jeans with a small child so close made him cringe.

He didn't have a problem *drinking* in front of him,

though. He used the glass his memories told him belonged to Mandyel. The thought filled his throat with sorrow, but the whiskey knocked it down. He offered Adam some water, but the boy refused with a distracted shake of his head.

A commercial came on. Adam leaned back and rubbed his thighs.

"You cold?" Henry asked.

"I'm never cold."

The back of the building was filthy. Not much contrast with the front, but noticeable. Francesco pulled into a space between an orange Chevy Spark and a rusty blue dumpster.

The TV blipped off when the engine died. Adam dropped his head. "Aww …"

Francesco got out and went to the emporium's rear entrance. Henry cracked his door open while the driver knocked on the blue metal door. Nadia opened it from the inside, and Francesco stepped back to hold the door wide.

"Let's go," Henry said.

He ran into Nadia's waiting arms. She held him tight, and he sagged into her. A notorious touch freak most of his life, physical contact was becoming more important, and Henry didn't want to let her go. Nadia leaned back and looked into his face. "Where have you been? Where's Mandyel?"

Henry cleared his throat and blinked his tears away. "He's dead."

"What?"

"Peterson killed him at the Purveyor's house."

She laughed and turned away, grabbing his hand and leading him into the store. "No, he didn't Henry."

"Everybody keeps telling me that. I saw the guy eat his fucking heart."

"Please. *Peterson* ate the heart of one of the oldest archangels?"

Henry skidded to a halt inside the retail space, his jaw dropping open. Wall to wall. Floor to ceiling. Packages and boxes.

Katanas on decorative stands. New and vintage clothing on racks and in plastic bags. A stack of VCRs still in the original packaging. VHS tapes still in the cellophane. A velvet Elvis *and* a Jimi Hendrix.

"Where the fuck am I?"

Nadia spun in a circle with a smile, her head tipped to the side as if she were listening to a bird on her shoulder. "Don't you love it? It's Mandyel's secret passion."

"A fucking junk shop?"

She stopped, her face clouding in anger. She raised her finger and opened her mouth in a snarl, then looked down with widening eyes. Her mouth fell open farther, and she looked at Henry, her finger falling. "Who is that?"

Adam looked up at Henry from behind his hip. "She's beautiful," he whispered.

"Oh, Henry. Who *is* this little boy?" She dropped into a demure squat with her elbows on her knees.

"This is Adam. Don't look into his eyes."

"Why shouldn't I? They're exquisite." She held her arms out, offering a hug.

Adam took the invitation. He launched into her embrace, burying his face in her hair. She looked up with wonder.

"Cute kid," Francesco said.

Henry looked over his shoulder with a nod. "Probably be your boss someday."

"No doubt."

"Pick me up," Adam demanded.

Nadia obliged with a grin, and Adam clung to her hip, his head on her shoulder.

Henry bent down to catch Adam's gaze. "Did you command her to pick you up?"

"I can't."

"What do you mean, you can't?"

"Not anymore since you pledged yourself to me. Not when I'm just a little boy."

"But you and Remmy said I was champion to another."

Adam shrugged and took another sniff of Nadia's hair, like a bride and her bouquet.

"Who's Remmy?" Nadia asked.

"A Tracker named Ramiel."

"*Ramiel?* The Ramiel from the auction?"

"You know him?"

"Henry, what the hell have you been doing?"

"Oh, you know. Stuff and things."

"Henry, I need more than that."

"I got a better idea. Get it from the kid. I got a man to kill."

Nadia turned and dropped Adam to sit on a glass case full of antique lighters. "And who is this man?"

"Petrov Obisev."

Oddjob whistled, and Nadia looked at the ceiling with a sigh. "Do you ever do little things?"

"Hey, I need to find him. You gonna help or what?"

"What do you want me to do?"

"I don't know, gimme the name of somebody who can get me close to him, and then, you know … babysit?"

"Yes!" Adam exclaimed.

Nadia sent an absent smile Adam's way. "It would be a pleasure to watch the boy, of course. And he'll be safe here. This store is not well known."

Henry looked at the glut of inventory. "Obviously."

Nadia leaned over the counter and slid a leather organizer across. She flipped it open. "I can give the name of somebody who might be able to help. He deals in weapons. The kind that a religious bounty hunter would use."

Adam kicked his feet to drum his heels lightly against the glass, grinning at his savior. Henry couldn't help but smile back.

Nadia tore off a scrap of paper. "Gaston Livre."

Francesco snorted laughter. "Frenchy Letters?"

Henry grabbed the paper and turned to the limo driver, stuffing the note in his pocket. "You know him?"

"Oh, yeah. He used to drive for Cloud Nine a couple of years ago. Got busted with a trunk full of fairy dust in Ireland. They pulled his ticket, and he's been hustlin' on the black market ever since."

"You know where he is?"

"You think I'm gonna drive you there, you're wrong."

"I'll pay you double time."

"Henry!" Nadia shouted. "You don't even know what that means."

"Done." Francesco stuck his hand out.

"And I get to ride in the front from now on."

The driver narrowed his eyes. "Deal, but I stay in the car."

They shook hands, and Henry cocked his head waiting for the sound of trumpets.

Nadia pulled Adam back to her hip. "We'll get this little guy some food, a bath, and some clean clothes."

"Gee, where you gonna find any clothes around here?"

"And I thought you were a comedian. Just go and hurry back. You still owe me a story."

Henry rushed forward and bent to plant a kiss on her cheek. He ruffled Adam's hair and spun away. Francesco waited with his arms crossed then shook his head and followed Henry back to the car.

The windows in the front weren't as dark. Henry raised his hood and pushed himself low. It was a big car, but he still ate his knees.

Probably would have been better in the back.

"You gonna kill Frenchy if he don't tell you what you want?"

Henry dug the brass phone out of his jeans and stuffed it into the kangaroo pouch on the front of his sweatshirt. "Probably, yeah. You think he deserves it?"

Francesco blew a sigh out through his nose and nodded. "I think he does. You know, fairy dust is only used on kids."

"I didn't know that. There's a fucking lot I don't know."

"Get used to it. There's a lot I wish *I* didn't know."

"You and me both."

Silence as they crossed the J. Moses East Bridge. Tires bucked over joints in the concrete, and traffic transformed into beaters and delivery trucks, both belching smoke and leaking oil.

Everything turned gray. The East Side was named after the race riots during the 1930s. Even though it was actually south-west of Burg City, when the Irish started moving in, they expanded and pushed the blacks out. Westside residents fought back, but after generations of racism practically supported by the city, they finally gave up.

Turned out to be the best thing that could have happened. The shipping industry moved to the northeast, where displaced families found new jobs and homes, leaving the East Side with nothing but an ironic name.

The bridge that connected them to the rest of the city was named after J. Moses. A black lawyer who spent his life fighting for the immigrant rights. After the last steel plant had closed in the 70s, East Side's only exports were cops and criminals.

"This is a rough neighborhood," Henry said.

"Nah, ain't nobody gonna look at you twice. You're too red."

"You got a point." *And what a sad fucking point it is.* "What about the car?"

"Buddy, from the outside, all they're gonna see is Penske yellow."

Henry counted five liquor stores, two gun stores, two pay day lenders, and seven pawn shops before Francesco pulled into a parking lot surrounded by an eight-foot chain-link fence. Not a single grocery store or school.

Old vehicles in various states of disrepair lined a lot that slumped in front of a wide stubby building that looked like an ancient dealership where hustlers once unloaded lemons on wheels. The blacked-out front windows looked like rotting teeth. A rebel flag fluttered on one side of the front door. A Nazi banner beat in the breeze on the other.

"Jesus." Henry sneered. "Is there anything fucking worse than a Burg City Nazi?"

"I dunno. Maybe Illinois Nazis?"

Henry chuckled. "How do you think I should do this?"

"I say kick the fucking door in and tear his dick off."

"That works for me."

Chapter Thirty-Two

HENRY THREW the door open and sauntered up to the building. His reflection grew as he neared, and he was stricken by his appearance. Tall and wide. Muscles showed through his clothes. A stark relief to the fat balding dickhead from over forty years of hating the mirror.

It threw off his groove. He stumbled the last few steps, and when he planted his left foot for the kick, his balance was way off. Instead of blowing the door and the frame right out of the crumbling block wall, it exploded in with a *WHANG* of bent metal and a shower of glass.

A pasty shithead in a tight yellow leisure suit and a David Crosby mustache looked out from between his raised hands. Tinted glass covered his IKEA desk and glittered in his thinning hair. The only light was a small lamp on the corner of the fake wood top, and Henry's shadow stretched like an inverted triangle.

Henry marched up with a village idiot nod and said in his best redneck accent, "Hey, man! I'm looking for a late model Caddy with a cassette player. I know a feller who's got a bunch o' tapes still in the damn plastic."

The shithead leaned back, blinking in confusion. He didn't seem concerned that the person who had darkened his door was a red demon with a hayseed smile. He kept his eyes on Henry and turned his head toward a door at the end of a small hallway. "Gus!" He slid his chair back until it hit the wall behind him. "You and Bardo need to get in here right fucking now!"

"Who's Gus?" Henry looked down the hallway, and his grin ramped up a notch.

A little greasy teenager with oily hair pulled back in a ponytail that exposed the angry acne on his forehead walked out like the world was his hourglass. He wiped grease from a rusty crescent wrench, and his jaw worked as he chewed a wad of gum with his mouth open. *Gus* in a script font sewn above his breast pocket.

The hallway darkened behind him, and Henry's grin slipped into a hesitant smile. A giant demon crowded through with his shoulders drawn in and his head pushed down into his chest. His knees bent to keep his back clear of the ceiling, and when he stood and spread out in front of the desk, Henry's smile fell into an open-mouthed frown.

Black eyes set deep in albino pockets of flesh. His nose was a pale button, and his underbite thrust jumbled fangs into the air, their crazy points all the way to his cheeks. As wide as Henry was tall, he was a foot over Henry's horns, and his fists looked like warty boulders.

"Hi guys," Henry said. "I'm here to talk to Mr. Letters. It's kind of private, so if you don't mind?"

Frenchy stood and looked at Henry from around the giant fucker's elbow. "Keep this piece of shit busy while I go get my dog." He pushed off Bardo and jogged up the hall.

"Hang on a minute," Henry shouted. "I just want to talk!"

Bardo pushed his sleeves up, and his face broke into a hideous smile. "Too late for that, buddy."

Gus pocketed the wrench and pulled out a shiny butterfly knife. He whipped it back and forth, clickety-clacking it into a blade, brandishing it with what he probably thought was a menacing expression.

Looks like the guy's got gas.

Henry didn't wait for the albino mountain to finish getting ready. He slammed forward with his best roar, and Bardo caught him against his chest with ten of Henry's claws digging deep into his ribs.

Bardo howled and toppled over the desk. Henry pulled his claws out and slashed Bardo's face as they tumbled. The lamp crashed to the floor, dying with a buzz. Papers scattered hither and yon.

Bardo closed his hands over Henry's head and threw him to the side with a roar. Henry crashed into the wall, punching through Sheetrock, hanging up in the studs. He swiped at the dust in his eyes, and Gus crossed the floor in a dazzling flicker. He stabbed Henry a dozen times before Henry could heave himself out of the wall.

Gus danced away, and Bardo took his place. He hit Henry directly on the top of his head. The room blurred, and Henry's knees ceased to exist. The carpet smelled like piss.

Gus dropped on top of him, stabbing and slashing as Henry dropped into the dark of his own mind with Bardo's grinding laughter following him down.

Aw, fuck. The dark. The SHADOWS!

Henry stretched into the shadows fast, and Gus stabbed the floor instead of his back.

Bardo spun around, his confused eyes shining wide like compact discs.

Henry made a circuit of the room, wrapping himself in the shadows at the base of the walls. He gathered speed then launched into the dim light like a bloody missile, hitting Bardo right above his kidneys.

The giant's hips popped forward, and his head whipped back.

Henry drove him into the corner where the hallway started, and a third of the wall collapsed.

The ceiling groaned, and Henry drove back into the shadows, grabbing it with both hands, throwing himself in a quickening arc. Gus stood in the center of the room, tracking Henry's progress with Rain Man's concentration.

When Henry burst back into the light, Gus's knife met him under the belly button. His speed tore the knife from Gus's hand, but not before the blade ripped through hoodie and flesh, blood flowing around his side and dripping down his ass crack.

He caught Bardo standing from the pile of splintered wood and vinyl paneling, right in the shoulder like a safety rocketing across the field for the tight end. Bardo left his feet, carried across the room on a slingshot of shadow, and he hit the outside block wall with his face to cushion the impact.

He's gonna be in the concussion protocol for sure.

Henry released the shadow and bent over the hole in his belly. Gus retrieved his weapon and stood with the dripping knife held out in front of him. Henry's legs quivered, and he dropped to one knee. Gus gave him that bilious smile then charged with a thrust at Henry's face.

Henry rocked back and lifted his hand with his fingers spread wide. The blade stabbed into his palm and punched through his knuckles, showering his face with blood. He closed his fist over Gus's knife hand then stood with a dark grin that reflected from the mechanic's wide eyes. He fell into the shadows, pulling the screaming man with him. Swaddled in the dark, wrapped in its comfort and warmth, he opened his hand and rushed into the light like bursting through the surface of a frozen lake.

He fell to the floor in a gasping heap. Slashes on his back closed with a biting heat that made him grit his teeth. He held his hands over the flow of blood from his gut and drew deep breaths as Gus's frantic screams faded to a whisper.

Bardo snored in a spreading puddle of black blood from his split forehead. Clear fluid leaked from his nose with every rasping breath.

A rumbling growl brought Henry's head around, and a Pit Bull with a thyroid problem stood panting in front of Frenchy's desk.

She was the size of a vending machine. Blocky and covered in jet black fuzz. Drool dripped from either side of her fanged mouth, and it steamed when it hit the carpet. Her eyes burned with a yellow fire. A glowing rope of blue fiber trailed from her barrel neck into Frenchy Letters' white-knuckled grip. She jerked against the rope, and Frenchy's feet dragged across the carpet.

Henry threw himself back, and the bitch lunged, catching his raised forearm in a gaping maw that puked smoking heat into his face. She clamped down, her teeth meeting through bone, and she thrashed her head.

Henry thought his arm was going to tear from its shoulder, tendons and muscle stretching to the limits. His forearm snapped, sending electricity buzzing through his elbow. He gouged his claws into her eyes, bursting them under his fingertips, and she only shook her head harder.

She's gonna tear it off!

Henry brought his fist down like a hammer on the tip of her nose, and she opened her mouth in a pitiful yelp. Henry readied himself to sacrifice his other forearm to her bite, when Frenchy shouted, "What the fuck?"

A shotgun pressed against the dog's neck, and the blast tore through fur and bone, knocking her body on its side with its feet kicking. Lava sprayed from the wound, setting the carpet and wall ablaze. Sizzling holes in Bardo's pant leg. The dog's head hit the floor, her growl a wheezing cough, her teeth still gnashing.

Francesco pointed the shotgun at Frenchy's face, and the shithead dropped the rope and lifted his hands.

Henry pushed his mangled forearm into the still bleeding cut in his stomach. He bent and picked up the dog's head like a thirty-pound bowling ball, his fingers in the torn eye holes. He staggered over to Frenchy and thrust the head at his chest, where her questing bite got a hold of his sagging pec through his Rayon shirt. He screamed and beat at the head with flailing blows, but it chewed into his chest, blood flowing around her mouth in a red flower.

Henry looked at Francesco over the shotgun barrel. "The Hell was that?"

"You're right about that. It was a Hell Hound. Just a baby one, though."

"That was just a *baby*?"

"Yeah, that's why the rock salt and iron shot did such a number on her. A bigger one would'a just laughed that shit off."

Frenchy screamed again and dropped to his back.

A rib snapped, and Henry winced in sympathy. Then he squatted down and dug his fingers into the Hell Hound's eyes.

Her jaw relaxed, and Frenchy gasped in relief, his face twisted in agony.

Henry leaned his knee onto the man's thighs. "I still need that Caddy."

"What?" Frenchy gasped.

"Where's Petrov Obisev?"

"Who the fuck is that? I'm dying here!"

Henry let go.

Frenchy howled.

Henry grabbed harder.

"All right, all right! He's at the cleaners on 33rd. Under the Burg City Credit Union."

"What, like dry cleaners?"

"Not that kinda cleaner, you halfwit."

"Hey, fuck you." Henry looked up at Francesco. "You know where that is?"

"Of course."

Henry let go of the smoking head and stood with popping knees. He danced aside as the fire licked at his calves.

Francesco grabbed his upper arm, guiding him to the front door and into the rainy East Side gloom.

Frenchy's voice unraveled into a gurgling whine. The bitch must have made it through the ribs. Henry dropped into the back of the limo, barely able to get his foot inside. Francesco shut the door and walked around to the driver's side, leaving Henry with a view of flames curling around the doorway and lighting the edge of the Nazi banner on fire.

That should make for pleasant dreams.

Chapter Thirty-Three

HENRY WOKE in the back of Francesco's car, snapping out of a dream about Amélie.

She had grown into a beautiful woman. Visiting Henry and Samantha at Christmas.

Standing at the kitchen counter with a green reindeer sweater, just like the one she wore in their family photo when she was five. She tipped a glass of white wine to her lips. A silver ring glinted on her finger.

Henry couldn't see the details, but he knew it had the snake and frog. She was hiding her true self from her family. He raised his own glass to hide his disappointment.

Then he stretched, his feet hitting the inside of the back door, and pulled his claws in to protect the leather and sat up with a yawn. The rain had stopped, and the sun was behind a bright blue sky.

The limo took up two spots in front of the Mexican restaurant next to Mandyel's thrift store. Francesco sat on the other side of the restaurant's glass near the front door, working through a mountain of nachos, a frosty margarita next to his plate.

Henry heard the pained voices of the city wash over him. He closed his eyes, and the cacophony of sorrow swelled. So many cries. Like overlapping radio stations. He imagined his mind was an AM dial, and he spun it. His mind filled with the static of wordless screaming, and he winced and spun the dial.

An old woman mourning the loss of her husband, taken by cancer. A father crying at the funeral of his little girl killed by a mugger. Henry spun the dial.

A man laughing with mad glee as he plunged a knife into his girlfriend's lover. Murderous plans painting vivid fantasies across his mind. Henry spun the dial.

The voices died all at once. A silence heavy with its emptiness and Henry sagged with a gasp. He opened his eyes, and the blessed silence held him. Tension flowed from his shoulders. He could think again.

He turned the dial in his mind, and the voices flooded his brain in a cramping crescendo. Sent him hissing and spinning the knob back to the empty spot on the dial.

This is Hush-Hush Henry with all the sounds of silence here on 666 AM. We'll take requests now. You're on, caller.

Henry made a phone out of his thumb and pinkie. "Yeah, can I get some peace and quiet, please?"

You got it, caller. Thanks for listening.

Henry giggled as he hung up his "phone" on an imaginary hook in the air in front of him. He rocked in an awkward dance of victory, wiping the tears from his eyes.

This being a demon shit should have come with a manual.

He took a rib-cracking breath and settled back with an explosive sigh, closing his eyes again.

Now, for this fucked up face.

He pictured himself standing in an empty room. Without the distraction of the city's constant murmur, the image sprang into his mind without effort. Two Henries.

One balding and paunchy, a sheen of sweat on his broad forehead, his hoodie and jeans hung on his stooped shoulders as if he were hoping to melt within the folds. Fat Henry stood next to Demon Henry, but as Demon Henry collapsed into human form, Henry opened his eyes, shook his head, and banished the fantasy.

Mandyel, Boothe, and Henry's own mind had betrayed him.

Demon Henry *was* his true form. The one his hate had chosen.

I can't walk around in the body of a dead man.

I'm a monster, and I've always known it.

He dropped his head in his hands, and Demon Henry appeared with sardonic disapproval. Mike Serafino stood in front of him. Demon Henry winked at him over Mike's head, then stepped forward into Mike Serafino as if stepping through a human-shaped door.

Good old Mike stood alone in an empty room.

The demon buzzed beneath the surface, bouncing around the confines of his new form like a pounding heart.

Henry stepped out of the limo, wearing Mike Serafino like a pair of sweatpants. Francesco stared at him through the restaurant window, holding a loaded nacho in front of his hanging jaw, his eyebrows practically up in his hairline.

Henry fired a finger gun at him and walked into Mandy's Export Emporium.

A bell over the door dinged as his shadow spread across the floor, and Nadia looked up from her leather planner. A wreath of cigarette smoke floated around her hair, the silver stem clamped in her teeth.

"Hey," Henry shouted, looking around like a seasoned shopper. "I'm looking for something in a summer pinstripe. Forty-three regular."

"Henry!" A blond bullet shot out from under a circular

rack of plus-size flower print dresses. He braced for impact, and Adam launched the remaining six feet to land in his waiting arms. He took a steadying step back and hugged the kid to his chest.

"I found him, buddy."

Adam looked up with shining eyes, and Henry fell into them, swimming in their weird beauty and thinking of Amélie. "You did?"

"Yup. Frenchy Letters told me where he is. Easier than I *thought* it would be, too."

Nadia stopped in front of him, eying Henry from toes to head. "How are you doing that?"

"What? Old Mike here? Not really sure, but that's pretty much the way I've done everything my whole life. I never stop to ask *why* a thing works, I just keep doing that thing and move on."

"I always needed the ring. I could never figure it out, myself. So, whatever you're doing, keep doing it."

He nodded with a grin and looked at the boy in his arms. "I think things are starting to go my way." The thought of Boothe dying in a Tracker's net bubbled to the surface, but Henry drove it down with an annoyed shake of his head.

Adam grinned back. He wore jeans and a loud Hawaiian shirt with a surfboard on the pocket. Henry bent to set the boy on his feet, but he ran back under the rack of dresses. Henry peeked in. Adam had a pile of action figures arranged in battle.

He stood back up, and Nadia pinched the shoulder of his hoodie with distaste. "Henry, this is gross. Let's get you out of those clothes, and into something a bit more … clean."

Henry took her hand and held it between both of his,

pulling it into his chest. "If I wasn't still in love with my wife, I might have taken that a little differently."

Her smile grew sad, and she pulled her hand free to reach up and lay it against his cheek. "And if you weren't still in love with your wife, I may have *meant* it differently."

She dropped her hand, sliding her first finger along his arm before turning toward a rack of suits along the wall. He followed and let her pick out his new outfit.

He knew better than to argue with a woman's taste.

He inspected himself in the mirror and couldn't help remember Charlie Mara walking into the cell as a naked demon, and returning as a fully clothed human. *Maybe the secret is to always be naked. Just add the clothes in my mind later?*

He wasn't ready to walk around naked, no matter what people saw. *Fuck that.*

He adjusted his tie and met Nadia's reflected eyes. They were hooded with worry, and she lit another cigarette with trembling hands.

"What is it?" he asked.

"Adam told me his story while you were away, and I can't help thinking you're making a mistake."

"Maybe."

"And that's good enough for you?"

"Not really." Henry cocked his head at the beautiful child playing with dolls. "But it's good enough for *him.*"

"You're putting your trust in an angel's spawn who has less of a grasp on reality than you?"

Henry grinned. "I know, right?"

"Henry …"

"No. I'm one step closer to saving my daughter, but every second makes the distance I have to travel grow by fucking *miles*. I'll do *anything*! Don't you fucking get it?"

Nadia stepped back. The surprise on her face drove his

rage into a bitter shout. "I don't give a fuck about anybody but *her*. Boothe or Mandyel? Fuck 'em! They twisted the truth to get what they wanted from me, and I'm finally doing things *my* way. And I'm gonna take this kid with me, and I'm gonna kill that man. And if he kills me instead, then *I. Don't. Care.*"

"Maybe *I* care."

"Who the fuck are *you* to care about *me*? You don't fucking know me, lady. You can pretend to be on my side all you want, but just like everybody else, you walk around like you got a secret, and you know what? Keep it. Because I don't give a fuck about *you*, either. The only thing I give a *fuck* about is my *DAUGHTER!*"

Adam pressed against the back of his leg, kneading the fabric of his slacks between his little fingers. Nadia dropped her face to smile at him.

Don't mind us, Son. Mommy and Daddy are just having a little disagreement.

"No, Henry. The only person you give a fuck about is *you*."

She jammed the silver stem back into her mouth and spun around to stomp into the back. A door slammed so hard, the glass in the display cabinets quivered, and a painting of angels playing poker jumped from its nail to slide down the wall.

Henry stood with his shoulders heaving. He opened his fists, and Adam's hand crept into his, clamping down in a grip much stronger than the child's frame would suggest. He looked down, and the boy returned his anger. His brows drawn together, and his lips drawn up in a snarl.

Adam turned to step toward the door, dragging Henry along like a newspaper boat in a storm drain.

Through the front door an into the blinding afternoon sun, he marched to the limo. Henry turned to catch Francesco's eye and twirled his finger around his head in a *let's go* gesture of impatience. The driver nodded and tipped his glass to drain his margarita. He dug into his pocket as he stood, dropping a handful of bills on his empty plate.

Adam crawled across the seat and drew his legs underneath him, watching Henry duck in and slam the door. The car rocked when Francesco dropped in, and the engine fired up with a rumble. As they pulled away, Henry couldn't shake the feeling that it was the last time he'd see her. He shrugged.

After what I said, it's probably for the best.

He ground his teeth and stared out the window.

Still burning those bridges.

Adam set his hand on Henry's forearm. He looked into the boy's eyes, and they hardened into ice. Henry could no longer tell how deep the water was. "You remind me of my father."

"Why? Because I'm a demon? Because I'm *ugly*?"

"No, because he was sad and angry all the time, too. Like he knew something bad was going to happen, and he couldn't let himself be happy for too long."

"Sounds like a smart man."

"Not anymore. He's dead, Henry."

Henry growled, and his demon form vibrated in his chest, stretching Mike Serafino like a flesh balloon. His anger flashed into a rage, and the light coming into the car turned red. Sparks glittered in the air like dust, and he felt a sudden but unmistakable heat pluming up from the floor.

"It makes me so *mad*," Adam said. His hands drew into small fists, his knuckles whitening with the pressure. His panted breath steamed out of his mouth in a billowing jet. Anger rolled off his brow like a fever, feeding Henry's rage where it grew to a blinding inferno in his mind, consuming his whole world.

The limo slowed to a stop in front of a tall black building. The Burg City Credit Union. The main entrance was black glass and revolving doors. Two flanking side entrances with stairs descended below the street. *Under the credit union.* Henry nodded and turned back to Adam, his throat closing with emotion, unfelt and unwanted.

The little boy swelled, and his human form went blurry. He turned to put one foot on the floor, and when he looked up, the boy ceased to exist. Wings burst from his back to spread across the cabin. Brilliant white with black tips, one pressed against the glass behind Francesco's head. The other rubbed the rear window. Silver-blonde hair flowed from his head like water, his eyes burning with a swirling white light.

His powerful hands with the fingers tipped in black claws, opened and closed in rhythm with his breath. Muscles rippled up his forearms all the way to his shoulders. His jeans and Hawaiian shirt charred into a curled shell that clung to him like a second skin, the crisp edges glowing with red heat. He growled, and the sound penetrated Henry's brain like a bear hiding in the brush, ready to clear the trail with one wicked slash of its monstrous paw.

The separation glass slid down, and Francesco looked at the back seat through the rearview. His mouth closed with a snap. "Nope," he said with a tight shake of his head.

The glass reversed direction and sealed at the top with a suck of air.

In Henry's mind, Mike Serafino waved goodbye.

The demon erupted, and it was almost orgasmic. He sucked in the air until his breast split with thunder, his Hell roar shattering each window on every car within twenty feet.

Screams and horns. Car alarms. Emotion carried on the breeze. It fed Henry's rage, and he thrust his shoulder into the street, tearing the door off its hinges in a twisting squeal of metal. A swirling tunnel of red light narrowed in his vision, leading to the bank's subterranean entrance.

Adam streaked past his head with the scream of a falcon, his wings pounding. Adam's burning wake washed over him, and Henry joined the half-breed's shrieking terror to streak down into the dark.

A door of smoked glass loomed at the bottom of the steps, and Henry pulled the shadows around him like armor. Henry's lips drew back in a grin, and he lowered his head as he charged.

Chapter Thirty-Four

THE SHADOWS SHREDDED AWAY from him as they exploded into the grand lobby under the Burg City Credit Union. A room heavy with a darkness that extended beneath the building above them supported by raw steel columns bolted into the ceiling. A reception desk in the center made of live oak clad in copper, soft cove lighting making its polished counter glow. Rich leather chairs in a half circle waiting area. Subdued lamps for reading.

What is this fucking place?

Dead silent and empty.

Henry skidded to a stop, his claws digging into the plush burgundy carpet. Adam careened in a spastic arc to land on the desk, his wings scattering paper into the air like glossy white leaves. He ran from one end to the other, his frantic steps slapping an echo like a snare drum.

Henry swung his head from side to side in confusion. The rage left him, and he shivered with a chill racking his spine. Like dialing his mental radio to an empty spot in the spectrum, he heard a buzzing in the background. Something trying to intrude on his station. Demanding his attention.

Adam dropped to the floor, wings wilting into his back, his little boy's face folding out of the demon's rage to look up at him with his exotic eyes wide and crying in frustration.

It was *Adam*. It was the *boy's* frequency overloading his antenna. Henry closed his eyes and spun the knob. The city's oppressive sorrow burst into his brain, bringing clarity to his thoughts. His own anger dropped to ride the symphony in his mind, and an undercurrent of satisfaction flickered in his attention.

Laughter floated out into the lobby. Low and dark. A sinister chuckle that paralyzed Henry.

"Where is everyone?" Adam cried.

Come rushing in here without a plan.

"Why aren't they here?"

Like a fucking little kid.

Adam's tiny fist pounding into his bare thigh. The laughter's rising strength as a shadow stretched from the depths of a hallway. Another shadow at its side. A third.

"Answer me, Henry! Answer me *right now!*" The child's commanding power washed over him, crumbling as it passed. Henry shook his head and pointed to the approaching shadows.

"Answer it yourself, kid."

A dusky man in an expensive suit and an open-mouthed smile stepped into the light. Dark laughter rose from his thick chest, and his eyes sparkled with genuine mirth.

Hennessy Lucius stood at the man's shoulder, a brass horn held out in front of him.

Oh, fuck.

The old man lifted his shoulders in a deep breath and pursed his lips.

God damn it.

Hennessy pressed the metal spiral to his mouth and blew.

Adam spun as a piercing note rang through the air. It doubled and tripled, blaring from the distance. Ringing in Henry's mind.

The little boy screamed, slapping his hands to his ears and falling to his knees.

Hennessy blew again, and when Adam screamed a second time, blood burst from his mouth in a bubbling gurgle.

Blood poured from his nose. Seeped from the corners of his eyes. He tipped to his side, gasping and coughing, his wide eyes fixed on Henry's. Horror and panic painted his face, and Henry scooped the boy off the floor.

Hennessy blew again, and Adam convulsed in Henry's arms, his eyes squeezing shut in agony as more blood pressed through his gritted teeth.

"STOP IT!" Henry screamed, looking at the mayor's brother with seething hatred. "You're *killing* him!"

"For God's sake, Hennessy. Henry's right." The voice dug into Henry's heart, and the third shadow solidified.

Pastor Owen dropped his hand on Hennessy's shoulder. "That was not supposed to happen."

Henry struggled to maintain his grip on the dying child in his arms. His grip on reality. Adam gasped and moaned, bloody tears tracking down his cheeks.

Confusion spun through Henry as the pieces slid together — Pastor Owen. How long had he been a part of this? How much had he orchestrated?

What the fuck?

"I don't know *what's* happening," Hennessy said. "Now

that he's found his champion, the horn should draw him to us. It should just *work*."

Henry gently laid Adam on the blood-soaked carpet, putting his right hand on the child's chest the way he had when Amélie had been rushed to the hospital with pneumonia. They thought she was going to die, and if she had, he and Samantha wouldn't try again. *Three strikes and you're out.*

He looked up at Hennessy, then at Owen, his vision dimming with the red cloud of his rage. "He doesn't *have* a champion, you dumb fucks."

Hennessy asked, "Then how is he commanding *you*?"

"He's not. He *can't*. I'm somebody *else's* champion."

Hennessy shook his head, but Pastor Owen's eyes sprang wide in understanding. "Of course. *Amélie.*"

Hennessy's faced wrinkled in disbelief, and he brought the horn up, pulling air in through his nose.

Henry flashed into the shadows, stretching across the floor to pool at Hennessy's feet faster than a thought. The old men sent his air into the horn, and Henry shot out of the darkness spreading out from the old man's shoes.

Time slowed as he sent all of his pain and frustration into the strike, his left hand rising from the shadows. He could still feel Adam's dying heat beneath his palm.

Every time he yelled at Amélie. Turned his back on Samantha in anger. Hurt somebody. Hurt himself. Adam's terrible panic, his eyes begging Henry to help. It all went into the muscles of his shoulder. Filling every fiber as his claws descended toward Hennessy's wrinkled forehead.

Pastor Owen threw himself to the side, suspended in the molasses flow of Henry's awareness. The suit on the other side, Petrov Obisev for sure, ducked and threw his hands up to cover his face.

Henry's claws sunk into Hennessy's flesh, parting his

skull like clay. Blood erupted in a sparkling wash. Tinkling in his ears like music as it bounced and rippled through the air, each drop a silver bell ringing out.

His claws continued unabated through the old man's face, the remains spouting out like a melon collapsing under the blast of a shotgun. Henry thought it was beautiful. If only the moment could last forever.

He shredded through Hennessy's shocked expression, then connected with metal as the horn sang its final note.

Pain exploded up Henry's arm.

A crushing wave blew Henry back as his left hand burst into flames. His fingers crumbled into ash as he flew, the light filling his eyes and his thoughts, drowning the scream that rose from the hollow of his soul.

As light consumed his senses, Henry felt nothing. Not the flight, nor the landing. In a final brilliant flash, the light dimmed, pulsing as it went.

And in the darkness, Henry felt only the pain of failure.

Henry ached.

A deep throbbing that spread from every joint. His left hand was swirling agony. His skin puckered with blisters. He took a deep breath, and it almost felt stolen.

Burning chains kept his chest from expanding. He looked down through swollen eyelids, breathing through his nose.

He smelled like a steakhouse.

Black charring like a dark star extending from the center of his chest and down the fronts of his thighs. His burned cock flopping over to show healthy red underneath the split crust from base to tip. Rusty iron links digging into the skin across his shoulders and stomach. Around both ankles.

He flexed, but the chains glued his arms and sides together.

Henry raised his eyes to the flickering light as it danced across the floor. They were in the Lucius family tomb at Prince Hill. Bloody pentagram on the floor and empty mirror, but no Hennessy. *Fuck him, anyway.*

In the center of the pentagram was Adam. Ropes snaked out from bolts in the walls to knot around his wrists and ankles, forcing the boy to spread out like the points of the star he was held to. His naked flesh was covered in drying blood, and he was wan and gray.

His chest fluttered with his breath, and Henry sagged in relief.

The crypt door opened, and the candles danced, guttering black smoke into the air. A pair of figures in Order From Chaos robes stepped inside. One was the familiar form of Pastor Owen in red.

The other was his new friend, Petrov Obisev.

They crossed to the mirror, making a wide birth of the bloody symbol on the floor. Obisev crossed behind the iron frame and slid the robe from his shoulders. The pastor followed, and the two men stood nude in the orange light.

The pastor's chest was a rainbow of ink. The cult's symbol surrounded by colorful demons swirling around his ribs, each one stabbing into his skin and bringing out a torrent of inked blood that flowed into the runes all around them. Obisev was a dark blue blur of ink from knees to neck to elbows.

Henry tried to speak, but his dry throat seized. He worked some spit from the depths of his asphalt tongue and tried again. "The fuck is this?"

Pastor Owen smiled bitterly. "This is what Plan B looks like, Henry."

Henry grunted a chuckle. "What, are you trying to summon that goat-foot bastard? I saw him the other day, and I gotta say. I wasn't that impressed. Kinda looked like a pussy to me."

Owen folded his robe and placed the neat pile at his feet. Obisev copied him, almost in perfect time like a military drill team.

"Yeah," Henry continued. "He just disappeared in a poof when he saw me. To be honest, I think it was penis envy."

Pastor Owen looked over with a pained scowl. "I never cared much for your comedy, Henry."

"Ouch, man." Henry nodded, continuing to wriggle his right hand under the chains, working it toward his lap. "That hurts my feelings. I mean, kill my kid and rape my wife, fine. But insult my comedy? That's just downright *mean.*"

Pastor Owen sighed. "Henry …"

"Too soon?"

"Henry. *I* didn't rape Samantha or kill sweet Amélie."

"Don't you fucking dare say their names!"

"Henry, it wasn't me who has caused you so much pain."

"Oh, yeah? Then who was it, fucker?"

Pastor Owen dropped into a squat, resting an elbow on his own knee. His other hand rested on Henry's thigh, and he looked up in sympathy. "It was *you*, Henry. That's what everyone's been trying to tell you."

"The fuck outta here, you son of a bitch."

"Son, it was your *voice* that made you a target. Your immorality that brought you to our attention. Your little followers who hung on your every word. As I'm sure your angel friend told you, your *choices* put this in motion."

Looking into his eyes took Henry's breath away. Exhaustion battled his mind, and his eyelids sagged.

"You evil fuck," he croaked. "Did you ever even *believe* in God?"

"Oh, Henry." The pastor's face split into a loving smile. "Who do you think this is for. God *wants* this child dead. He wants to be safe in his own home like anybody else. Just like *you* did. And if the result is for my power to rise here on earth so that He can remain on his throne in Heaven, so be it. He will prepare for a battle that I allow Him to wage, all the while waiting for me to ascend and demand payment due."

Henry grunted with the effort to move his hand the final few inches that would put the chain in his grasp. He closed his fingers over the burning metal and *heaved.*

Black dots swirled in his vision, and he let go of hope as the chain remained unbroken.

Pastor Owen reached up and stroked his cheek. "Close your eyes, Henry. We just need the blood of a Paladin. It doesn't have to be *his* Paladin. Or his blood." He pointed to the boy spread out on the floor, and Henry caught his breath, his chest constricting with a loss that hadn't yet happened.

"Sleep, Henry." The pastor's voice echoed in his mind, and the power of his command followed Henry into slumber. "There's no need to watch, my son. You've seen enough."

Henry's guilt was swallowed by his relief, and once again, he let himself turn away from his problems.

Chapter Thirty-Five

A SMALL STAGE about a foot off the floor. A single microphone on a silver stand. A circle of light shining against the brick-wall backdrop like the opening of a portal.

Henry sat by himself at a small round table right up front. He glanced around, and the rest of the audience sat waiting for the next comic, they're faces open in anticipation. Wait staff dodged through the crowd, bringing fresh drinks and removing the empties.

As one, the faces focused on the stage, and their hands shot up in applause. Thunderous and joyful, peppered with whoops and whistles. Henry turned to see what could have possibly churned them so much.

Mike Serafino stepped out with a grin and a wave. He shielded his eyes against the spotlight, pointing to someone off to the side. Then he grabbed the mic from its stand, jamming his hand into his pocket. Same way Henry had started almost every show of his life.

He looked down at the floor, and the applause tapered down to a pocket. Mike raised his eyes to lock gazes with Henry. The applause died, replaced with expectant silence. "The fuck are you doing?"

A titter washed over Henry from the crowd. He looked around, but all eyes were still on the stage. Henry turned back, and Mike was still looking at him, his eyebrows a question. He stepped forward and put his hand on the empty stand, leaning on it the way Henry remembered doing a thousand times. "Seriously, what the fuck are you doing?"

"What do you mean?"

"That kid's gonna die, Henry."

"So."

"*So?*" Mike shrugged, and the crowd snickered. "If you don't do something, that kid will fucking lose his soul."

"There's nothing I can do."

"Then what about your daughter?"

A pop of laughter and Henry waited for it to die. "There's nothing I can *do*," he whined. He couldn't figure out how to make them understand.

"We're not talking about her *dying*, Henry. She's *already* dead." Roaring laughter, and Mike talked over them. "She's in Hell, buddy. The devil himself has her in his arms."

Wailing laughter like they had heard the planet's greatest punchline. Mike dropped his hand, and the mic stand wobbled in a spiral as he paced the stage.

Henry leaned forward. "You don't understand," he shouted over the rolling laughter. "There's nothing else I can fucking do!"

Mike spun, disgusted anger twisting his face, and the crowd erupted in a collective guffaw. "Goddamn it, Henry! I'm sick and fucking tired of your bullshit."

Henry felt anger redden his cheeks.

The laughter rose to a maniacal wail.

Pain at the edges.

Panic filled the breaths in between.

Henry argued, "Hey, fuck you! You don't know what it's like."

"*I* don't know what it's like? I *am* what it's like, you fucking simpleton!"

Joy turned to pain. Screams of laughter became wails of anguish. Mike charged to the edge of the stage, leveling an accusatory finger at Henry's face.

"You can't *barely* try and then give up, you cocksucker! That bus ain't gonna back up to let your wheezing fat ass catch it. You gotta *run!* Nobody gives a flying fuck about your troubles but *you.* That little boy isn't sparing a single thought about how hard your charmed goddamn life is! Do you think your daughter gives *one absolute SHIT* about your *struggle?*"

The air split with applause, cutting through the cries and moans of pain. Henry shrank in his chair, trying to duck under the judgment at his back. He just wanted everybody to shut up and leave him alone.

"But that's all you ever wanted, isn't it?" Mike's voice was a near whisper. The applause and screams fell to match. "The impact without the responsibility. But I'm here to tell you, buddy. You're fucking *nothing.* All the money and all the fame. The laughter and the awards. That shit … *that's* what you wanted more than *anything.* And the thing that you *claimed* to want more than anything? The love? Whatever. The world held its hand out to you, and you spit in it. Over and over."

Henry denied him. Wiped the tears away and *denied* that any of it was even happening.

The screams grew louder.

Mike wiped his own tears away, and looked at Henry with grief. "There's a guy pushing a boulder uphill, and he barely has the strength. And you know what? You're not that guy." He slipped the mic back into the stand and leaned against it with his shoulders drooping. "You're the fucking boulder."

In a blink, Henry stood where Mike had been, leaning against the microphone, looking out over a crowd covered in flames. Writhing in agony.

Amélie sat in the center with Adam in her lap. They held each other in a desperate embrace and looked at him with terror-filled eyes. Pleading. Begging.

Henry nodded and took a breath against the weight of his own guilt. He pulled the mic back out and held it up, whipping the cord behind him to give himself room.

"Stop me if you've heard this one."

THE CROWD'S screams washed over him, the crackling roar of the flames blowing heat across his face. He opened his eyes, and the mirror's surface rippled with the fire shining in its depths. Hell was on the other side of the reflection, and Henry thought he heard Amélie's voice screaming out from her torment.

He snapped awake to find Adam writhing on the floor, his eyes fixed on Henry's face. Pastor Owen stood chanting on the other side of the pentagram, a knife raised in front of his chest like an offering.

Dark words issued from his mouth like bile.

The glyphs in the vines of the Order From Chaos symbol given voice, and Henry knew if he listened too closely, insanity would follow.

Obisev stood in front of Henry's knees, echoing the pastor's chant. His voice rose into ecstasy as the mirror's surface bent into the crypt, and a tentacle dripping lava to the stone floor broke through, twisting in the air. Questing like a blind snake.

"Adam," Henry shouted. "I need your help, buddy!"

The boy stilled, and stared into Henry's eyes. Even during this torture, he shone with beauty. Despite the demon that had manifested in the car, this little boy was a true angel.

"Come on, buddy. I need you to sing. The song of the Tracker, okay? I promise you I'll get you outta here. I'm a Paladin, remember?"

A Paladin.

Henry froze.

A champion.

Henry smiled.

No chains can stand before my claws.

The crowd's laughter echoed in his mind.

Holy shit!

Adam nodded, his eyes wide in understanding.

Henry twisted and wriggled, drawing his hand out from under the chain inch by inch. His fingers finally popped free, and his claws pushed against the thick links, sinking into the metal with a grinding squeal that set his teeth on edge.

He smiled and tensed his shoulders.

The boy's song filled the chamber, winding in and out of the dark chant.

Pastor Owen faltered.

The questing tentacle paused, stretching out in shock. An oblivious Obisev continued, his worshiping face aimed at the ceiling.

The pastor shook his head as if waking from a stupor. He winced and covered his ears, the knife clanging to the floor. "What is this?"

The tentacle withdrew, and the pastor's eyes widened

in despair. "NO!" He ran to the mirror, sliding on the bloody floor, bracing himself with a hand on either side of the frame.

A rumble in the earth.

A tearing in the air, and the roof split open.

A Tracker's light filled the tiny space, blinding and glorious.

Obisev dropped to his knees, covering his head in terror.

Henry jerked his claws up with everything he had, and the chains shattered to fill the air with sparkling rust. He lifted his claws above his head as he stood, and drew them down in a swipe that tore Obisev's arm off in a jet of blood that washed across Henry's feet.

Another slash, and the man's head rolled back, held on by only a scrap of flesh from his neck.

His body fell to the side, and blood sprayed the floor in a wave. The pastor danced away, his eyes wide with horror, filled with the glow of the Tracker's arrival.

Do not be afraid.

Henry dropped down and slashed the ropes holding Adam to the floor. He worked the blackened stump of his left hand under the child's head, and pulled him to his chest, rocking him back and forth.

"HENRY!" Pastor Owen screamed. "What have you *done*?"

You are safe now.

"I made a *choice*, motherfucker!"

The pastor stood up straight, tears streaming down his cheeks. His shoulders hitched with a sob, and he turned away from the Tracker's light to face the rippling reflection of Hell.

Pastor Owen dove into the narrowing portal, and the

mirror's image emptied with a flash of red light and a swirl of inky black smoke.

The fucker was gone.

Henry closed his eyes and curled over the child in his arms.

You will suffer no more.

Henry shook with fear. Dread welling up into his stomach. He hugged Adam to his chest, and when the boy squeezed him back, pride swelled to replace the fear.

The Tracker's net fell on his shoulders, gentle and soothing.

But this time Henry surrendered himself to the angel's mercy.

Chapter Thirty-Six

GRAY LIGHT FILTERED through the branches above Henry's face. They swayed with a wind he couldn't feel, and his chest tightened with sorrow. Without a breeze cooling his cheeks, the Tree's movement seemed so sad.

He took a breath and pushed from the trunk with a stretch. The knuckles of his right hand popped and crackled. His left hand did nothing. He looked at his bandaged stump and sighed, pushing the horror down with an audible swallow.

I'll never hold a mic the same again.

"We took care of *you*, Henry, but the hand is gone forever I'm afraid."

Henry looked up with shocked joy spreading across his face. "Boothe? How the fuck did you make it out?"

Boothe smiled and reached down to help Henry stand. He waved the hand away, and stood on his own.

Boothe's smile split into a grin. "I have Ramiel to thank for that. He shielded us in his light, and the fight passed over us as if we weren't even there."

"What about Ezra?"

Boothe's face tightened with sorrow. "He didn't make it. Killed by a bolt of dark energy sent down the hill by the good pastor."

"Aw, fuck. I'm sorry."

"Be sorry for yourself. For some reason, he loved *you* more than *me*. But I may be starting to see why."

Henry ducked his head. "Pastor Owen got away."

"We know."

"But I saved the boy."

"Yes, you did, Henry. Mandyel's faith was not misplaced."

"Henry!" Adam rocketed into him like he had at Mandy's store. Henry held him tight against his chest. "Ugh, you're squishing me."

"Sorry, buddy." Henry inspected him. White shirt and shorts, he kicked his bare feet to bounce off Henry's thigh. Not a scratch on his perfect skin.

"What have you been up to down here?"

"Randall's teaching me to play chess."

"He is?"

"Yeah, and I have his queen in a corner."

Randall's voice floated around the tree from the stone table. "A master in the making, Henry."

Henry nodded, and his relief made his knees shake. His grip loosened, and he covered his emotion by setting Adam down and patting his butt. "You go on back to the game, okay? I need to talk to Boothe."

"Okay, Henry." He grinned and ran off, his pale hair flopping.

Henry took a deep breath and turned back to Boothe. "It's time to get what I'm owed."

"And so it is, Henry. But there is one more thing you must do."

He grabbed Henry's arm and guided him to the path

leading away from the Tree. He put his hands behind his back and looked up at Henry from the corner of his eye. "The boy tells me you have learned to alter your form. Why walk around in the demon's skin?"

"Because this is my true self, I guess." Henry said it like it he'd found the answer in an encyclopedia. He lifted his shoulder in an embarrassed shrug.

Boothe laughed, his teeth gleaming. He shook his head. "You are a strange one, Henry. You have no problems learning what we try to teach you, but only after much argument. Everything on your terms."

Henry shrugged again, uncomfortable under Boothe's scrutiny. "Yeah, well, speaking of *terms*. What else do I have to do?"

"Kill the boy."

Boothe continued a few more steps before realizing that Henry had stopped. He turned back with his eyebrows lifted in polite attention.

"Is this another of your fucking tricks?" Henry whispered.

"I'm afraid not, Dear Henry. The boy is a threat to God. To all of *humanity*."

"He's just a kid, for fuck's sake." He couldn't think, and the betrayal tasted like salt.

"No, he is a weapon. You saved him from the Pastor's sacrifice. Eliminated him as a threat. Filled with the boy's power and Hell's Army at his back, he would have been nigh unstoppable. Lucifer would have traded anything to see Heaven overthrown. Even command of his realm."

"How is he a threat?"

Boothe sighed. "I don't expect you to understand, but there's been a battle between Heaven and Hell for a very long time. Between God and Lucifer. Adam is a threat to *everything*. Not just *tipping* the scales, but *removing* them altogether. It is not Adam under another's control that terrifies us so. It is Adam under his *own* control that defies thought. *That* is why he must die."

Henry looked over his shoulder. Adam sat across from Randall, his face still with concentration, the tip of his tongue held between his teeth. He remembered every tiny hug. The understanding look in the boy's eyes. The moment when he had realized they both were safe. He shook his head and sniffed back his tears. "No fucking way. *You* kill him."

"But I can't, Henry. Only a demon can do it. And you're the only one he really trusts."

"Fuck that. He trusts you, too."

Boothe opened his jacket and slid it off, spinning it over his shoulder to hang behind him. "You still don't understand, do you?"

A glow behind Boothe's neck grew as a pair of white wings spread out to wash Henry with the breeze he'd been craving under the tree. Henry staggered back, and his mind emptied of rational thought. Everything he thought resolved now crumbled away.

"Fuck this. Fuck *all* of this. How did *you* manage to become an *angel?*" He spat the last word out with all the disgust he could muster.

Boothe smiled, one eyebrow raising in a confident smirk. "Never underestimate the power of redemption." His face smoothed to something grave. "And that's what you're being given right now. A chance at redemption. Kill the boy and you get whatever you want. Your daughter. Your life back on Earth. We can even make *you* an angel, Henry. You can go back like none of this ever happened, but you have to do this. This one little thing."

"But … that little thing is a kid."

Henry's voice came out in a desperate whine. He didn't

care. The time to give a shit about how he looked or sounded was over.

"No, Henry. He's already been infected with the seeds of hate. If you could go back in time and kill Hitler as a child, wouldn't you? Any decent person would. Imagine Hitler, but on a cosmic scale. Destroying everything, Henry. Every thing. His hate is already turning him."

"No, *you* don't understand. He doesn't hate. He's fucking *hurting*. I've spent time with him. He's only a boy. A *good* boy. Please …"

"Henry, this is the only chance you'll have to get your daughter out of Hell. Are you really going to let her suffer for an eternity?"

This angel. This *demon*. Every moment Henry had tried to convince himself that Boothe deserved an ounce of sympathy … Henry ate it all down, buried it under the black hatred brewing in his heart.

And now to beg?

"Please," Henry gasped. "There's gotta be some other way."

"I'm sorry." Boothe shook his head, and even *looked* sorry, but Henry knew better. "This is what must happen."

Boothe furled his wings and spun his jacket around to slide his arms inside, then shrugging it up to fit. He reached into his pocket and pulled out Heaven's Blade, the knife Henry had won at the *Draconis Arcanum* auction.

He held it out, and Henry took it with numb fingers. It seemed to twist away from his touch, and he knew just how it felt. It was repulsive to hold such a thing, knowing its intent. To kill an angel. He looked past the Tree at the crumbling cityscape of the tormented souls lost in the Forgotten.

He remembered finding Amélie in there, her ghost flitting among the ruins. Remembered that neither Randall nor Boothe had entered the mist.

Maybe they can't?

Henry slid the sheath into the bandage surrounding his stump with a grimace. He looked at Boothe and forced his hatred and anger to recede. He drew a calming breath. "Okay. I'll fucking do it."

Boothe sagged in relief, a nervous smile twitching the corners of his mouth. "Thank you, Henry."

"At least let me say goodbye, okay?"

"Of course, Henry."

They walked back to the Tree in silence. His shadow fell across the board, and Adam and Randall looked up in unison.

"I lost," Adam said.

"That's okay, buddy. You can't win 'em all."

Randall caught Boothe's eye, and God's newest angel nodded. Randall leaned back, covering his smile against the back of his hand, like a gentleman stifling a yawn. Henry wanted to stab them both in the face.

Henry ruffled the boy's hair. "Hey, how about you let these guys get back to their own game, and you and me take a walk. I've been on my ass too long."

"Okay." The trust in his expression made Henry want to weep. What would this boy feel when he discovered yet another betrayal?

Henry steered him toward the Forgotten, and Adam explained the game of chess. Henry pretended to listen, but when he felt they were far enough away, he squatted down and grabbed the boy by his shoulder, forcing him to meet his eyes.

There was power in the child's strange gaze. Command, and a light. Raw and untamed.

What will this child become?

"Adam, you have to listen to me, okay?"

He nodded, his eyes wide and still full of trust.

"You see the mist we've been walking toward?"

Another nod.

"When I tell you, I need you to run there as fast as you can. Into the mist and don't stop, okay?" From the corner of Henry's eye, he saw Boothe stand and button his jacket. "Adam, *please!*"

The boy stepped out from under Henry's hands, shaking his head in confusion.

Henry slid the knife from under the bandage, slinging the sheath off to expose the blade. Black motes of power crawled along the edge like ants, and a bone-numbing cold crept up his arm to the elbow.

Adam jumped back with a hiss, flinching from the blade's dark power. "I don't understand."

Tears sprang into the boy's eyes.

Boothe moved toward them.

"They want me to kill you, Adam. With this knife. They want me to do it because I'm the only one who *can*."

"You can't kill me, Henry. You *saved* me!" He lunged forward, ducking under the knife to grab Henry in a hug that banished the seeping cold from Heaven's Blade.

"I know," Henry whispered into his ear. "That's why you have to run."

He pushed the boy away, and Adam stepped back, shaking his head. Sobs racked his shoulders. He wanted to stab himself in the neck. Bleed out in the dry grass and never have to disappoint anyone ever again.

Boothe broke into a jog. "Henry?" His voice strident with concern.

Henry leaned forward and shouted into the boy's face. "Run!"

Adam jumped back, shock freezing his body. Tears pouring down.

Henry pushed the boy away and screamed, "RUN!"

Adam tore off like a shot, his wail of pain trailing over his shoulder.

"Henry!" Boothe shouted. "What are you doing?"

Henry pushed to his feet. He held the knife in his fist and closed his eyes. Imagined it slicing through Boothe's throat. After all, it was made to kill an angel. He opened his eyes to watch Adam recede into the distance.

The mist parted in front of the tiny sprinter, closing over him as he disappeared into the Forgotten.

Wings thundered behind him, and Henry didn't bother turning around.

He wrapped himself in the shadows, pulling them from the base of every wilting bush along his path. Every rock casting darkness under the gray sky. Every scurrying creature stuck in Nowhere, a Hell of its own between worlds.

He shot away from the light, rocketing through the black that stretched to fill the spaces between one breath and the next, and he launched into the Forgotten with Boothe's enraged voice racing behind him.

"HENRY!"

TO BE CONTINUED ...

Get the Epic Conclusion...

Can Henry redeem himself and save his daughter, or will he be damned for all eternity as *monstrous*?
Get Monstrous Book Three

A Special Request

Thank you for reading *Monstrous Book Two*.

If you enjoyed this book please consider writing a review of it on your favorite bookselling site so other readers might enjoy it too. Just a couple of sentences would mean a lot to me.

Thank you!

SB & DWW

About the Authors

Sawyer Black writes dark and violent fiction for people who secretly love puppies and rainbows. In addition to being a U.S. Army veteran, he's also a beardsman. In fact, that's where all his ideas come from. The beard. Speculative stories about struggle and triumph and brutal emotion, written mostly for his ideal reader, his wife of nearly twenty-five years. He's an independent woman who likes cigars and margaritas, and he holds the deep belief that the earth is round.

David W. Wright is the co-author of edge-of-your-seat thrillers including the best-selling post-apocalyptic series *Yesterday's Gone*, the paranoid sci-fi *WhiteSpace* series, and the vigilante series, *No Justice*, as well as standalone thrillers *12*, and *Crash* which was recently optioned for a movie.

David is an accomplished, though intermittent, cartoonist who lives in [LOCATION REDACTED] with his wife and son [NAMES REDACTED.]

He is not at all paranoid.

He is "the grumpy one" on *The Story Studio Podcast* with fellow Sterling and Stone founders, Sean Platt and Johnny B. Truant.

You can email him at david@sterlingandstone.net

We swear, he almost never bites. Unless you feed him after midnight.

~

For any questions about Sterling & Stone books or products, or help with anything at all, please send an email to help@sterlingandstone.net. Thank you for reading.

Also By Sawyer Black

The Monstrous Series

Soulless

Monstrous Book One

Monstrous Book Two

Monstrous Book Three

Stand Alone Novels

Zoomers vs Boomers

Analog Heart

Born To Die

Also By David W. Wright

Cold Vengeance

Cold Vengeance

Cold Reckoning

Hidden Justice

Hidden Justice

Hidden Honor

Hidden Shame

Hidden Virtue

No Justice

No Justice

No Escape

No Hope

No Return

No Stopping

No Fear

Karma Police

Jumper

Karma Police

The Collectors

Deviant

The Fall

Homecoming

Yesterday's Gone

October's Gone

Yesterday's Gone Season One

Yesterday's Gone Season Two

Yesterday's Gone Season Three

Yesterday's Gone Season Four

Yesterday's Gone Season Five

Yesterday's Gone Season Six

Tomorrow's Gone

Tomorrow's Gone Season One

Tomorrow's Gone Season Two

Tomorrow's Gone Season Three

Available Darkness

Darkness Itself

Available Darkness Book One

Available Darkness Book Two

Available Darkness Book Three

WhiteSpace

WhiteSpace Season One

WhiteSpace Season Two

WhiteSpace Season Three

Stand Alone Novels

Crash

Emily's List

Threshold

The Secret Within